WONDER GUY

a tale from the files of the
Fairy Godmothers' Union, True Love Local

by

Naomi Stone

**This book is dedicated to all
the dreamers of impossible dreams**

Additionally, I'd like to thank everyone who inspired, informed and in other ways helped with the creation of this book, especially my wonderful critique partners, Lizbeth Selvig, Nancy Holland and Ellen Lindseth - all terrific writers in their own rights, and my patient editors,
Abby Rose and Penny Barber,

The 4th Saturday Filkers and Friday Gamesday players (you know who you are) for help keeping my spirits up, the many friends, family & angels who helped keep me solvent,
Jerry Corwin, for help with the pesky business of keeping a roof over my head, and feline helpers:
Tigger, Ash, Skipper & Pippin.

This book would not be the book it is without each and every one of you.

WONDER GUY

a tale from the files of the
Fairy Godmothers' Union, True Love Local

by

Naomi Stone

Chapter 1

"Hi, Greg!" Gloria Torkenson's grin flashed past like sunshine off a moving car--hot and bright, but gone in an instant.

A full-body electric jolt slammed Greg Roberts to a stop. All thoughts of his mission vanished. Behind him, the screen door into his mother's kitchen clapped back in its frame. He hadn't expected he'd find Gloria here this early.

She turned back to her discussion with Aggie, their heads together over sketches they'd strewn like battle plans across the tabletop. Probably the latest artsy-craftsy project she had going with his mother. Aggie, as usual, too absorbed in talk to notice her only son, never looked up.

The topic of their conversation didn't register. His gaze locked on the creamy column of Gloria's neck where it emerged from the low collar of her blouse. Her throat formed a subtle line sweeter than any asymptotic or hyperboloid curve he'd studied as an undergrad. The murmur of her voice undercut all logic to turn his tin-man core into something closer to a lion. Her faint perfume of rose blossoms and citrus and her sun-gilded hair pulled his attention like iron-filings to a magnet.

Their conversation belonged to the world of e-commerce and public forums. Amazing how Gloria existed in that mundane context, yet embodied a whole alternate universe of her own where ordinary laws of physics did not apply and her eyes held alchemical powers to ignite heat in a stone.

He'd waited too long, content simply to be near her. Speaking of his feelings had never seemed right. They'd been little more than children when he'd first noted affection sprouting into something more. Back then, she'd only begun to turn from girl to woman.

But now the only world he shared with Gloria was this common one. He turned his attention finally to the discussion.

"This is your best idea yet," Aggie said, her wheelchair hitched in close under the specially designed worktable replacing the former kitchen table. "I know where we can order more of this clear vinyl."

"Terrific." Gloria pulled her chair in, the legs scraping against linoleum as she scooted closer and wrote rapidly in the margins of a sketch. "How many should we make for a start?"

"Hmm. A few different colors. What's our market?" Aggie rummaged in a pile of sample books on the shelves behind her and opened one displaying vari-colored swatches of fake leather.

Greg shelved a useless sigh. At least Gloria had acknowledged him. His mother had yet to look up since he'd entered the house. Not that she'd have missed the slam of the screen door.

From the sketches visible over Aggie's shoulder, and their talk of clear vinyl, he understood the new project. They planned to add window pockets to their designer cell phone holders. Most of their customers were women. Pretty rhinestones, appliqué or beadwork decorated the majority of their customized "Cell Shells," but this design might appeal to a wider audience.

"Pink, sky blue, yellow, violet..." Gloria jotted as she spoke.

Daring to broach the girl-talk walls felt like taking his life in his hands, but he was going in. Greg found his voice.

"Don't forget us men. We've got cell phones, too." He nodded at the sketches. "Guys will like these. They can carry an ID card in the window pocket, or tell the world you're on their last nerve--but not in pink or baby blue."

"Oh, hi, dear." Aggie turned to smile absently at him.

"Okay, okay." Gloria wrinkled her nose, sticking her tongue out at him in a gesture she'd used since they were six-year olds. Since then, it had only grown in its powers of provocation.

"Black, brown, red..." She turned back to Aggie. "Navy blue and forest green. How many is that?"

Before either Aggie or Greg answered 'nine,' the door behind Greg rattled under someone's fist.

"Oh, that must be Pete. I asked him to meet me here."

9

"Come in!" Aggie called at the same moment Gloria spoke.

Greg stepped aside, further into the kitchen, and nodded a mechanical greeting to Pete Jensen, Gloria's fiance.

Greg had no explanation for the way he bristled like a wild boar around the fellow. He couldn't put his finger on anything specifically objectionable about Pete. Pete constituted an enigma to be studied, maybe not actually dissected, but certainly observed closely. There had to be more to him than met the eye. How had this bland specimen managed to win the heart and hand of the incredible Gloria--the sassiest, brightest, sweetest girl in the world?

☆☆★☆☆

Gloria gathered up her sketches, her excitement bubbling over. This project might be the one. The one to get her out of her stuck-in-limbo-between-career-heaven-and-grindstone-hell job as an administrative assistant. The one to show her father how wrong he was with the way he dismissed her hopes and dreams. She tucked the notes into a thin leather portfolio and the portfolio into her shoulder bag.

Pete liked her ambition. She shot him a welcoming smile as she gathered her sweater up along with the bag. She'd been lucky to find a solid, respectable guy who made her feel like a glass-bauble safely wrapped in cotton wool. She liked his friendly smile and his nice suit. Pete had a nice, solid, responsible job as a junior accountant with a firm allowing plenty of room for him to grow to be a senior accountant. He treated her right, often making small romantic gestures like sending flowers and chocolates. Pete represented everything she wanted, certainly more than her father thought she deserved. Pete was perfect.

"Bye, Aggie. I'll be back later and we can get started on the prototypes." She bent to give the older woman a warm hug. Since she'd lost her own mother at the age of twelve, Aggie had been there for her in more ways than she could count. She'd needed her kind neighbor's support after being left alone to take on too much responsibility in a household her father neglected.

She hugged Greg too, hovering there like her personal domesticated Sasquatch. She tousled his caramel blond hair, though she needed to stretch to reach it these days. "You need a trim, my boy."

"Do I?" He looked up as if he might see his own head. Well, maybe he saw his hair hanging across his forehead.

"Definitely. You're looking scruffy again. Don't you want your professors to take you seriously?" Sometimes dealing with Greg seemed like dealing with a child. How could he be so smart in some ways, a graduate student in computer science no less, and yet miss so much?

"They do take me seriously, and half of them are scruffier than this. Haven't you seen pictures of Einstein?" She'd heard him before, venting his frustration at having to live in a society obsessed with appearances, valuing hulks who carried inflated pig bladders across a field more than they valued a technical genius. His tone now evoked the whole rant.

"You know what I mean. Aren't you applying for grant money? They don't just look at your ideas. You'll have to meet with people. They'll look at what kind of person you are, no matter how brilliant it is to make a computer go super fast."

"The speed of light. Photonic computing is the obvious next step for laser technology."

"Yes, that. You listen to me this time." She exchanged a frustrated glance with Aggie, who'd long since given up on reminding her son of these things. How could the boy be smart enough to think up speed of light computers and be absolutely helpless when it came to living in the real world? What would he do when she wasn't around to look after him?

"I always listen to you." The intensity of the look in his mild brown eyes made her gut do a jig.

"Well, we've got to go. See you later." She turned to her date, who'd stood at the door, without speaking to anyone while Gloria made her goodbyes. "C'mon, Pete."

The neatly dressed and trimmed Pete held out his arm for her, and finally gave a wave to Greg and Aggie. "Good night, folks."

☆☆★☆☆

"Did you need something, hon?" Aggie drew Greg's attention back to the familiar kitchen.

He turned away from the door through which Gloria had vanished with the obnoxiously well-groomed Pete. "Oh. Right. Did the delivery guy leave my bread with your grocery order?"

"Why didn't you check the bread box?" Aggie gestured to the counter behind him. "It's in there, crowding my sesame semolina loaf."

"Thanks, Mom. I'd better get back to work." Greg grabbed his loaf of whole wheat. "I got a three day weekend and still put off grading papers until the last minute."

He waved to Aggie and left before she started looking too pointedly back at her project. He headed across the back yard, where the low-slanting rays of the sun cast their lingering glow, to his apartment above the garage. He did have papers to grade, and at five o'clock, he had the whole evening to finish his task.

First, he'd better hit the road. He needed a good ten miles of furious pedaling right now. It was hard enough that he didn't stand a chance with Gloria, but seeing her go off with someone else intensified the ache. He had to stop thinking about her. Pretty soon she'd be out of his life. The thought knotted his gut. No granny knot easily pulled loose, but a good, solid square knot that wouldn't let go.

He usually welcomed the quiet of the garage, dim and dusty, but safe harbor for Aggie's specially equipped SUV and his bike and gear. This evening it seemed too empty, despite the surrounding gear and his apartment waiting above. No life. He'd left all the liveliness behind at Aggie's. Here, he'd welcome even the company of a mouse. Maybe he should get a dog, make sure he'd come home to a warm welcome rather than this hollow space that might as well be a hermit's cave.

Setting the bread on top of the deep freezer, he grabbed his helmet from its hook on the pegboard and turned to lift down his prized Trek Valencia 24-speed road bike.

A tinkling, like bicycle warning bells, sounded at his ear, startling him so he nearly stumbled, only catching himself before he knocked into the little old lady who stood at his side.

Jeez Louise! If this were a cartoon, he'd have to climb down from the rafters to get back into his skin.

"Whoops." She laughed. "We almost had ourselves a collision there."

He stared, mouth slightly ajar. He'd be politically incorrect to think of her, a no doubt empowered senior citizen, possibly as militantly feminist as his mother, as a "little old lady." She looked as if she might blow away in a strong breeze, stood hardly as high as his shoulders, even with the ostrich feather arching above the gaudy purple hat perched on her snow-white hair. Despite the twinkle in her eye, something in her demeanor warned him to mind his manners. How else to think of her, but "little old lady?"

At least she gave him a moment to recover from his near-rafter experience. "Sorry," he said, "I didn't see you there." He dangled his contour-styled helmet by the chinstrap, having forgotten why he wanted it.

"Oh, I wasn't there." She gave a charming, tinkling laugh, which awakened an answering grin in him. She evoked images of every birthday-present-giving, story-telling, cookie-baking grandma he'd ever imagined.

"So, where were you?" Had she been waiting for him out of sight?

"Somewhere else. I just popped in to help you with your little problem." She waved a hand upward, to the ladders lying across the garage rafters and his apartment above. "Why don't you ask me up?"

"I'm on my way out. What problem? One of the pre-test problems? You're not in the advanced computing class are you?" No way he'd have missed her among the students he helped as teaching assistant to Professor Morrissey.

"No, no, dear." She took his elbow, a strong grip for someone of such frail appearance, a grip he'd sooner have expected from a bar room bouncer. "Why don't we make ourselves comfortable while we discuss it? I wouldn't mind a nice Mountain Dew Code Red."

How the hel--heck had she guessed what was in his fridge? Greg replaced his helmet on its peg. It looked like his ride would have to wait.

"Are you one of Mom's friends?" He managed to keep 'weird' from modifying friends. His mother had grown up on a commune, and knew more than her share of dropouts, burnouts and one-time hippie freaks.

The pressure on his elbow increased and he found himself moving to the stairs leading up to his apartment.

"I'm here because your mother made a request handled by my Society," she chatted in her bright, Sunday-school tones, staying close to his side as they mounted the stairs.

"Society?" He dug in the pocket of his windbreaker and found the jangling bunch of keys there.

"The Fairy Godmothers' Union, True Love Local."

"What?" He turned to face her, key in lock. His tone rose a couple steps in pitch. "Is that some kind of dating service?"

"Now, now. It's not like that at all. Your mother is only worried you'll stand aside and let Gloria marry someone else. She's concerned you'll lose your chance for True Love."

His nerveless fingers would have dropped the key if he hadn't already stuck it in the lock. What did this strange little old lady know of his feelings for the girl next door? Feelings he'd never mentioned to Gloria, or his mother and would rather not admit even to himself. How could he possibly speak of anything that confused him so utterly? He had no words for how he felt about Gloria.

Ever since Gloria had accused him of being clueless regarding matters of emotion, he'd tried to pay more attention to his feelings. This was a new one. Interesting. Elevated heart rate, cold sweat, fast, shallow breathing. It would be much the same if he'd come face to face with a tiger in the wild. All this from mentioning 'true love' in conjunction with Gloria's name? Yep. Must be fear.

He drew a deep, steadying breath, finding his voice at last. "What has my mother said to you?"

"She said, 'I sure wish my boy would grow a pair and tell Gloria how he feels.' This brought the matter to our attention." The feather on the gaudy cap brushed his nose.

Greg sneezed.

The sprightly woman reached past him and turned the key.

He fell forward, half stumbling into his apartment, fumbling in body and mind alike. The lady followed before he'd decided whether to invite her.

"Uh, have a seat?" He gestured to the loveseat arranged with a pair of comfy chairs around a coffee table, and the pair of stools at the kitchenette counter, which, with the loaded bookshelves, managed to fully occupy the small apartment. He steadied himself with a hand on the counter. This would probably make more sense if he let her explain herself. He hoped.

"Can I get you something to drink?"

"The Code Red would suit nicely." Her eyes *twinkled* as she smiled.

"Uh, right." He snagged the last two cans out of the fridge, passed one to her and wiped the condensation off on his slacks. He sat on the comfy chair opposite the loveseat where she perched. He had to get this conversation on track somehow.

"So, you're one of my mother's friends?" Must be. She had to be confused. Her bustling manner had fooled him into thinking her something out of the ordinary.

He popped the top of his can.

"No, no, dear. No, I'm here on your behalf. Let me introduce myself." She fumbled in a small beaded handbag, pulled out a white card and handed it to him. "I'm Serafina, your fairy god-mother."

Just as it said on the business card: *Serafina, Fairy Godmothers' Union, True Love Local 521.*

"I...see." But he didn't. This made no sense. It must be some kind of joke by one of his mother's definitely weird friends.

"You will. Don't worry." Serafina took a dainty sip of her Code Red and snorted as the bubbles hit. "It's simple, really."

"I hate to rush you," Greg took a swig of soda and leaned forward in his chair, "but I'd like to get out for a ride before I start grading papers."

"Don't worry, dear, this won't take long. I know how you can win your love."

"You're here to rescue my love life?" If it weren't so outrageous, it would be laughable.

"Yes." She went on in perfectly sober tones, "You're a good boy. You've probably been telling yourself you want only what's best for Gloria and you're happy for her because she's found someone she wants to marry. We both know you're only fooling yourself."

The words jabbed him like a fork. Soda sloshed from the can he clutched too tightly. He wasn't fooling himself. He was a good boy, er, man, and he did want what was best for Gloria. This was too much.

"Look here." He fumbled for something to say.

She continued as if he hadn't spoken. "You've loved Gloria since you were twelve and you want her for yourself."

"It doesn't matter what I want." He spoke with a degree of force that surprised him and waved his can of soda, gesturing wildly, spattering the vicinity.

Serafina never flinched as a flying droplet narrowly missed her face.

"If Gloria doesn't want me, we'd never be happy together." The words escaped him like a cry from some forgotten fragment of his soul.

"Just so," Serafina continued, unperturbed. "But you've never given her the chance to want you. You've always been there for her, like a brother. She thinks she knows everything there is to know about you. There's no mystery."

"She does?" He slumped heavily into his chair and drained the last drops from his can.

"That's right. We need to use a little fairy godmother magic on you to get her to look at you in a new light."

Gloria thought what? This was crazy. The old woman was crazy. What she said was crazy. Only a crazy person would do anything else but show her the door.

"I'm listening," he said.

Chapter 2

Where people gathered, Elysha, who considered herself a genuine people person, found ample opportunity to stir up the kind of energy she feasted upon. Invisible to human eyes, she strolled among the tables under the banner reading *Christ Church Memorial Day Picnic.*

The sun shone warm, the cooling breeze blew soft, and picnickers filled the park surrounding Minnehaha Falls. They sat around laden picnic tables under the pavilion and on blankets scattered across the oak-shaded lawns. They stood around barbecue grills, ran after Frisbees, lounged in portable chairs, strolled along paths, and hiked the trail beside the falls.

A woman with gray strands threaded through her brown hair frowned, etching the lines of the expression into her face, at a paunchy, slightly balding man sitting beside her at a picnic table. His back rested against the table, one elbow propped among half-emptied bowls and trays. His gaze followed the actions of two young women tossing a yellow Frisbee back and forth across the expanse of lawn between them.

The older woman, watching her male companion focus on the younger women, radiated insecurity. As good as an invitation for Elysha. She whispered into the woman's ear, "He'd rather have her than you. See how he looks at her, so young and beautiful? He doesn't look at you like that anymore."

The woman's frown deepened. She slapped the man's shoulder. "You're making a fool of yourself. You think she'd look twice at an old fart like you?"

"What?" The man's face showed only puzzlement as he turned to his companion. "What are you talking about, Laura?"

Elysha hovered near, smiling as she drank in the growing conflict. The woman's fear and defensiveness, the man's growing annoyance. He'd been paying only casual attention to the Frisbee players. Now, as his partner called his attention to their youth and beauty his interest in them only grew. Delicious. A tiny push from Elysha and Laura had exacerbated the situation, feeding into her own insecurities.

Appetite whetted on the petty jealousy, Elysha wandered away from the arguing couple. The younger children at the picnic looked up when she passed, but then looked quickly away. Her passage made a shadow on their games.

She paused near a scrawny young male who sat alone with his back against the bole of an oak, in the shade of its broad-spread branches. He seemed nearly adult, but not near enough to be accepted as such by the older humans. Resentment--and

21

something darker--fumed from him. Elysha drew up beside his tree, leaned over his shoulder and whispered, "None of them care for you. You might wander down the creek and into the woods and never return. No one would notice."

"I could take a swan dive over the falls onto the rocks and nobody would notice," her prey muttered. "Not until they have to deal with the mess."

His darkness deepened, thickened like a pudding, weighted with a deep conviction that he deserved none of the notice he craved--so rich. She really shouldn't. Elysha savored the treat.

"Well you don't care for them either, do you? Who needs them?" she whispered.

"Donny!" A child's voice called out across the lawns. "Get over here!" A bare-kneed, bare-footed, tow-headed girl of perhaps ten years ran toward them across the emerald velvet of the grass. The teen looked up, his sour expression shifting to something softer, if non-committal.

"You said you'd push me on the swings. C'mon." The waif shied at the shadows where Elysha drew back. Donny rose.

"Oh all right." His tone complained, but without conviction. "Got nothing better to do."

"What are you talking about? Didn't you get some barbeque chicken? There's ice cream sandwiches in the cooler." Their voices faded as the young man trailed away in the wake of the voluble girl.

Oh well. Something interesting might yet come of this one. Elysha's whispers had a way of sticking in a person's mind.

Hmm. She caught the sweet perfume of self-righteousness wafting from a knot of women who stood around a grill where a large man in t-shirt and *Kiss the Chef* apron flipped burgers.

The women looked of an age to be the parents of some of the children racing around. She drew close enough to hear their conversation. Mmm, yes. Bolstering their imagined superiority by clucking over the misfortunes of a neighbor. Tasty.

☆☆★☆☆

"You're familiar with moving pictures?" Serafina asked, tilting slightly toward where Greg sat across the coffee table. "Marvelous what they can do with them these days."

"Um, yes?" Not just out of left field, this change of subject must have crossed county lines. Well, he could still show her the door, in a minute or two.

"Did you see the one where the ordinary young man suddenly acquired superpowers, and the young lady he always secretly loved noticed him when he appeared as a mysterious masked hero?"

"Yeah." The one? A whole list came to mind. "You're not thinking I--?"

"Yes." She spread her lace-gloved hands wide in her enthusiasm. "That's just what we'll do. A dashing costume, a few crimes stopped, and Gloria can't help but be intrigued, and when she learns it's you--"

"It all falls flat." Greg rose to his feet and paced the small area between their seats and the kitchenette. "I can't tell you in how many ways that's a bad idea. Wait. Let me try. One, I'm not a superhero! I'm not cut out to be a crime-buster. Two, I'd look like a fool in a costume. Three, Gloria is too sensible to go for some stranger because he's dressed up like a superhero. Four, This is Minneapolis. I've lived here my whole life and never even witnessed a crime in progress, let alone been in a position to stop one."

"Stop, stop." The tiny woman fluttered a hand at him. "You're going too fast. The first thing is, you will be a superhero. I'll give you a superpower and a costume."

"What? Lady, you seem very nice." The fight whooshed out of him with an exhaled breath. He dropped into his chair and leaned toward her across the table. "It's nice of you to want to help save my love life, and all, but you're confusing fact and fiction. Just because they do it in the movies doesn't mean..."

The words faded in his throat as she rose from the sofa--and not in the ordinary way. She remained seated, legs crossed demurely at the ankles, but floated a good three feet above the cushions.

He set his soda can carefully on a coaster on the coffee table. He blinked a few times, goggling at the unbelievable, but each time his eyes showed him the same sight. A falling sensation swept through him. His legs might have gone out from under him if he hadn't already been seated.

"Uh." He cleared his throat at the squeakiness of his voice, and continued at a more normal pitch. "Okay. You'll give me a superpower." Either she was crazy or he was. Better play along. "What did you have in mind?"

"I thought you might like to pick something for yourself." Wrinkles, like an excess of dimples, framed her smile. She floated back to a normal altitude relative to the chair and picked up her soda. Nodding to his bookcases, she said, "I noticed you have a large collection of those picture adventures."

"Comix? Graphic novels?"

"Precisely, the comical books. I thought you would have a lot of ideas for a nice, impressive superpower."

"Let me think." How surreal. Should he take this seriously for one minute? Or make an appointment at Mental Health Services?

But he did have a lot of ideas. Super strength? X-ray vision? Super speed like the Flash? Spider powers? Should he suggest one of the X-Men's powers? The Fantastic Four's? The Incredibles? Both Elasta-Girl and Reed Richards did pretty well with that stretchy thing, but they worked with teams. He should pick something to work as a stand-alone power. He should have his head examined.

"I don't know," he said finally. "There are a lot to choose from, and, like I said before, what good would a superpower do anyone when I've never encountered any crime around here?"

"There's crime here." Her wrinkles lost their resemblance to dimples as her mouth tightened. "It's a matter of being in the right place at the right time. With my help, you will be."

His mental review of comic book history slowed. So many superheroes' girlfriends seemed to live on the brink of death. The nasty thought kicked his growing interest to a dead halt. "I won't have you putting Gloria in danger."

"Now, now. Your Gloria is in danger every day, walking down streets where big metal cars hurtle past, living in a world with more diseases and toxins than you'd have the patience to listen to me name, where the weather can turn deadly and a certain percentage of the surrounding population are predators." She must have seen his face going pale as his heart tightened in his chest. "I promise I won't make things any worse."

"Even if this is for real, I can't use superpowers just to impress a girl. With great power comes great responsibility. I'd be morally obligated to use it for the common good if I had that kind of power."

"Pish and tosh, young man." She sniffed. "You've been watching too many of those silly movies. True love is the source of these powers. You can use them to impress the girl and for the common good. Benefiting the common good is a bonus. There wouldn't be any such powers without the magic true love generates in the world." She leaned across the coffee table and patted the back of his hand. "Since there are so many powers to choose from, why don't we try a few out and see which one you like best? No need to be hasty."

"I'm going to need super speed to get these papers graded tonight after I go biking." he spoke half to himself, trying the thought on for size.

"Very well." Serafina drank her soda, swirled the last few drops in the can and set it on the coffee table. "Just say 'Speedo' to call on your power and 'Whoa Now' when you're ready to go back to your secret identity."

"Secret identity?"

"You'll wear a costume. For the element of mystery." She winked. "Let me know what you think." Her words echoed through the small apartment. She'd vanished.

If it weren't for the dent in the cushions of the sofa and her empty soda can on the table before him, she might never have been there.

He considered the definite possibility he'd suffered a psychotic break. Maybe he'd sat on the sofa himself, drunk a can of Code Red, and moved to a new seat here while hallucinating this whole bizarre conversation.

"Speedo?"

Peculiar sensations, like a hive of bees bodysurfing his system, swept through him. He glanced down, jerked back. Bright red leotards garbed his legs. He jumped to his feet and his chair flew backward to land with a crash. "What the..." He rushed to the mirror in the bathroom and the wind of his passing set the curtains fluttering in the windows. The neat stack of the Introductory Computing class's final papers at one end of the coffee table went flying around the room like as many huge ghostly leaves.

But his image in the mirror drove everything else to the background. Red leotards were only the beginning. The form-fitting costume showed off the muscular benefits of his daily biking. He wore bright scarlet, from the masked hood to his gloved hands, arms, and torso, where a swath of yellow flared from his belly out to his shoulders in a red lightning-bolt sigil blazoned across his chest. Derivative, but not bad.

"Holy cow." He wanted to laugh out loud at the sheer corniness of it. He looked like a refugee from a comic book convention. At least he didn't have a cape. "This is ridiculous."

If Gloria saw him dressed like this, she'd laugh herself silly. Except, with the mask, he might be anybody. Anybody with sculpted marble calves and six-pack abs, chiseled jaw and impressively wide shoulders. Maybe she wouldn't laugh.

He'd never looked at himself as if at a stranger. Biking was a healthy hobby, but he did it because he liked to move--it helped him think--not because he wanted to look good in tights.

He was a man of science. His world had been turned upside down, tossed in the air and given a good shake. The universe was supposed to behave in logical, predictable ways. Now it seemed like quicksand might lurk at any step. This was all impossible, from the first appearance of the little old lady who claimed to be a fairy godmother to this.

This figment of an over-active imagination staring at him from the mirror.

Or his existing models of reality were inadequate. Examine the facts. If something happens, it's not impossible, it's new data, calling for new theories and new models to better understand how it's possible.

Before he formed any new theories, he needed to make a few tests, figure out whatever new rules might be at work. First, check out this speed thing. See how fast he could go. How far. How long he'd be able to keep it up. Since he didn't want to risk his expensive Trek bike, he'd better conduct his experiment on foot.

Greg moved with exaggerated caution, wary of slamming headfirst into the apartment door or tumbling down the stairs in a headlong rush. Clutching the banister all the way, he made it safely downstairs and peered around the corner of the door out to the yard. What would people think if they saw the red-costumed "hero" exit his mother's garage? He'd never hear the end of it, let alone losing the advantage of a secret identity.

Finding the coast clear, he took off in such a burst of speed no one would have seen him if they'd been there. A wake of flying dust and debris swirled along his path. As it was, he made it down the alley before taking a single breath. He grinned. He hadn't felt so foolishly proud of himself since he caught the dodge ball at a crucial moment in a middle school game, winning for his side.

No time to savor the feeling. He put on his brakes, but stopping proved trickier than anticipated.

Oh crap! His momentum carried Greg past his feet and sent him tumbling into a somersault. Asphalt, garages, dumpsters and fenced yards seemed to whirl around him until he slid to rest, breathless and flat on his back, where the alley joined the cross street. He'd have skinned himself to the bone on the gravel and crumbling asphalt if his costume and gloves hadn't proved so resistant to damage. The Hanson's ginger cat, Max, looked down at him from between the slats of their fenced yard, clearly not impressed with Greg's athletic prowess.

"Like you'd do better your first time out," he told the sole witness to his fall, as embarrassed as if Max might spread the story. For a moment he lay still and gathered his rattled bones and rattled thoughts.

Brushing himself off, he rose to his feet by careful stages. He looked around to check out the cross street before going further. Not much traffic. Good. The fewer witnesses or obstacles, the better.

Greg darted down the road. Kind of fun, the wind in his face, the world spinning by so fast he might achieve escape velocity, outrun the wind or chase down his dreams. Pounding rock 'n roll played on his mental radio. Exhilarated, he ran circles around a squirrel daring to cross the street. He'd probably busted all the land speed records for a man on foot, without even pushing himself.

He'd come a mile in no more than a few seconds.
Maybe that really would impress Gloria.

He stopped again, taking care to decelerate
gradually as he reached Lyndale Avenue, where
he stood for a moment and looked up and down
the street. Long past rush hour, the few cars on
the road moved at a steady clip. A young woman
walked her standard poodle around a corner, leaving no pedestrians in sight. He may as well go all
out, see what he could do at full throttle.

Greg ran down the deserted bike lane at first,
but, as he pressed for his top speed, it seemed as if
everything moving around him stood still. He ran
rings around a cyclist and must have been only
a blur to the helmeted rider, like being invisible,
like the world belonged to him to do with as he
wished--a heady rush of power.

A child dropped a fast food wrapper out the rear
window of a family sedan. Littering constituted
criminal activity, all right. A chance to apply his
superpowers for the greater good. Greg snatched
up the crumpled scrap and popped it back in
through the passenger window onto the lap of the
man seated there and made it halfway down the
next block before anyone would have had time to
notice his passing.

Ahead, off to the side of the road, under one of
the maples lining every street, he spotted movement, a cat twisting in midair. An open-mouthed
teenaged girl stood nearby, alarm widening her
eyes. *Never fear, citizens, Speedy-Greg to the rescue!*

Greg hardly paused as he scooped the animal
deftly out of the air and deposited it gently on its

31

feet, then ran off before teen or cat reacted. The small act left him with a warm glow. Maybe the cat would have landed on its feet regardless of his intervention, but he'd made sure of its safe landing, and made the day that much better for the teen and the cat alike.

Buildings, cars and people became a blur as he rushed on. He rolled the world away under his pounding-along-at-blurring-speed feet. It had only been a couple minutes since he'd left the alley and he'd already crossed 494 into Richfield.

Amazingly, he wasn't even breathing hard, but he needed some goggles and his jaw burned from the wind. At this rate, he'd be in Burnsville in another couple minutes. Fascinating. His perceptions must have sped up, too. He couldn't get over the way the cars on the road seemed to stand still. Incredible. His fingers itched for a notepad to record his observations.

He eased up on his pace, gradually slowing until he ran beside the cars at their own speed. He caught a few looks of surprise from passengers and drivers. He waved to them in passing. Finally, he slowed to a stop at a bus shelter and plopped to a seat on the bench, congratulating himself on stopping without disaster. He needed to find a scrap of paper to use for some notes. He eyed an old flyer taped to the side of the shelter. Still not breathing hard. Wow.

A buzzing sounded in his ear. Greg waved a hand, shooing whatever away. The sound persisted, too steady and mechanical to be an insect.

He felt around the ear of his hooded mask, found a small projection and pressed it.

"There you go."

Her voice, the little old lady, Serafina.

"I forgot to mention the radio connection, young man. I called to let you know there's a crime in progress. Right now, in Richfield, the backyard at 6699 Bryant."

"I'll be right there," Greg said without thinking, or stopping to remind himself he wasn't really a hero. Already he moved at top speed, easily dodging the nearly stationary cars, buses, trucks and people dotting his path.

Crime? Since when did he rush to the scene of a crime? What did he think he could do? His doubts echoed in his ears, but he answered them. At this speed, he certainly had the power to do something, and do it before the bad guys even noticed him.

No time to think things over. No time to second-guess himself. It took no time to cover the few miles of side streets lined with small suburban homes as he rushed toward danger. Greg darted past the last garage standing between him and the designated backyard.

Maybe a dozen people filled the yard, men, women and children.

A blonde woman whose strapless dress bared sunburned shoulders stood clutching a toddler and a gangly girl close against her. Her face contorted in a clash of anger and fear, the children gaped, frozen expressions angling toward tears.

A man with buzz-cut gray hair and an impressive beer gut sat at the picnic table with men who might be his brothers. He held a barbecued rib halfway to his mouth, fingers greasy, alarmed eyes on the intruders.

Most of the adults sat around the table. The man at the grill held his hands in the air, still wielding a barbecue fork on which perched a skewered brat.

Most of the children huddled nearby, around a slip 'n slide game. A boy clad in sky blue swim trunks snaked down the slide on his belly. By perceptible inches.

Three men with guns stood positioned around the periphery of the gathering. They wore nylon stocking masks. Two were of medium height and build, one larger, all looked old enough to know better. He scowled at the intruders with an unaccustomed sense of determination locking his jaw. Last summer there'd been news reports of a gang of robbers targeting backyard barbeques. *Looks like they're back.*

In moments shaved fine from a second, Greg tore past the masked men. He pulled weapons from their frozen grasps. The largest man held the shotgun with such a determined grip only Greg's momentum enabled him to tear it free. A glance behind him showed the beginning of their reactions, eyes widening, mouths opening. The snap of breaking fingers didn't catch up to him until he'd already collected two thirty-eights and the sawed off shotgun. The sickening sound almost slowed him.

The frightened eyes of the children and people at the picnic table firmed Greg's resolve. He frisked the men for other weapons, found a couple knives and another gun, and then dumped the hardware into a plastic wading pool where a lone yellow ducky bobbed.

It took the work of another instant to unstring the rope from a clothesline at the side of the yard and tie the robbers' arms and legs. Everything he handled seemed unwieldy. Inertia created more drag at this speed. The clothesline might be an anaconda, the guns cast in lead.

Greg didn't stop until he'd positioned himself behind a huge oak in the next yard over to make sure the situation stayed under control. The world caught up with him, quickly followed by a couple screams and the thuds of falling bodies as the bound robbers toppled. More screams and shouts.

"Oh my god!"

"What happened?" Several people exclaimed at once.

"Where are their guns?"

"Call the police."

"Jesus, my hand. My hand!"

"It was a fast man," A child piped.

"Here they are," cried another child, "in Dougie's pool."

Greg bit his lip to keep from cursing as a six-year-old boy pulled a dripping handgun out of the pool. A woman snatched it away immediately and the boy started crying, adding to the din.

He obviously needed to work on his weapons disposal strategy. What was he thinking? No way would he make this a habit. He'd had fun playing the hero, and had to admit it gave his heart a lift to stop those thugs, to see the kids and families safe and take part in their relief. It made the evening light glow a bit brighter, made him stand taller. But he still needed to grade papers in time to get them back to the professor in the morning. High time he returned to his real, if somewhat duller life.

When he darted out of concealment and down the alley, his earlier urgency had left him, and Greg didn't go as fast as possible. He went no faster than a car, slow enough to be seen.

He changed course halfway home. If he meant to turn in his costume and superpower when he got home, he still wanted to try one thing while he had the chance. Foolish, maybe, but he'd been a comics fan forever and if he missed this chance to play around with it, he'd kick himself later. It worked for The Flash, so it should work for him. Greg headed for Lake Calhoun.

Approaching the lake, the scene might have been a landscape painting of a June evening, a picture of perfect serenity, calm waters reflecting the clear evening sky, lush trees ringing the water like a green feather boa around the bare shores of the lake. A few sailboats glided on the lake, and plenty of people walked, skateboarded, biked and picnicked around the shoreline despite the lengthening shadows. Reaching the shore, Greg pushed himself to full speed.

The physics of it worked in theory. Moving at over a hundred miles an hour, water shouldn't be able to get out of his way fast enough and would support him as he ran across it, like self-propelled water-skiing.

He crossed the lake in an instant.

Even with his speed-enhanced perceptions, he'd made it across the water before he had a chance to appreciate the experience. Kind of a letdown. He looked back to the lake, wondering how to remedy the problem. A straight course allowed only a fraction of a second on the watery surface, but nobody said he had to take the straight path, not when he had the option of taking the scenic route.

This time Greg started the same full-speed dash across the water, but bent his route into a circular path around the inner curve of the lake. He raced around the circumference, far enough from shore to easily avoid the relatively motionless waders, children splashing in the shallows and the moored boats. This was more like it. He moved further from shore and wove his way around the sailboats.

He reversed direction, jumping the small waves his earlier steps had kicked up. Legs pumping faster than he'd ever have believed possible, the water's surface lay like rippled stone beneath his feet. He sped around the lake like a kid running for the sheer joy of it. Like he'd done with Gloria and the other kids on the block before he'd learned to read and discovered other worlds. The wind burned his face. He gave a shout as he ran, never stopping, until a renewed buzzing sounded in his ear.

He slapped the button and, startled into a too-sudden halt, tumbled like a skipped stone until he lost momentum and splashed into the drink, sinking like that same stone.

Spirits dashed by the cold dunking, Greg rose splashing and coughing to the surface. "What?" he sputtered, choking back a few words Aggie'd taught him to avoid in polite company.

"Tut, dear. It's an emergency."

"What?" Sobered, he spoke more calmly, still treading water.

"There's a house not far from you. The family's on vacation. It's being burgled even now." She gave him the directions.

Greg treaded water faster and faster, against continually greater resistance, working his way up like a corkscrew emerging from the cork, until he sped across the surface at full speed.

Chapter 3

"So, that went pretty well, don't you think?" Pete drove as they headed home from the Red Lobster where they'd joined his parents for an early dinner. The homecoming traffic of Memorial Day weekend vacationers had dwindled by now, leaving the streets and highway nearly empty.

Gloria stared into the deep shadows along the road and into the reflections on the windshield, watching the passing lights. She should say something before it got awkward.

"Sure," she answered with brightness more habitual than related to the topic of discussion.

Her mind strayed to the project she'd left on Aggie's worktable. She'd retained nothing notable from the dinner conversation. Pete's parents seemed nice. They'd been pleasant in manner, soft-spoken and dressed straight from the *Sears* Catalog. His father, Pete Senior, hadn't spoken much other than to say hello, offer Pete congratulations and agree with his wife.

Pete's mother, Marion, had talked a lot, mostly about her church groups--people Gloria had never met--and so relentlessly, Gloria hadn't had any opportunity to comment or question. After the initial greetings, talk of their engagement was cut short when she and Pete admitted they hadn't set a date and weren't ready to talk actual plans. Gloria's mind had wandered away to focus on a better appreciation of her buttery scallops while Marion chatted through the meal.

"Your parents sure seem like nice people." What more was there to say? She didn't blame them for being boring. Not everyone could be a brilliant conversationalist. To be fair, she might have seemed dull to them too, if she'd found a chance to talk about the new project that she found so exciting. Not everyone would be interested in her entrepreneurial dreams.

"Yeah. They are. Mom's real active with the church. Her groups do a lot of good work, help a lot of worthy causes. She'll probably get you involved once we're married."

"Um." She called on the patience she'd learned through years of dealing with her father, though something in her reared up in defense. Why would he spring this on her so late in the game? "I'm not Episcopalian." *Even if I were, I've got plans of my own for how I spend my time.* "I thought you weren't very religious?"

"I'm not. I've been putting all my energy into building my career, but I used to go along with the folks on Sundays, and will again when I can."

She caught his puzzled puppy look and reminded herself you don't fight with someone while whipping down the highway at 60mph. She consciously relaxed her jaw. This wasn't a fight. They were both reasonable adults. "I was raised Unitarian, and I'm not planning to convert."

"Oh." Like it had never occurred to him someone might object to switching faiths with zero notice. "I guess it's okay. It doesn't matter a lot to me. I'm just not sure how Mom will take it."

"Did she assume I'd change my religion when we got married?" Gloria didn't usually give much thought to religion, but the idea of someone else dictating her beliefs got her back up like a Halloween cat's.

"We never talked about it. I never thought to mention it. Maybe she assumes you are Episcopalian. Doesn't make any difference to me. If this is an issue, why didn't you bring it up at dinner?"

"I didn't want to interrupt your mother." It took some effort to keep any snark from her tone, and Gloria set her jaw to keep from saying more. She took a deep breath. "I suppose I might go along sometimes to services at the Episcopalian Church, but it's not what I believe in."

"Maybe that would be best. Mom knows you're not a regular churchgoer. She wouldn't have to hear about the Unitarian thing."

The thought of concealing her beliefs didn't sit any better than having them dictated to her. "If we get a place here in South Minneapolis they won't expect us to go to their church out in Roseville, will they?"

Pete had his own apartment, his own life here in South Minneapolis. It was sweet how he wanted to stay involved with his parents, but he'd never

41

suggested before that he might want to move back to their neighborhood and go to church with them every Sunday. How much else might Pete still spring on her? She'd spent too many years twisting her dreams to fit around her father's requirements. She didn't want someone else's parents taking over her new life.

"It's not far by highway." He took the exit ramp faster than she liked and braked hard at the stop sign at the cross street.

"Pete, c'mon. You don't have to cross town to go to the same church as your parents do you? You're a grown up now."

"Well, I thought it would be better if we got a place in Roseville. I've been living near work because it's cheaper, but we'll need a bigger place anyway."

"You know I need to look in on my father. He's not responsible."

"We can get professional care services to look after him. He might even be better off in a care facility."

"He's an alcoholic, not an invalid." Obviously, she didn't know Pete as well as she'd thought. Maybe things were moving too fast. On the other hand, it might be nice to have other people share some of the load of looking after Dad. She hated the quickly buried thought, but sometimes her father seemed like her own personal albatross.

"Maybe what we need is a second car." Pete pulled up at the curb outside the two-story stucco house where Gloria had lived most of her life. "If we get a place somewhere in between here and

Roseville and you have your own car, you can see your father as often as you want and I can go to church with my parents."

"Oh, Pete." Her shoulders loosened in relief. She hadn't lost her fond dream of a secure home and future. "Just when I'm starting to think it's hopeless, you come up with an answer. You're my hero."

After turning off the engine, he scooped her close. "Got time for a kiss for your hero?"

She melted into it. Pete's kiss reassured her. One hand cupped her face, his lips brushing hers, sweet as a familiar face at a party full of strangers. He didn't press her, just let her enjoy the simple pleasure of the moment.

For a few seconds, and then time to get moving. She had things to do. She swung the door open and jumped out. "Have a good night, you." Gloria turned back, leaned into the car with one hand braced on the roof. "I'm going to run across to Aggie's for a while and finish up the prototype I started. Do you want to stop in and see it?"

"Nah. I've got an early day tomorrow. You have fun."

She'd hoped, like a child offering a crayon drawing to the teacher, for a word of praise, but she'd expected none. Guys. He didn't get the arts and crafts stuff that meant so much to her. To be fair, she had as little interest in the world of golf he'd watch for hours on TV--and maybe she shouldn't attribute it to his being a guy. She didn't get Jo's interest in *World of Warcraft* either.

The car moved away almost as the door thunked shut behind her. Instead of heading up the walk to the three-bedroom bungalow she shared with her father--who'd have passed out on the couch this late in the evening--she cut across the lawns and around to the back of Aggie's house. The climbing roses on their trellis and the scent of fresh-mown grass perfumed the mild June evening. Gloria, paused, savoring the quiet darkness. She shivered. The breeze had cooled considerably with the setting of the sun.

All the talk of moving across town was too confusing and troubling. She wouldn't just be leaving Dad. Face it, escaping the depressive aura he carried with him like a black cloud would be nice, but she'd also be leaving home. She'd be leaving the overgrown back yard where Sooty and Puzzler were buried, where memories both sweet and melancholy stirred every time she noted the place. She'd be leaving the garden where she'd planted the rose cuttings Aggie had given her. She had the sensation of standing on the deck of a ship, watching the shores of her old life begin to slip away, seeing familiar faces grow smaller. The thought threw a fist-sized ache at her, striking just below the heart.

She'd be leaving Aggie, who'd been much more than a good neighbor to her since Mom died. She wouldn't see as much of Aggie or the ever-present Greg. It would be a lot harder to work on her and Aggie's joint projects if it meant driving across town.

Silly. She wouldn't say goodbye. She'd still come around, still visit Dad, still work with Aggie. Maybe she wouldn't do it as often as she liked. What if her life carried her in a new direction and she drifted away from her old life, her old friends? Well, that would be sad, but life got sad sometimes, right? Partings were unavoidable. She'd said goodbye to her mother, to her pets, and moved on. She could do this. Ignore the ache. It would pass.

Gloria gave a quick rap at Aggie's kitchen door before pushing it open and entering.

☆☆★☆☆

"What a dork." Gloria glanced up from cutting rounded rectangular shapes out of clear vinyl as Channel 11's News at Eleven cut to an artist's rendering of the witnesses' descriptions. It showed a comic book hero in a red leotard. Ridiculous.

A ten-year-old boy talked into the mic held by the on-scene reporter. "Yeah, that's him. I didn't get a good look, he moved so fast, but he's the one stopped the robbers." The boy stood in a suburban backyard, with a wading pool and a picnic table behind him.

"There you have it, folks. It seems Minneapolis can thank a Real Life Superhero for stopping this latest attempt by the Backyard Barbecue Bandits." The reporter, Bob Richards, spoke in capital letters so often they'd made a running joke of it around Aggie's worktable.

Greg muted the TV as he stood and cleared his plate from the single corner of the kitchen counter

45

left free of craft projects and supplies. "Who's a dork?" he asked. "The kid? He's just--"

"Not the kid. The guy who dresses up in a costume to make everybody think he's some kind of superhero." Gloria rolled her eyes in unassailable argument. Wasn't it obvious? Sometimes Greg seemed awfully slow for a smart guy. "People shouldn't pretend to be more than they are. You take what life hands you and you deal with it."

"But he is a hero," Aggie broke in, mild as milk with honey. She sat across from Gloria at the worktable, cutting pieces from ultra-suede in various colors. "He saved the day. Those men had guns. Somebody could have been hurt if he hadn't stepped in."

"It might have been the hero who got hurt, or he might have gotten somebody else hurt," Gloria insisted. "He should leave that sort of thing to the police. They have the training for it."

Aggie muted the competing sound of the television, leaving Gloria's voice echoing loudly in her own ears.

"The police weren't there. They can't be everywhere." Greg spoke over his shoulder in his usual matter-of-fact tones as he scraped the last bits of lasagna from his plate and turned to wash up in the sink. "I bet those people who didn't get robbed after all are glad somebody stepped in."

"Whatever." Gloria sniffed in lieu of argument, turning back to her project. No point arguing with people who didn't see something so obvious to her.

"What would a hero have to do to impress you?" Greg dropped back onto his stool and leaned across the counter toward her and his mother at the kitchen table-turned-workshop.

"I don't know. Something big. Establish world peace? Save the environment?" She waved her bit of vinyl in the air as she spoke and did nothing to hide the exasperation in her tone. Why hadn't he let the argument go the way he usually did? "Cure cancer, feed the world's poor?"

"C'mon. Even Superman couldn't do all that." His grin bared straight white teeth framed by deep dimples. Greg should grin more. Except for now, when it just annoyed her.

"That's my point. It doesn't do any good to rely on make-believe heroes." Gloria frowned to show him how seriously he should take her. "There are too many problems in the world. Every one of us needs to be out there every day, doing everything we can. It takes all of us to deal with it."

What was up with Greg? He didn't usually bother to argue. Gloria looked him over. Same as usual. Same scruffy, too long hair. He'd spilled lasagna on his plaid button-down shirt and left a stain near the collar.

Greg laughed. Laughed at her.

"You're taking this too seriously," he said, brushing aside a lock of stray hair from across his eyes. "Some guy in a costume stops a robbery and you think it's a bad thing? You think he's somebody to make fun of?"

"It looks silly." She turned back to cutting the final corner on her carefully shaped bit of vinyl as if turning aside should settle the matter.

"You say the same when it comes to anything out of the ordinary." Greg leaned closer across the counter. "But you know what, Gloria?" He waited until she met his unusually intense gaze, "Being silly or being out of the ordinary doesn't make it a bad thing."

☆☆★☆☆

Greg grinned to himself as he crossed through the backyard to the garage. The surrounding trees shaded the yard to deepest night but his feet knew the way. He should probably be more upset. Gloria had called him a dork after all, but he'd been used to the same kind of talk from her since they were kids.

Funny how she wanted to deny anything special in a guy who moved so fast no one saw him. Funny the way she so badly wanted everything to be practical and predictable that she didn't appreciate something out-of-the-world extraordinary when it appeared in her own hometown. She'd seen the laws of the physical universe transcended like hundreds of years of science meant nothing, and what did she focus on? A silly costume.

At least she'd stopped in after her date. He found it strangely reassuring to know she'd be going home and sleeping alone in her own bed tonight.

Entering his apartment, Greg threw his keys down on the counter dividing the kitchenette from the main room of the small space. He'd been in the habit of forgetting to lock up when he went to the main house to see Aggie, but today's adventures served notice of the criminal element operating in town. Before tonight, he'd never witnessed a crime in progress. Crimes might be reported on the news every day, but they'd never seemed real before this.

Reviewing student papers at super speed had taken a fraction of the usual time, although some of the pages ended up singed from friction fires he quickly smothered. Greg needed an explanation for Professor Morrissey. He'd say he'd set them down too near the stove. At any rate, he'd finished in plenty of time to join Aggie for a late supper of leftover lasagna.

He eyed the stack of newly graded papers piled at one end of the coffee table. The charred patches hardly showed, but, yeah, friction fires went in the "minuses" column in assessing the usefulness of super speed. Add the wake of debris he stirred up behind himself whenever he went all out. He'd heard of tornadoes driving a straw through solid wood. Or was that an urban legend? What if the wind of his passing put someone's eye out with a straw, or some other bit of detritus?

He slumped onto the love seat, all he'd been able to fit into the tiny apartment to serve as a couch. Growing up in Aggie's pacifist household hadn't prepared him for dealing with violent men or situations. He didn't regret stopping the criminals, but his own ferocity in the process alarmed him. A sick taste rose to his throat as he remembered the sound when he'd yanked the guns from the robbers' hands--those finger bones snapping like so many dried twigs. It came back to mind like an accusation of brutality. If the robbers got lawyers and learned his identity, they'd probably sue him. Another good reason for secret identities.

He'd enjoyed super speed, but it included too much unintended havoc, and everything he did ended before he got half a chance to enjoy the good parts. As much as he'd liked running across the surface of Lake Calhoun--even his dunking had been kind of fun--he'd better try something different in the way of superpowers.

How was he supposed to contact Serafina? He wasn't wearing the costume hood with the built-in radio. He needed to talk to her about this.

He hitched his butt off the couch, digging in the front pocket of his slacks for the business card she'd given him. He drew it out, slightly foxed and bent but still legible, though it included no contact information whatsoever. He tapped it a couple times, flummoxed.

"So how do I reach you?" he muttered.

"You only need ask." She sat on the chair opposite him, still clad in her lace-trimmed purple suit and the hat with its jaunty feather.

Greg levitated a few inches. "Jesus!"

She tsked. "I won't tolerate profanity, young man." The corners of her smile drew into a disapproving moue.

"Fairy godmothers are Christians?" He settled back in his seat.

"That has nothing to do with it. It's a matter of respect for your elders." She pulled herself even more upright, lace-gloved hands folded before her.

"Sorry, ma'am. You startled me." Best to humor her.

"That's better." She twinkled at him again. "You wanted to speak with me?"

Oh yeah. "Right. The super speed was great, but it's not quite the right thing for me. It's too easy to cause accidents at high speed."

"Say no more, dear boy." She held up a dainty hand. "It's gone. Did you have something else in mind?"

"I'm not sure yet." Maybe he should have thought this through before calling her. Only he hadn't realized he was calling her. Why pursue this whole mad idea anyway? He'd been crazy to think a superpower would impress Gloria. He did have a life of his own. Why not leave this stuff to the police? But, those people the robbers held at gunpoint looked so relieved when he'd stopped the robbery, and those kids seemed so impressed. It had been kind of fun to foil the gunmen without them seeing him. It felt good to be able to help. Just remembering made him feel a bit taller, a bit stronger, a bit closer to being an actual hero.

When he'd been a kid, he'd daydreamed about what he'd do with superpowers. He'd taken the comics as his guide. Heroes stopped criminals. They stopped monsters and super villains. There wasn't much call for defense against monsters and super villains here in the Twin Cities, and today was the first time he'd ever encountered actual criminals in the area. What kind of superpower would be most useful here and now?

He mused aloud, "Maybe I could figure out what people need from a superhero if I were able to go around invisibly and observe things, see what kinds of problems come up, and then maybe foil crimes without doing any damage in the process."

"That's very thoughtful of you, dear." She smiled like a teacher approving a clever child.

"Thanks." Though, who knew what he might learn as an unseen observer that he wouldn't learn by paying attention to the people around him? At least he'd do less damage invisibly than he'd done moving at Mach whatever it'd been.

"You're very welcome. Now say 'Zone Out' to activate your power and 'See Ya' to return to normal."

"Okay, then. No costume this time, I guess?" Greg chuckled, trying to visualize it.

"Oh, there is." Her smile brightened her tone. "But no one will see it." Her words echoed over the empty chair.

Chapter 4

Gloria unlocked the back door as quietly as possible. Dad had probably passed out by now and it would be easiest if she didn't wake him...but the key scraped in the lock, and jangled against the others on her keychain as she pushed into the house, and the hinges creaked as usual. It didn't matter, with the television blaring from the living room. The news by the sound of it.

"That you, Glory?" Dad's voice, shaky, with a whining edge.

"Yeah, Dad. You still awake?" Not that she suspected him of talking in his sleep. She made her way through the kitchen and dining room to the front of the house where her father kept his usual post on the sofa in front of the television.

Ike Torkenson looked older than his actual age, with his deeply lined face, thinned hair gone gray, a big man who'd shrunken in on himself after injury stopped him from working in construction. He seldom bothered to shave and tonight made no exception, leaving his chin heavily stubbled in gray. Gloria breathed shallowly. He wore the same worn jeans and flannel shirt he'd worn yesterday and it seemed he hadn't bothered to bathe today.

"Why're you getting in so late?" Not looking at Gloria, he leaned forward over the coffee table, chose a beer can and waggled it, then another, until he found one in which some liquid sloshed.

"It's not late." She kept her tone light, but loud enough to cut across the weather report. "I went for an early dinner with Pete and his parents, then stopped by Aggie's and worked on a project for a while." She kept moving, hanging her jacket in the front closet, placing the portfolio of her sketches on the end table beside the wing chair also facing the television. She stood over the chair and looked at the TV screen without seeing it. She held herself braced like a dam against her own reactions.

"Pete's parents, huh?" Ike hitched around to face her squarely.

"Yes. They're nice people." Here it came.

"Bet they are. Too nice for the likes of us. You'll see." He frowned and drained the last bit of liquid from the can he'd found. "People pretend to like you, to be nice, but they don't think you're any better than you are. Like Aggie next door. When's the last time she invited me over? No. Last time she says, 'You clean up your act, Ike, or don't come over.' Thinks she's better than me. Probably mad cuz your mom, Evie, her good friend was killed while I got drunk at your birthday party."

Any attempt at talking seriously to Dad hit her like dashing through a hard, cold rain. Time to shake off the results yet again.

"Dad, you say the same thing whenever you have too many beers, which is every dang day. Aggie doesn't blame you. She doesn't like your drinking. Neither do I, and Pete's folks are not too nice for me." Fretting for something to do, Gloria sat in the wing chair and pulled her portfolio of sketches onto her lap. "They seemed perfectly happy to welcome me to their family. They're Episcopalian. Pete's mother is real active in the church."

"Episcopalian, huh? Churchgoers? Think you're going to fit in with them?" He glanced at the coffee table, as if wondering whether he'd find another can still holding a few drops.

She plucked at the zipper of the leather case on her lap. *Do not engage.* "Why shouldn't I?"

"Why should you? What do you know about their sort? What do they care about our sort?" His voice mimicked the scorn such people must feel for her. "A girl quits college after one semester, marrying their boy with his business degree?"

She turned to him, sick of his same old crap. She could shake off only so much before it soaked her to the bone and she had to deal. "Stop it. I quit college to take care of you. You couldn't do for yourself after the accident."

"Yeah." His remaining gnarled hand clutched the worn-shiny arm of the sofa. He scowled at her. "Rub that in."

"I'm not." Why did he always get so defensive? "It's just the way things went. But now, when I want to get married, you make like I'm not good

55

enough, like you want to stop my chance at happiness."

"I still need help," he muttered, so quietly she had to strain to catch the words.

Hopelessness, almost despair, crossed his stubbled face, tugging at her heart. Wasn't that exactly what had kept her at home, stalled her career for these past few years while Greg finished college and went on to grad school?

"Poor daughter you are," he went on. "You'll move away and leave me on my own. You don't care what happens to your old worthless papa."

"You're not being fair, Dad. You know perfectly well how much I care. Didn't I leave college to help you? I wanted my art degree, and now you throw it back in my face. Like I'm not good enough for Pete because I have less education?" She glared at him, surprising herself with the bitterness souring her tone. Sometimes she resented him, but resented herself more for the heart that trapped her here. If it were a paw, she'd chew it off.

He opened his mouth to speak, but she charged ahead. "Well, you're not as helpless as you make out. You got your prosthetic four and a half years ago. I helped when you needed it, when you first lost your arm, but you've had plenty of time to adjust and you'd be able to get along fine if you hadn't given up on yourself. Look at Aggie. Look at how much she does." She gestured in the general direction of the house next door.

"Don't you hold her up to me." He slammed his empty can down with a clatter on the coffee table.

"She's had MS her whole life and never knew different. What am I worth if I can't do the only work I ever knew?" With some fire in his eyes, at least he didn't look so helpless. Ah.

"Dad, do you want me to believe you're an idiot who can't learn a new skill to save his life? Or to give his only daughter a life of her own?"

With a jerk of his shoulder, he turned back to the glowing screen.

Gloria looked to see what he found so interesting.

They'd gotten actual footage of the guy in the red costume. Jeez. He ran across the surface of a lake like an ordinary person would run over solid ground. The first clip showed only a red streak. The slo-mo version followed immediately. The camera zoomed in on the man, moving like a great cat, well-muscled limbs sliding through the air like water sluicing over a dam. The rippling play of muscle under skintight red fabric fascinated her. Whatever had been next on her mental agenda never made it to the surface of thought. Not too dorky after all, until he stopped, slid bouncing across the water and slumped beneath the surface like a skipped stone, all in slow motion.

She laughed, along with her father, the old issues forgotten for the moment.

☆☆★☆☆

It must have been some kind of trick. Gloria sat on the edge of her quilt-covered bed among a pile of pillows and brushed her hair, teasing out the tangles her blond curls loved to get into. Nobody could run across the surface of a lake. It must be some publicity stunt. Someone staged the whole thing. She tried to imagine how. People on water skis traveled across the surfaces of lakes all the time.

She shook out the now shinier curls on the right side of her face. No, that wouldn't explain the speed--he'd just been a red streak until they slowed down the footage. Maybe it was a trick of the cameras. She hadn't been there in person. She started the fifty strokes to the tresses on the left. Yeah. It had to be some publicity stunt, film students trying to prove something, play a joke. Publicity for some movie, maybe. Maybe this guy in the red costume had an underwater accomplice. Someone pacing the runner, staying under him with a submersible something.

A comforting thought. Her momentary conviction that the truly impossible had happened, something beyond understanding, made the whole world seem flimsy as a stage set. If a person couldn't rely on the world to behave the way it was supposed to behave, what could she rely on? What else might happen? Anything might be real, anything at all.

If she allowed superheroes, that opened the door to super villains. If the laws of physics didn't apply, the whole world might come undone. Her familiar bedroom might melt away like a dream. Everything could go floating off into space, or dissolve in a mist. Didn't some people believe the world to be an illusion anyhow? *Maya,* that's what the Hindus called it. She set her boar-bristle brush on the bedside table and shook her head with abandon, shaking the wild thoughts away, shaking her shining curls into a single mass, and then ran her fingers through it to be sure she'd gotten out all the tangles.

Yes. Clearly, someone pulled some cinematic trickery. But that guy, the one in the costume... Wow. A frisson of delight shimmered through her at the remembered vision of him in motion and the supple flow of his well-defined muscles. She needed little imagination to guess what lay beneath his revealing, skin-tight costume. His legs had moved like pistons in a well-oiled machine. The sight ran on a continuous loop through her mind's eye. Imagine running her hands over those pumping limbs, sliding along his arms, down his sides to waist and thighs, or facing him and cupping his strong jaw between her hands as he moved.

She sighed. The shimmer deepened, shivering through her limbs, stirring where they shouldn't for a woman engaged to someone else.

Mmm. She snuggled in under the quilt and top sheet. She wasn't married yet, or dead.

☆☆★☆☆

Tuesday morning, Greg carried the front wheel of his Trek bike with him tucked under his arm as he entered the lab on the fourth floor of the University's Computer Sciences building. He leaned the wheel against the wall behind the front desk. The rest of the bike stayed chained to the bike rack on the front plaza. He didn't usually take the double precaution.

As a teaching assistant to Professor Morrissey, Greg got his own key to the computer lab and his own locked drawer in the front desk. Classes might be over for the semester, but end-of-term business didn't end with delivering the batch of final exam papers he'd dropped in the professor's in-box on his way to the lab.

Now was his chance to check out the invisibility thing. He'd been too tired after Serafina vanished last night. This morning he'd been concerned with getting to campus and delivering those papers to the professor first thing. Now, before any of the other grad students turned up to use the lab, made a perfect opportunity for testing his transformation. He'd go out on the campus, try wandering unseen among others and still have time to get back.

He stowed his empty book bag in his drawer and glanced around the lab. Morning sunshine slanted in across rows of tables bearing monitors and CPUs snaked together with lengths of cable. Everything seemed in order, but he walked down the rows to make sure people had powered down all the unused equipment. He adjusted the blinds to keep the sunshine from falling directly across any of the screens.

Standing at the window, looking out over the quad and past neighboring buildings, Greg spoke the magic words, "Zone Out."

He didn't feel any different. He lifted his hands before his face and they failed to appear. No legs or feet, only the bare linoleum floor and the power strip running along the nearest row of tables. On seeing nothing where his parts should be, a flash of vertigo hit him. Forget looking for a mirror.

"Weird." At least he heard his own voice. He turned back to the room. Invisible feet shouldn't trip him up. He could maneuver around obstacles as long as he saw them. Everything around him remained perfectly visible, though it shouldn't, logically. If his eyes were transparent to light, how did his retinas capture an image? He had no idea how this magical stuff worked. At this point he'd take it as it came, amass data first, analyze later-- despite his temptation to experiment on himself.

Voices sounded in the outer hall. Someone approaching. A key turned in the locked door to the lab.

Will and Eric. Greg stood quietly in place, back to the windows without blocking any of the morning light. Will entered ahead of Eric, who struggled for a moment to free his key from the door.

Both of his fellow Teaching Assistants were in their mid-twenties, near Greg's age, but there the similarities to him and each other ended. Eric, the shorter and stockier of the two, wore his light-brown hair trimmed close to his scalp. He caught up to the slightly built, tall, bearded and bespectacled Will at the first row of computers.

Will continued talking the whole time. "But quantum theory states they're only probably there, so each Eigen state in a quantum computer might potentially hold--"

"I heard enough about this in class, genius. When are you going to remember your Magic decks? You promised me a rematch."

"One of these days," Will drawled. "Did you remember the extra blank disks?"

"No." Eric looked around the apparently empty lab, nodded to the front desk. "I'll bet Greg's got some in his drawer."

"Yeah, but it'll be locked. Now who's the genius?" Will had mastered the art of the vocal sneer.

Eric brandished his set of keys, jangling them. "I've got the drawer above his. If I unlock it, pull it out half-way and reach under I can manually turn the latch on his." He spoke as he went around the desk.

Greg stood frozen at the windows. Interesting. Which was worse? His own eavesdropping or the guy breaking into his locked drawer to steal from him?

"You sound awfully sure that'll work." Will trailed after Eric.

"Empirical methodology." Eric shrugged. He unlocked and opened his drawer, bent, fumbled around for a moment. Greg moved closer, edging along the windowed wall for a better vantage. Eric opened Greg's drawer, lifted aside the limp book bag and pulled out a package of new writable disks.

"Neat trick." Will reached for the package, "Greg won't mind if we borrow a few."

Yeah, that's why I keep them in a locked drawer. Greg clenched his jaw to keep from speaking.

"Oh, just keep 'em." Eric closed Greg's drawer, reached under his own half-opened one, probably latching Greg's lock. He closed and locked the upper drawer. "He'll never know. The space case will think he used 'em himself, and go buy some more."

"Well, if you think so..." Something like guilt crossed Will's face before he took the package and headed for the computers.

"I think so. Let's get to work, here." Eric headed out from behind the desk, crossing in front of Greg, whose invisible foot extended, seemingly of its own volition, just in time for Eric to stumble over it.

"What the hell." Eric lurched forward, and would have fallen on his face if he hadn't caught the edge of a table. He righted himself, looked back to the desk, scanning up and down. "What'd I trip over?"

"I don't know. Your own foot?" Will looked over from a computer station another row down.

Eric shook his head and muttered something too low to hear, but turned to follow.

Greg held his breath until both passed out of earshot. What had he been thinking? He might have been caught. But so what? It wasn't a crime to be invisible. Eric had stolen from him. That was a crime. Greg had been buying more disks, adapters, cable and other small bits of hardware than he'd been using. It'd never occurred to him he couldn't trust his fellow grad students. Maybe eavesdropping was wrong, but it didn't compare to theft.

Surprised at the heated tone of his own inner voice, he took a deep breath. *Let it go.* He had data to collect. Greg managed to exit the lab without knocking into anything or making noise. Fortunately, his fellow TAs had left the lab door standing open.

Now to check out the campus--with maybe a brief stop in the men's room. Greg averted his eyes as he passed the mirrors over the sinks. He'd seen a couple different movie versions of *The Invisible Man*. By his theory, the title character's eventual descent into madness wasn't due to the chemicals. It happened because he believed if no one saw him, he wouldn't be accountable for his actions. Greg would have to keep the issue in mind to avoid falling into the same trap. Easier to do if he avoided mirrors showing nobody there.

He'd gotten as far as the first stall when a voice alerted him. He wasn't alone. He'd treaded softly even after leaving the lab, not wanting to spook anyone with the sound of disembodied footsteps, and the door to the men's room had closed silently behind him. Whoever spoke in hushed tones in the stall at the far end of the row must not have heard him come in.

"I'm telling you, I need more time." The man's voice rose in both pitch and volume. "The projects aren't complete. End of Term just applies to the undergrads. Don't you want the whole package?"

Greg backed quietly to the door. He entered again, this time striding in, making some noise before taking a stall. The man in the end stall fell silent. Good. Greg didn't want to be guilty of nosing into somebody else's private business, even inadvertently. The other guy flushed and departed before Greg finished his own business.

After the pit stop, Greg made his way downstairs. What good was an invisible superhero here? He looked over the shoulders of students studying at the scattered tables in the open area where four floors of the building bellied up to the slanted skylight windows above.

When he found someone on the wrong track with a problem, he waited until they got up or turned away. Frustrated students had a tendency to head for the snack wagon or the restrooms. He circled the problem area, highlighted a statement or turned the pages of the textbook to the section offering a clue. He might as well be visible if he wanted to act as a study aide, just talk to people directly.

Greg visited the snack wagon and wiped down some surfaces the busy attendant hadn't had a chance to polish, but the fellow seemed to have everything else well in hand. Might as well venture outside and see what else he could do.

Considering how many had finished with both their classes and finals, a lot of people remained on campus. It looked like most of them had come to the quad in front of Northrup Auditorium. The June day beamed sunshine on people lying out with books, playing Frisbee, standing or sitting around on the lawns in groups chattering like flocks of birds, or sprawled under oaks burgeoning with leaves already near their full growth.

First test: walk from one side of the area to the other without bumping anyone. Harder than it might sound, considering the people darting around after the Frisbee and those who chatted as they walked together, hardly noticing the entirely visible people around them.

He'd made it nearly halfway across the lawn when a girl jumped to her feet and raced in Greg's direction after a sheet of paper flying, dipping and turning in the air. It had too much of a start on her and seemed in danger of being whipped into the path of an oncoming light rail train rushing up Washington Avenue.

He easily caught a corner of the page and whirled around, guiding its flight on an almost natural looking path, to secure it among the shrubs lining one of the walkways between buildings.

"Oh, thank God!" The girl caught up to the restrained sheet of paper and tweaked it free from among the new leaves and twigs.

God huh? Smiling, Greg looked over the young woman's shoulder. The sketch captured an oak's limbs in bold lines contrasting with the careful detailing of the textures of bark and budding leaves.

He stood still as she returned to a sketchpad and the jacket still marking her place on the lawn. Most of the undergrads looked hardly more than children to him these days. This girl reminded him of Gloria back in their middle school days, a fresh-faced blonde whose lively features clearly showed her dismay when the sketch flew from her and her relief when it caught in the bushes.

He'd have been just as capable of helping her if he'd been visible, and the artist might have thanked him and struck up a conversation rather than thanking God. Yet, in the act of helping her maybe he'd taken on the role of God's assistant, playing the invisible helping hand, making things a little better even if he got no credit or recognition for his deed. Should this count as a pro or a con for invisibility?

The question warranted further investigation.

Greg took only a few steps further onto the quad before halting at a sharp buzzing in his ears. Putting a hand to one ear, he asked, "Serafina?"

"Yes, dear. This is urgent. Go at once to the middle of the pedestrian level of the Washington Avenue Bridge."

"Why?"

"Now. The young man is planning to jump."

Greg's gaze shot across the green lawns of the mall to Washington Avenue. The road ran east-west across a bridge spanning the Mississippi and linking the main campus to the west bank, the law school, art school, library and other buildings.

He ran. Not as fast as yesterday by any means, but biking had given him strong legs and good wind. He treated the people in his way as mere obstacles. He dodged around a gaggle of coeds ambling toward the auditorium. He ducked aside from a young man who dove across his path for the Frisbee. No one reacted. No one saw him, but his steps thudded on the earth and sidewalks and the impact of his feet pounded through him. His heart thumped double-time and his breath rasped in his ears. At the far side of the quad, he jumped over a sunbathing woman in shorts and halter-top. He hurdled the low wall and bike rack bordering the sidewalk to the pedestrian level of the bridge.

He sprinted to the bridge. Go right? Or to the left of the covered central walkway? A jumper would have to be at one of the outer rails, right? Breath coming faster now, Greg spotted a small crowd gathered on the upriver side of the walkway, half-way across the bridge's span. They formed a half-circle a respectful distance from a figure perched precariously outside the railing...

The river stretched wide between its banks at this point, murky water curling lazily below. Far below. Greg put on a burst of extra speed. People had died here before, after jumping from this bridge. He ignored the broad vista of the winding water and the tree-covered slopes below as he pounded down the walkway, dodging others headed the same way. He narrowly avoided a bicyclist. Maybe some remnant of his super speed remained, but it seemed to take too long to cover the remaining distance. Greg shoved past a man in the half-circle crowd to reach the guy who'd climbed out over the railing.

"Hey!" The shoved man looked around, scowling like a bulldog.

The thin young man outside the railing seemed hardly more than a boy. He startled at the shout, and wavered, leaning out over the river. Facing the water below, only a white-knuckled grip on the railing behind him kept him from falling. Clad in a worn white t-shirt and jeans, his blond hair lank, the potential jumper's baby face looked drawn and pale with strain.

At his lurch, the crowd gasped, swaying forward as one. The next moment the young man cried out and everyone stilled.

"Don't come any closer." He looked out at the crowd through eyes showing the full circle of their whites.

Greg moved unseen inside the circle of watchers. He paused, steadying himself with one hand on the steel rail until he quieted the harsh rasp of his breath. He inched ahead, keeping to one side, approaching the young man from behind.

"Donny!" A dark-haired man with a stubbled chin called out from the edge of the crowd nearest the railing. "What's going on? C'mon away from there and we can talk. This isn't cool."

With Donny momentarily distracted, Greg edged nearer. Donny didn't see him, but Greg moved with care to make sure he didn't make any sudden noise and startle him.

"I failed." Donny's voice rose in a wail. "Don't you get it, Toby? It's over for me."

"Hey, it's not over." Toby took a step toward them.

"I'll jump!" Donny shrieked and Toby froze. "One more step and I swear I jump. It is over. No med school for me. Not with my Chem grades. That's it. Nada. Nothing. There's nothing for me..."

His voice trailed off and he slumped forward as if he'd lost his last drop of strength. His knuckles, white with gripping the railing, relaxed visibly.

Abandoning caution, Greg jumped toward him just in time to catch Donny's T-shirt collar when he started to fall from the rail toward the muddy waters churning so far below.

When his collar cut into his throat, Donny choked and straightened, arching back, and Greg managed to shift his grip, catching the young man under his arms. He strained, grunted, hauling the surprisingly heavy young man backward over the railing.

Greg didn't stop to wonder what it must look like to the crowd: some invisible force hauling the boy from the brink of death. He pulled Donny back and lowered him, unresisting, to the sidewalk. He might have succeeded at his jump for all the life he showed now. As if loosed from a spell, everyone else finally surged toward the rail.

Greg jumped away from the rush. He ducked aside to avoid being trampled when a woman who'd been further along the railing hurried to the fallen Donny. Greg suffered a few knocks before he managed to get outside the crowd--at least no one knocked him off his feet in their eagerness to help. He backed farther away at the sound of sirens wailing on the road below the pedestrian level of the bridge. The police would be here soon. He should get going.

Greg had ample opportunity to practice his dodging skills, avoiding police and an emergency medical team making their way to Donny along the crowded walks. He returned to the Computer Sciences building at a much more leisurely pace than he'd taken to reach the bridge.

He hoped Donny got whatever help he needed to keep him from going back to the bridge some night when there'd be no one around to stop him. Of course Donny would get help. Obviously, he had people who cared for him, that Toby fellow, all the strangers who'd been ready to help. He must have family and other friends. Greg had done his part. The rest would be up to others.

Gloria was right about one thing. The world couldn't rely on superheroes to solve all its problems. The whole Justice League of America wouldn't be enough for the job. Still, she might have been surprised and gratified to see how many people had stepped forward wanting to help when somebody needed it.

He'd be curious to hear what the reporters said about this one. No one knew his part in Donny's rescue. What would they make of it? A surge of adrenaline and Donny's unconscious self-preservation instincts? They wouldn't commend any superhero for this one.

The whole episode was kind of a bust, as far as becoming a romantic hero for Gloria's sake. Although that didn't seem like such a big deal at the moment. In fact, he felt kind of good. If druggies got a high like this from their various substances he kind of understood the attraction.

Cursing, he stumbled aside as a bicyclist approaching from behind nearly ran him down.

Chapter 5

Gloria sent out the invitation to Friday's staff meeting and minimized Notes. So far, so good for this morning's calendaring tasks. She'd triaged Mr. Carlson's email and updated the Research Documentation Procedures file with the changes he'd requested. He wouldn't be back to the office until after lunch. She sat up straighter in her swivel chair, stretched and looked around her workstation. Her cubicle stood near the window outside Mr. Carlson's office, where she liked to gaze out at the sky when she got the chance, and at the surrounding buildings and the small corner park twelve floors below.

She opened her web browser. This was her chance to update the Cell Shells website. Aggie had formatted pics of the new designs for the web last night. Gloria would just download the image files from her thumb drive.

She'd gotten the process down to a science, setting up new pages for their site, inserting images and product descriptions and modifying the PayPal code for each new item. She did it without thinking, letting her mind wander for the first time since getting to the office this morning. As usual, it wandered to thoughts of the future. To her happy dream of what it would be like to be married and move away from home, to be part of a nice family where people didn't fall asleep drunk on the couch in the living room.

She could kick herself for letting Dad talk her into staying at home, saving money, rather than getting an apartment of her own. While she did have the refuge of Aggie's house and their craft-work, the housing arrangement sucked her vital energy like a mosquito sucked blood. Maybe it made her an evil, selfish person, but she didn't want to play governess and housekeeper to a grown man who'd given up on his own life long ago.

She felt like thin cloth torn down the middle. She loved her home, her neighbors, the place she'd always lived. Yet she didn't want to dwell in her father's miasma of not-giving-a-damn. She didn't want to live with his unsubtle messages that she deserved no better. The constant struggle to keep from giving in and agreeing with him took too damn much work.

Things would be different with Pete. He cared enough to keep things nice and keep himself up. He kept his apartment pristine. He probably made a better housekeeper than she did. Of course his place seemed kind of bare, seemed like he didn't own anything not strictly utilitarian. She'd enjoy bringing some homey touches to the house they'd get together.

She'd love to make curtains modeled after the page she'd marked in her *Better Homes & Gardens Home Decorating* magazine. She'd use the pretty Madras print she'd found during her last visit to the fabric store, and make matching throw pillows and choose a nice pallet of colors for paint and wallpaper. Their place would have an extra room for her home office slash workroom, and the house would be in good repair. Not like home, where anything she couldn't fix by herself stayed broken, the gate on the back fence, the leak in the porch roof, and the stuck garage door.

She sighed as she pasted the PayPal code for the final sample--the black leatherette, with sample text saying *World's Best Dad*--into the HTML page. Maybe she and Aggie would start pulling in real money. Then she'd be able to do her craftwork full time from home. Not that being an administrative assistant for ABM's Research and Development Department Head constituted a bad thing. Mr. Carlson was easy to work for, easy to keep happy. But maybe that was the problem. The job didn't challenge her.

She could keep up with the demands of her job and make daily updates to the Cell Shells site and do sketches for new designs and take time to gab with Jo or with Kathleen's administrative assistants while she was at it. Shouldn't she be doing work that took everything in her power to give?

Her phone buzzed. Gloria caught sight of the extension number on the unit's display. *Speak of the devil.*

"Gloria? Hi." Jo had a way of talking like letting you in on a private joke--it gave Gloria a lift just to hear her voice. "How's everything with y'all in R&D?"

"Oh, hi, Jo. I'm good. It's all good. What's up?" Gloria settled back in her chair, swiveling gently side-to-side, crossing her ankles as she stretched out her legs.

"A couple things. I ordered the cake, it will come out of the HR budget, but you'll have to pick it up. Will you have time before the party?"

"Sure. If we go out for lunch I could pick it up on the way back."

"On the way?" Jo laughed. "I suppose. If we get lunch in Uptown, Gelpe's Bakery might conceivably be on the way."

Gloria chuckled. They'd never get back downtown from Uptown in the time allotted for lunch. "Now that you mention it. I still need to pick up a card for Ron too."

"Good luck tearing him away from his project long enough to attend his own birthday party."

"I've got my people trained." Gloria buffed her nails against her blouse. "Celebrations take priority. So, what was the other thing?"

"Oh, I just wanted to ask you about some missing 1099 tax forms. Maybe they're done and not entered into the system yet?"

"I entered the 1099 forms into tracking back in January." Gloria straightened in her chair, turning back to the computer, bringing up Excel. Maybe she had overlooked some? "Which ones are missing?"

"I started running a report on our own employees and forgot to filter out the contractors, or I'd never have noticed we don't have tax forms for the Inspired Logic Corporation or IntelligentD-Zine. Kathleen lists them as resources for some of her projects."

"Oh. That explains it." Gloria relaxed again, shifting the phone to her other ear. "Kathleen takes care of the forms for her contractors. I just do the forms for Don's contractors and the regular 1044s for our in-house research team."

"Ah. I'll call her about it, then." Jo sighed through the line. "Or, more likely, leave her a message and never hear back. I swear that woman never holds still."

"Yeah." Gloria grinned at the understatement. Kathleen Pedersen seemed to live for her job, fully involved and always on the go. She should be as involved in her own work. "Where shall we go for lunch, then?"

☆☆★☆☆

Ambling back along the route he'd raced before, Greg considered his options for the day. He still needed to meet with Professor Morrissey and get some lab work done this morning. He'd had enough of the invisibility thing. Even now he had a hard time concentrating while keeping a constant lookout for bicyclists and random Frisbee players.

Just to escape them, he cut across the lawns. They spread like a long green carpet running between Northrup Auditorium and Washington Avenue, flanked by the classic old red brick academic buildings with their white-pillared porticos. Despite enabling him to save Donny, invisibility had too many drawbacks to want to keep it for his superpower.

On his way back to the Church Street entrance of the Computer Sciences building, in the relatively narrow walkway between buildings, he dodged a couple more bicyclists, but once inside he relaxed vigilance. He might like to lose himself in the world, to observe how people lived when they thought no one was around--if he didn't feel so embarrassed by playing voyeur--but he needed to stand out. Invisible hands didn't get noticed and Gloria would never notice him while more invisible to her than ever.

Half the morning had slipped away and he had yet to meet with Professor Morrissey. His advisor would need his help on a few more end-of-term tasks, work perfectly possible for Greg to do without the addition of any magical superpowers and work that would produce at least a nod of recognition.

Greg found the main reception area of the department deserted. He made his way past the front desk to the hallway where the professors' offices were located. He spotted Professor Morrissey standing in the open door to his office, talking with Professor Stevens. Greg approached them and stood politely by, waiting for his advisor to finish his conversation and notice him.

The conversation turned a dark corner without either of them seeming to notice him. *Oh, right. They don't see me. I'm invisible.*

"You can't do this," Professor Morrissey said, voice rising as if he'd breathed helium. "I'll go to the Dean."

"You don't want to do that," Professor Stevens drawled. "A man with your habits. I might have to speak to your wife…"

"Cora knows worse about me than a little flirtation with an undergrad."

"I saw you at Rick's place." Stevens smiled like a wolf looming over its prey. "Your wife might understand a coed, she might even understand the 'coed' being a boy half your age, but maybe she won't understand the drugs. I'm pretty sure if we speak to the Dean, he won't be so understanding about any of it."

"I don't want to shout my affairs from the rooftops." Morrissey stiffened, voice turning cold. "But I'm not hurting anyone with my after-school activities. Selling students' research before they can publish their results will ruin their chances at grant money. You're talking about destroying the futures of our students."

Stevens made a brushing-off motion. "The same people who are buying from me will probably hire them right out of grad school. Think about it, I go down, you go down."

Greg stood frozen. Too late to avoid hearing way more than he wanted to hear. Way too late to sneak away and return openly, pretending everything was normal. He couldn't ignore this. His own research might be at risk, his own grant application, and those of his friends. Morrissey was right about one thing. If someone published the stolen research first, it would set a student's career back, possibly by years.

He and the other graduate Teaching Assistants had research projects continuing through summer session. His project consisted of preliminary simulations testing integration of laser technology with computer processing, and would form the basis for his grant proposal.

Even after Eric's larcenous behavior earlier, Greg wouldn't want him losing his work, let alone anyone he liked better losing theirs. While Morrissey had always seemed like a nice person, he'd have to be more than nice to throw his own career to the winds for the sake of saving the research of a few grad students.

Even now, he'd fallen silent in the face of Stevens' cold-eyed smirk.

"I see we understand each other." Professor Stevens turned away.

Greg would have to stop Stevens if Professor Morrissey wouldn't. But how? What evidence did Morrissey have of Stevens' scheme? Who was Stevens' customer? And how the heck could Greg even begin to find out?

Following Stevens around waiting for a clue was out of the question. It might be hours, or days, before the man did anything revealing. Maybe he'd better confront Morrissey for some answers. Except, he'd hate to embarrass the man by letting on how he'd overheard the conversation with Stevens. There must be another approach. Time to get visible again. He'd overheard enough should-be-private conversations to last him a lifetime.

He left the office area, found a deserted stretch of hallway and spoke aloud, "See ya."

Ah. Greg's hands and feet appeared again exactly where they should be. He'd never been so glad to see the familiar evidence of his own presence in the world. Good solid feet in their worn running shoes, good strong hands with their scattering of light brown hairs, knobby knuckles, and cleanly trimmed nails. Perhaps foolishly happy, because he'd felt them all along, he clenched his fingers and flexed them open again a few times. He ran a hand through his hair, assuring himself all his parts were still attached.

He made his way down the hall to a back stairwell, ducked through the door to pause on the landing, listened to the hollow echo of the stories-tall space for a moment before calling softly, "Serafina? Ma'am?"

"Yes, dear?" A quizzical look on her face, she stood above him on the flight of stairs leading to the next floor.

"This invisibility thing isn't working for me," he told her, reminding himself exactly why. It made him feel like a sneak is what it did. He'd rather deal with people face-to-face. Avoiding collisions with people who didn't see him made it too much work. Plus, for Gloria to see him as a hero and a man of mystery, she first had to see him.

"Say no more." Serafina winked at him. "I understand perfectly. What would you prefer?"

Good question. Sneaking might be a good way to find some answers to the questions the situation with Stevens had raised, but he should be able to handle this with some simple human detective work. The superhero business called for something more. A superhero was supposed to step in where ordinary human abilities weren't enough to save the day. A superhero had to be something out of the ordinary, and Greg had to admit he'd gotten a kick out of feeling capable of extraordinary things, like a singing in his blood. He could get used to this.

"Would it be too much to ask for the same powers as Superman? I mean, I know it's a lot--nearly everything about him is super: his strength, his perceptions, his speed."

"Not at all." Serafina raised a forefinger as if it were an exclamation point. "What an excellent idea. Very versatile. I'm sure it will prove helpful in a great many situations." She gave him a smile he might expect from a doting grandmother. "Just say 'Super-ize Me' to activate the power and 'Back to Me'" to return to normal. I think you'll like the costume. I noticed a lot of golden browns and greens in your apartment and used the same palette. Oh, I should mention, with the similar powers come similar limitations."

Before he responded, which would have required closing his gaping mouth, she'd vanished.

He closed his mouth, glancing around to find the stairwell as deserted as when he'd first entered. What did she mean by limitations? He should watch out for kryptonite? Nothing like that around here.

☆☆★☆☆

Eric and Will looked up at Greg when he returned, fully visible, to the lab. Eric stood leaning over the monitor at a station in the back of the room while Will hunched over the keyboard.

"Ah, there you are," Eric drawled. "Saw your bike wheel and thought you must be around somewhere."

"Just down in the office." Greg paused at the front desk, looking hard at Eric. He seemed different. After witnessing his trick of stealing stuff from Greg's drawer, he saw something rodent-like he'd never noticed before in Eric's features.

Eric turned back to his computer, taking no further notice of Greg.

Did Greg even know this guy? Eric attended half the same classes as Greg since they were undergrads together. They'd hung out with the same crowd, grabbing lunches and doing late night study sessions, ditching it for gaming tournaments. Had they ever talked about anything other than classwork, computers or gaming? Greg opened his drawer, grabbed his book bag, and then set himself up to work at one of the stations near the front of the room, well away from Will and Eric.

He didn't know much about Eric beyond his preference for games with a strong strategic element. Maybe he came from an underprivileged background or one where possessions were shared freely. Aggie had told him things about her commune upbringing he'd found hard to understand. Even so, taking without asking seemed an act of contempt.

Maybe Eric considered their friendship superficial and felt justified in taking things from Greg? That didn't make it okay, but Greg couldn't work himself up to be angry over it. The crime seemed too petty. Did superheroes bother with the truly petty criminals? It seemed beneath them.

Still, he didn't make any more income as a TA than Eric did and was no better able to afford to buy disks or the other equipment he needed. His needs deserved as much respect as anyone else's. Maybe a petty crime deserved a petty response.

Greg made a mental note to buy a mousetrap, then turned to concentrate on running another simulation. He managed two productive hours of work before he thought of getting some lunch.

☆☆★☆☆

"What's with the traffic?" Gloria and Jo headed to the bakery, walking from the side street where they'd finally found a spot to park. "I've never had this much trouble finding a parking spot on Hennepin Avenue."

"Some kind of parade." Jo, taller than Gloria, saw over the heads of the small crowd lining the main road.

"Let's get closer." Gloria led the way, finding gaps between the small clusters of people, some in office dress like themselves, some in slacks or jeans with shopping bags or small children in hand. They reached the street in time to see banners unfurling, accompanying a fanfare of trumpets.

"What's all this?" she asked, distracted by tumblers tumbling by, jugglers juggling their way past, and a fire-eater producing a great spout of flame as he crossed in front of them.

"Hear ye, hear ye!" A herald clad in a purple and gold tabard over purple tights stepped out in front of the similarly garbed trumpeters. He unrolled a long parchment scroll, reading from it in tones of great importance. "His majesty, King George of the Renaissance Realm declares his intent to hold court on the shores of yon Lake Calhoun. Come join in the festivities and make merry sport with us."

"Oh, fun." Jo's exclamation was half sigh. "I wish we had the time."

Gelpe's Bakery stood on the far shore of Hennepin Avenue with an entire parade flowing like a river between the curbs. Gloria resigned herself to being entertained--and late getting back to the office.

"Ooo. Belly dancers." Jo gripped Gloria's arm, pointing.

"Wow. How do they do that?" Gloria gawked at a woman who danced ahead of the others, her belt of golden coins flashing and jingling with the rapid swing of her hips, while, remarkably, she balanced a scimitar, pointy edge up, across her head of dark curls. "I'd be scared to even try--probably cut something off."

The drummers passed so close conversation became impossible. Jo nodded in time with their beat.

Behind the dancers and drummers marched a column of men and women in elaborate costume. Gloria stood fascinated by the gowns and doublets, damask corsets, floppy hats, dashing cloaks and swords, slashed sleeves, puffed sleeves, velvets, brocades and satins. She'd love to dress up like a member of the royal court, keep company with the wilder characters. A wizard strode along in flowing robes. A fairy with glittering beaded bodice and wild, out-flung wings danced by. Scurrilous pirates brandished swords and men at arms bore spears held high, their pennants catching in the spring breeze.

The King and Queen followed on horseback, surrounded by armored knights. The Queen's crown and underskirt of cloth of gold glittered in the sunshine. Gloria sighed over the ropes of (okay, probably fake) pearls, memorizing details of the elaborate sleeves and overskirt. Why didn't people dress like this anymore?

She glanced down at her sensible business-casual ensemble. "Suddenly I feel like a peasant."

"I know what you mean." Jo laughed beside her, her spiky dark hair motionless in the breeze.

Taking up the rear, an elephant followed with ponderous steps and swaying trunk. Its keeper rode in a howdah on its back. A banner hung down its sides reading, 'Free Elephant Rides at the Lake.'

"I wish we didn't have to get back to the office." Gloria pointed out the banner. "How fun would that be?"

"Maybe next time." Jo shrugged.

"Maybe there won't be a next time. I've never seen them do this before." Wishing for something she couldn't name, Gloria looked down the street to where the leaders of the parade had already turned a corner toward the lake.

"I have." Jo's green eyes gazed off at some point in her memory. "Every once in a while the Festival people put on a parade like this and do an afternoon's show at the lake." She turned back to Gloria. "It's some kind of promotional thing."

As they spoke, Gloria glimpsed some motion at the edge of the crowd. What?

A child--a little sandy-headed girl no more than three years old--pushed a baby stroller bigger than herself into the street, moving on eager feet toward the elephant. Where was the mother? A father? Gloria scanned the crowd, spotted a woman holding back a little boy who howled in protest, straining to follow the girl with the stroller. With her back to the street, the woman couldn't see what the boy reached for. The drums and pipes and trumpets of the parade made it impossible to call out and bring her attention to the stray child.

Gloria darted into the street, heading to intercept the girl with the stroller before the tot reached the elephant. The animal was probably perfectly tame, used to being around children and crowds on a regular basis, but her heart went to her throat at the sight of the tiny girl rushing toward those massive feet. The girl had a head start on her, being further down the street in the direction the parade moved, but Gloria made good time. She'd nearly reached her quarry when out of the crowd, a red Frisbee flew straight at the pachyderm's eye.

The beast reared back, lifting its trunk to block the flying object, trumpeting, throwing its surprised master from the howdah. Gloria caught up with the little girl and pulled her into her arms as the elephant dropped back to the earth, the impact shaking the ground. The beast swung its massive body and trunk back and forth as if to ward off further attacks. A thin, wailing cry rose from the stroller. The elephant's wild trunk passed within a hand's breadth of Gloria's head. Heart in throat, on watery limbs, she backed away, pulling the girl and stroller with her.

Chapter 6

When Greg's thoughts finally turned to lunch, he set his simulation to run on auto and headed up the backstairs of the Computer Engineering building. The roof would be a good place to test his new powers. On the landing to the access door he paused long enough to say, "Super-ize me," before stepping out onto the graveled surface of the roof into the sunshine and a crisp breeze.

He twisted the outer handle, making sure it wouldn't lock him out, then closed the door behind him with a gauntleted hand. Serafina had sure taken the gold and green theme to heart. He wore gloves the golden color of ripe wheat. His arms and legs were clad in some stretchy skin-tight fabric of the same color, with a slight sheen glimmering in the sunshine. He wore knee-high boots green as grass, like the jerkin covering his torso. A golden 'M' stood emblazoned on his chest. Make that a 'W,' given he saw it upside down. 'W?' What did it stand for? 'Weird?' 'Whacky?' Might he be the latest in a line of fairy godmother-created heroes, starting with A, B and C?

He flexed his toes, bouncing on them, going higher each time.

He had a craving for the scallops with cashew nuts and basil they made at Rainbow Chinese. Would it be wrong to use his new superpower for the personal advantage of getting clear across the city to his favorite restaurant in Uptown for lunch? It would save time if he didn't have to bike there, and he'd like to get as much work done as possible this afternoon.

He bent his knees deeply and jumped as high as possible, startling a pigeon whose flight path he intercepted, leaving the rooftop far below. A lot depended on whether Serafina interpreted Superman's powers according to the early years, when he only leapt tall buildings, or the later years, when he actually flew. Greg stretched himself, reaching skyward with both hands, straining for flight.

Wind whistling around his ears, he continued to ascend long after the impetus from his leap must have been exhausted. He bent slightly at the waist, angling around to level out and head west, away from the University. Flying--flying!--one arm stretched out before him.

Now this was magic, no mere function of impetus and momentum. He'd forged a whole new relationship between earth and air, between mortal man, the wind, the sky and the clouds. The wind stroked his face, touching the planes of his cheeks and jaw around the edges of his mask, combing back his hair like a lover's hand.

As if swimming, he angled himself through the supportive currents of the sky. He dove upward until he flew wrapped in the moist cloak of a cloud, and lifted to further heights still until he looked down upon the cloud towers and billows as if walking among their shimmering halls.

Wow. He passed high above the tallest buildings in downtown Minneapolis before veering south along Hennepin Avenue. The city spread below him like a quilt pieced together from the squares of neighborhoods and parks, its predominant color drawn from the greenery of trees lining the streets and filling the parks. All looked brighter and fresher and more alive than any satellite photo he'd ever seen. All right. This was great. He zoomed in on the smallest details even from this height. Telescopic vision. Probably x-ray vision, too, but he'd wait to check that out.

Looking ahead, he aimed toward his goal, seeking out the restaurant. As he hunted for a discreet place to land, he spotted some unusual activity along Hennepin Avenue. Vehicular traffic had been diverted from the road and a section extending north from Lake Street churned and glittered with what looked like a parade. From blocks away and high above, telescopic vision zeroed in on the belly dancers. He scanned the length of the route, taking in the costumes and performers, the sounds of drummers and pipes, the scents of mighty steeds--and of elephant.

As he scanned for a spot to land, a red Frisbee caught his attention. It sailed toward the pachyderm. The great beast reared up on its hind legs, trumpeting in alarm.

☆☆★☆☆

Heart pounding in her ears, breath coming short, Gloria didn't dare close her eyes as she backed away. She clutched the squirming girl protectively close, pulling the stroller and its occupant along with them. People screamed and shouted. The elephant's trainer had fallen to the street on the other side of the beast now stomping and rearing again as other members of the parade rushed toward it.

Why did those idiots wave their spears around? It scared the elephant. Bad idea. Bad, bad idea.

Backing away, her foot hit something unseen behind her. Gloria stumbled, tried to catch herself, but fell with the girl across her lap. The stroller tottered, but righted itself beside her while the infant wailed its protest.

Gloria nearly swallowed her heart as the elephant skittered sidewise, away from the men with spears, toward her and the children. No time to get out of the way. She squeezed her eyes shut. Then, as a sudden hush fell, she opened them again.

A man stood between her and the huge beast looming above. It looked like a shoving contest between him and the elephant. He stood braced with his back against the beast's foreleg.

Strain showed in every line of a beautifully muscled body clad in skin-tight gold and green. He seemed to be winning. The elephant lost traction, skidding backward as the man pushed. Gloria had never seen anything as wonderful as the hero in gold and green. The contours of his form appeared as subtly turned and unyielding as the limbs of a tree. The firm shapes of his clenched jaw and the determination in his eyes made her catch her breath. Her heart skipped a double-time beat when his gaze met hers for a moment.

While the hero held the animal in place, the trainer rushed forward and stood at the beast's head, apparently talking into its ear. The beast shied again when the men wielding spears started forward. The hero in gold and green drew a deep breath and blew out again, a gust at near hurricane force, driving back the well-meaning spearmen.

What part of the Renaissance featured comic book heroes? Gloria wasted a moment of precious time staring, mouth agape, at the impossible, incredible, wonderful man, and only then scrambled hastily to her feet. The tot she'd rescued pointed and clapped as if it were all part of the show. Gloria dragged the child away, the awkward stroller impeding her progress. It jolted over a chunk of asphalt thrusting up from the road, probably the same thing she'd tripped on before. The bump aggravated the infant's wails.

"My babies!" A harried-looking woman rushed toward her from the now cheering crowd. "Give me my babies!"

Gloria put the stroller between herself and the newcomer. She'd used her last nerve. No way was she going to deal with an over-wrought mother on top of everything else. "You're welcome," she grumbled, thrusting the stroller and girl toward the woman. Eager to escape the scene that had sent her heart scrambling for a steadier beat, Gloria turned and walked away, too overwrought to spare a glance back at her hero. Needing to touch base with the familiar and normal, she searched for Jo among the faces of strangers.

☆☆★☆☆

Whatever the trainer did at its ear, the elephant gradually grew calmer. It stopped pulling and pushing against Greg's hold. It lowered its trunk until, at last, the beast rocked placidly in place on legs as large and rough as tree trunks.

Greg stepped away and turned to find a cheering crowd. Dumbstruck, he stood frozen. What should he do? A glance around gave him the answer. Judging by the clapping and cheering, the crowd seemed to think him part of the show. He made a flourish with his arms and took a bow. The cheers grew louder.

He held up his hands, acknowledging the applause, praying for it to stop. His face grew hot. He wasn't used to this much attention. He'd always been a behind-the-scenes kind of guy.

Thinking to get the hell away from there, Greg stepped away from the pachyderm only to be swarmed by belly dancers. They draped themselves on his arms, petted every part of him in reach and crowded so close he feared it would take violence to escape them.

"Er, thanks, ladies." He found his voice. "That's very nice. I hope you'll excuse me." He edged and sidled between them, angling for freedom. "Duty calls. A hero's work is never done."

"Oh, don't go so soon," cooed a redhead in a cobalt-blue gauze skirt and golden bangles.

"No, stay. Come along to the lake," said the brunette whose thick curls hung long enough to frame her very ample cleavage.

"Please," coaxed all the blondes: short and tall and scantily clad in what seemed an entire rainbow of gauzes and silks and a plethora of finger cymbals and bells and beads.

He lightly lifted the brunette as if she weighed no more than a Chihuahua, and set her aside, managing a step forward.

"Ooo. At least tell us your name," she begged.

"Um." Name? What should he call himself? The wisdom of maintaining a secret identity seemed only too clear at the moment.

"I know." The redhead traced the golden 'W' on his chest with her forefinger, making a caress of it. "The 'W' stands for 'wonderful.' He's Mr. Wonderful!"

"No, no. That's not my name," he protested, peeling himself free of another one by picking her up and setting her aside. "You can call me Wonder Guy."

"Wonder Guy," they breathed in unison as he stepped back, eluding the reaching arms, and leaped high into the air.

☆☆★☆☆

"Are you okay? Jo asked when Gloria caught up to her on the sidewalk outside Gelpe's. "I thought that elephant would stomp you to mush."

"So did I." Gloria took a deep breath to steady her still shaky nerves. "I'll never look at Dumbo the same way again."

"Was that guy for real? It looked like he pushed the elephant away from you. Was it part of the act?"

"The elephant didn't seem to be acting." Gloria shuddered at the memory of the beast looming all too close above her. "I'd swear the guy really pushed the elephant away. It sure didn't give him any help."

"Oh wow. And what a hunk." A dreamy look crossed Jo's face. "I wonder who he is?"

"Me too." Glancing back, Gloria spotted the bevy of belly dancers surrounding the hero. Her hero.

"Why are you frowning so hard?"

"Am I?" Gloria forced a smile. "Sorry. I don't know what I was thinking."

Certainly not jealous thoughts of belly dancers. Even though the hero they petted had saved her. If anyone should get to show her gratitude, to pet and pamper him, it should be her. It wasn't fair. She sighed. She didn't have time for this. "How late are we?"

"We should have been back in the office ten minutes ago, but we might as well pick up the cake since we're here." Jo led the way to the shop.

☆☆★☆☆

Man. Greg flew with super speed to the deserted alley behind the Rainbow Chinese restaurant. No way had he been prepared for the reaction of the crowd--or those dancers. He didn't know whether to be flattered, embarrassed, titillated or horrified. Maybe all at once. Alone, he breathed easier. The pounding of his heart eased. He leaned against the brick wall behind him and said, "Back to Me."

Good. He smiled to find himself clad in his familiar button-down plaid shirt and beige slacks. He ran a hand through his hair. No more mask or gloves. Normal was good. All he wanted now was a nice normal lunch of scallops with cashew nuts and basil. But first, "Serafina?"

"Yes, dear?" There she stood beside him, wrinkling her button nose at the overfull dumpster nearby.

"This is great so far. I love flying... and the way Gloria looked at me earlier." How would he say this without offending her? "Just one thing... Didn't I say I don't want Gloria to be endangered by all this?"

"Yes, you did and I commend you for it." Serafina patted his arm, took it, steered him toward the mouth of the alley. "But I wasn't responsible for what she did, dear. Your young lady has her own ideas and her own heroic impulses. If she hadn't been there, following her own path, there's no telling what might have happened to the little girl and baby Gloria ran to save."

He'd missed that part in all the confusion. "She saved a little girl and a baby?" Gloria had put herself in danger to go after those kids? And she'd done it without any superpowers. She was the hero here.

"She kept them from being in the wrong place at the wrong time--and you were in the right place to save her when she fell. It all worked out very nicely and you got there on your own. Very good, dear." With another pat, she released his arm.

He'd only followed his impulse to go for lunch. How had he managed to be in the right place at the right time? He closed his mouth on the unasked question. Serafina had vanished again. Before he asked her what happened to the keys and wallet in his pockets when he switched to his Wonder Guy costume. A rumbling stomach reminded him he still hadn't gotten his lunch. At least he had his wallet now. Greg blinked, emerging from the alley into the sunshine and headed for the front of the restaurant.

He held a Styrofoam take-out container when he returned to his guise as Wonder Guy and took flight from the alley behind the restaurant. An odd crunching sound had accompanied his leap into the air. He twisted a hundred feet above the alley, focusing his enhanced vision on the scene below.

A crater two feet in diameter and a foot deep occupied the spot from which he'd jumped. In the center were the impressions of two feet. He had an uncomfortable feeling his own feet would fit those prints perfectly. Crap. *Equal and opposite reaction, buddy.*

And what could he to do about it? He hoped not too many drivers used the alley. Uh oh. The concerns flashed by as he cut back to Hennepin.

Wonder Guy

There'd been so much commotion around the parade, he wouldn't have noticed the sound of asphalt crushing beneath his take-off jump. And what about the roof of the CC/EE building back at the U? When he first took off, he'd been distracted. The sheer wonder of being in flight struck him anew every time he went aloft. He reached the scene of his earlier victory over the elephant before completing the thought.

Enhanced hearing brought him the curses of the driver who'd just clunked across the monster pothole Wonder Guy had left as evidence--or a memento--of his adventure there. The impressions of his feet remained all too clear in this second take-off crater.

Why didn't Superman ever have this problem? Maybe he was doing his take-offs wrong? Maybe comic books weren't reliable guides to all the ins and outs of superpowers. Maybe he needed a running start? Airplanes got up to speed before they lifted off.

He imagined the resulting black, gooey, tarry mess if he used heat vision to melt the asphalt. This wasn't the only pothole on Hennepin Avenue. He should leave fixing it to the experts of the Highway Department. In the meanwhile he turned back toward the University, take-out box in hand, his pleasure in flying not at all dimmed.

☆☆★☆☆

Gloria drove up Lyndale to avoid the congestion on Hennepin. Jo sat in the passenger seat with the sheet cake on her lap and chatted about the trouble HR had finding qualified researchers to replace the few who'd left the company recently.

Gloria murmured a few mmm hmms and ohs, but as she maneuvered the familiar route past familiar streets and buildings her thoughts strayed, taking the direct route back to the moment when her gaze had met the eyes of the hero in the golden mask. Brown eyes, she was almost certain. In the shadow of the elephant, it had been hard to distinguish their color, but there'd been no mistaking the snap of electricity when his gaze had turned to meet her own. His look, hot and intent upon her, had awakened an answering spark that sent shockwaves straight to her core.

Before this, the sweetness of Pete's kisses had seemed sufficient. Love meant understanding and consideration. Love meant being comfortable with a person. Other descriptions of love were a bunch of exaggerated hype, the songs, poems, stories of undying passion, all that 'climb the highest mountain, swim the deepest sea' crap. She didn't get any of it.

Until now. His look had slammed into her like falling out of bed. Like falling out of a dream to find the breath knocked out of her, her head spinning, but not caring because she was awake to a day full of amazing possibilities. Who'd have thought she had the capacity to feel like this? So jazzed, so powerfully alive, so ready to grab onto something with both hands and never let go?

Gloria drew a deep breath and sighed, gripping the steering wheel tight as she waited at a red light, tapping the foot not dedicated to the brake.

Jo shot her a questioning look but didn't stop detailing the pros and cons of each applicant who'd come through the HR office this week.

But this was crazy. Crazy and selfish. Pete would be hurt if he knew she dreamt about a look in the eyes of another man. What did she want to do? Fling her plans and her whole future to the wind because she'd imagined a look in the eyes of a stranger? Maybe she had imagined it, but she hadn't imagined how it made her feel. But again, what good was passion, with nothing in the real world to support it? Oh, this was crazy. *Stop it, Gloria.*

The only thing to do, the only practical thing, was get back to work. Keep her mind on the road. Pay attention to Jo. How rude to daydream like this while her friend talked. If the day seemed to go gray when she followed her own advice, Gloria attributed it to clouds moving in, though the sky remained as clear as it had been all morning.

☆☆★☆☆

Greg followed Interstate 35W north, headed back toward the university. If only he'd had the chance to spend more time with Gloria. Why hadn't he swept her up in his arms instead of tackling the elephant? Because if he'd swept her up, he'd have needed to grab the toddler and the baby in its stroller too, and might have dropped one or more while juggling to hold them all. No, he'd done the right thing. No one got hurt.

And he'd caught that look in Gloria's eye--a look holding something more than simple admiration or gratitude. Something electric. She'd never looked at him like that before. If he'd managed to escape the belly dancers sooner he might have spoken to her. 'Are you all right, Miss?' He imagined asking in his best George Reeves style, hands fisted on his hips. Maybe things were better this way. The 'mysterious stranger' must have made an impression on her.

He flew with little attention to the road below him until he noted a car merging from I35 onto I-94 East. The compact sped up to merge ahead of a semi-trailer but at the same moment, a pickup truck angled to merge in front of the semi from the center lane. The two merging vehicles were on course to collide directly in front of the big rig, involving it in their accident.

Amid a blaring of horns, heart slamming into his throat, Greg dove, placing himself between the compact and the pickup truck just in time to buffer their impact. He held the vehicles apart by main strength, the reek of gas and the road rising hot into his face as he drew a deep breath, but the rescue still had a ways to go. His arms felt like coiled springs, bracing against the tension of tons of hurtling steel on either side. The force jolted through his entire frame. He flew between the faded red pickup on one side and the dusky blue compact on the other, matching their speeds, keeping them apart for the long moment it took the drivers to react.

The driver of the pickup, a jowly, heavyset man wearing a faded Vikings sweatshirt, dropped back into his lane long enough to give the driver of the compact a chance to shoot ahead. The woman, in a business suit and close-cropped brown hair, took the opening with a look of mixed shock and annoyance. The driver of the semi slowed enough for the pickup to complete its merge a moment later, dropping in between the compact and the semi.

Greg shot back in the air, deliberately not picturing the mangled metal and bodies that might have smeared the highway if Wonder Guy had been slower. Thank God. Thank the fairy godmothers that he'd had the chance to help. Lucky the drivers had kept their cool. Must have been a shock to find not only another car suddenly in one's path, but also a costumed superhero. Still, if anyone had reacted badly he, or his mighty alter ego, would have lifted one of the cars out of the way.

Drat. Admittedly a small enough sacrifice, but in his rush to stop the collision, he'd lost his takeout box. Chances of his lunch surviving in any recognizable form seemed too low to bother looking for it now. It all went to show what came of mixing personal errands with superhero business. His stomach grumbled again. He'd have to stop at home for a PB&J.

Greg flew straight to his apartment above Aggie's garage. He had sandwich fixings in his small refrigerator. He let himself in through the window over the backyard, left open for the spring breezes and the alley cat who condescended to visit him occasionally.

When he lifted the sash it shot up much harder than he'd intended, cracking the glass in the frame. Damn. He squeezed in. He'd have to deal with the glass later. In climbing over the bookcase below the window, he knocked into it, sending it flying, scattering books across the floor. And that, he'd deal with that later, too. He felt like a gorilla in a china shop, or whatever. He'd thought to use his enhanced speed to get quickly in and out and on with his day, but no.

Greg moved with exaggerated care to avoid bumping anything else on his way to the kitchenette. If he switched back to normal, he'd miss this chance to practice applying his powers to stuff less durable than elephants and cars before he had to do so in a more public way.

How had Superman managed in his Clark Kent guise? It proved surprisingly hard to gauge the strength it took to do small, ordinary things like open the refrigerator without tearing the door off its hinges, or open the peanut butter without crushing the jar in his grip. Let alone applying peanut butter and jelly to bread without mashing the bread to a paste. He threw a couple of botched attempts out the window for the squirrels and birds before he produced a sandwich that held together long enough for him to eat it. He followed it with half a carton of milk. It might not be scallops with cashews and basil, but it hit the spot.

Recalling the potholes he'd left behind on his earlier take-offs, Greg didn't dare attempt leaving through the same window by which he'd entered. He left his apartment taking great care of the door and lock mechanism and practically tiptoed down the stairs and out to the alley, where he relaxed, shaking off the sensation of being three sizes too big for his apartment. Nobody'd care if he harmed the weeds beside the garage, out in the open air with plenty of elbowroom. Now to try taking off again without adding a new crater to the ruts of the alley.

Stepping as lightly as possible, he started off at a run, faster and faster, aiming high, building up to super speed as if flinging himself, like a Frisbee, into the air. He took flight in time to soar above any cars passing the mouth of the alley and twisted to look behind him, zeroing in with super vision. The alley looked no worse than usual, no fresh new potholes anyhow.

Even at super speed, Greg had only gotten as far north as Franklin Avenue before a now familiar buzz sounded in his ear.

"Hurry!" Serafina's voice urged him. "It's a home invasion."

Chapter 7

No sooner did Serafina impart the address than Greg bent his angle of flight toward Prospect Park, steering by the 'witch's hat' tower standing on the highest bit of ground in the city.

The house proved to be an older Tudor-style structure shielded from the street by trees and hedges. He circled above. What now? Ring the doorbell?

At the same moment he remembered the option of x-ray vision, his super hearing brought him the sound of flesh striking flesh and a woman's muffled cry.

Greg spun in the direction of the sound. It came from the upper story of the house. Focusing intently revealed shadowy figures through the walls. Guns showed clearly in the hands of the two standing in the center. A slight figure crouched over someone lying unmoving nearby.

He crashed through the window, tearing it from its frame before he thought better of it. Who would pay for the damages?

He landed in the large, well-upholstered bedroom in full superhero regalia.

"What the hell," someone exclaimed.

It didn't take super vision to read the situation. The guns in the hands of two unkempt youths swiveled instantly from the fallen man and crouching woman to take aim on Greg as he alit inside the destroyed window.

He had barely time to flinch before one of the guns fired.

Something struck his chest and he stumbled back a step. The impact wasn't what he'd expect from a bullet, and something--a ricochet?--smashed one of the bedside lamps. Holy shit. Had a bullet bounced off him? Oh man. No time to think about it now.

The other gunman's eyes widened when the first shot had no effect. He cocked his weapon.

Greg easily wrenched the gun away and crushed the barrel in his fist.

"Jesus," the shorter young man backed away as he shouted. "Did you see that, Bob? He's not just dressed like a comic book hero." He turned and ran for the bedroom door, his companion not far behind him.

Greg caught them both by the backs of their collars before they'd gone more than a few feet.

"Excuse me, ma'am," he addressed the crouching woman. She looked up from beside the fallen man, eyes wide in a face looking older than it probably did on most days.

Greg gestured to the man beside her. "Does he need medical assistance?"

"I don't know." She seemed to recover herself, shocked features growing more animated. "That one," she pointed to the taller of the youths in Greg's grip, "hit George over the head with the gun. He's breathing okay, but he won't wake up."

"Call 911," Greg told her. "Tell them to send the police and an ambulance. Then bring me something to tie up these," he scowled at his captives, wanting to give them a good shake, not wanting to call them men, "these thugs, until the police get here."

She nodded, starting to move. "There's another--"

At a slight sound behind him, Greg whirled, his prisoners still in hand. The bullet meant for his back struck one of them in the chest.

"Howie," screamed the young woman in the doorway. She trained her gun higher, on Greg's masked face. She took a step back. "Look what you made me do."

"I didn't mean--" He went numb. What had he done?

Her features contorting into a Greek tragedy mask, she pulled the trigger.

He released the wounded thug, flung up his hand at super speed and caught the bullet, which became a flattened dollop of metal in his hand. He dropped it to the carpet.

The girl stared, at Greg, the dime-shaped bullet, her fallen partner.

The captive struggled against Greg's grip.

"Run, Jenny," he yelled to the girl. Her stunned look faded, but rather than take his advice and run, she knelt beside the fallen youth who'd taken the bullet she'd meant for Greg. She leaned over him, running her hands over his chest.

"Is he dead? Oh God, oh God. Are you okay, Howie? It wasn't supposed to go like this."

The older woman approached, cell phone in hand. "The police are on the way. I told them to send the ambulance."

"He's breathing." The girl looked up, tears in her eyes.

Greg's captive squirmed against his choking grip. "Let me go!"

The older woman wore a flowered dress, but a dressing gown lay across the end of the king-sized bed. She pulled free its long cloth belt.

Jenny turned her tear-streaked face toward the woman moving to hand the sash to Greg. "You weren't supposed to be here. You said you were going out of town."

"Jenny? Jenny Stevenson? What are you doing here?" The girl's identity seemed to register with the older woman for the first time.

"You were supposed to be out of town. You and Mr. Zimmer. We needed some cash. No one was supposed to get hurt. Oh Howie."

The thug in hand lashed out at Mrs. Zimmer when she handed across the tie. Greg shook him into dazed compliance.

Should he tie up the girl too? She had tried to kill him. She'd fired the shot that had laid Howie out on the floor, but she showed no sign of attempting flight, sitting beside her wounded companion as if her legs had collapsed under her. Superman and Batman always knew what to do.

The lady of the house sat heavily on the end of the bed. "We decided to catch a later flight. Why? Why would you do this?" She focused on the girl. "Why break in here? With guns? We're neighbors. I used to babysit for you when your mother worked."

"You wouldn't understand." Jenny's bloodied hands pressed against a seeping wound in Howie's chest. He wasn't dead, at least. He moaned and stirred under the ministration.

"Why wouldn't I understand?"

"You don't know what it's like! You've both got jobs. You can afford a vacation in Europe. My dad lost his job a year ago and my mother's only got half the hours she used to have. We're going to lose the house. We can barely keep food on the table. We can't afford a new cheerleader's uniform for me. You're the one who insisted to the school board that the team needs new uniforms. You can pay for mine."

"I had no idea." Mrs. Zimmer stared at the blood with widened eyes and held her hands fisted in her skirt.

"You didn't want to know. You could have figured it out easy enough if you paid attention." Jenny spoke over her shoulder. She bent forward across Howie, brown hair veiling her face.

109

Greg hadn't noticed the sound until now, but the wail of sirens grew louder. Two injured men, one bound felon, two emotional women. The last item filled him with more dismay than the rest combined. This situation had moved beyond the scope of superhero duty. Greg scanned the room with his x-ray vision, making sure the weapons were accounted for.

"Will you be all right now, ma'am?" He took a step back toward the broken window.

"Do you plan any more mischief?" Mrs. Zimmer asked the girl.

"I have to stay with Howie," Jenny answered with a look of resignation.

"We'll be all right." The older woman told Greg. "Thank you for stepping in." Her gaze strayed to the broken window frame. "Oh no. What am I supposed to tell the insurance people?"

Greg made his exit before he'd have to answer. The ambulance and police cars pulled up in front of the house as he jumped out the window and flew up and away out the back. The clear cold air slapped his face, breaking him free of the spell of confusion.

He hadn't meant for Howie to be shot. He shouldn't feel so guilty. He hadn't pulled the trigger. Except, if he'd just held still, the bullet to his back wouldn't have done any harm. Come to think of it, that girl might never have staged a break-in if her family wasn't desperate, if her accomplices weren't stupid enough to go along with her or if she'd had some guidance. No one would have been hurt if the Zimmers had left according to plan. The lines between criminal and victims were supposed to be more clear-cut. He told himself he'd done his part, but left feeling as if nothing at all had been settled.

☆☆★☆☆

When Gloria got home from work, she stopped first at Aggie's without waiting to change out of her business-appropriate blouse and blazer over her neat black skirt. She'd long been in the habit of going to Aggie's before going home. It had to be a carryover from her middle school days when Dad had still been working and didn't want her returning to an empty house. Back when he'd managed to lay off the drink until he got home, before his injury.

It had been a good arrangement then, and it still worked now. Aggie seldom went out in the afternoons, and when she did it took planning, making it an event Gloria always heard of well in advance. She could count on Aggie to be there, count on a welcome at the cluttered worktable where they'd shared countless projects over the years. They'd made everything from crocheted can holders and fingerless gloves, to ceramic whistles, to the current designer cell phone holsters, one of Gloria's own ideas.

Her mentor did twice the work on the business end of things as Gloria did. She didn't have to keep a regular day job, and had more time for it. Aggie was the one who had found their team of piecework seamstresses, recruiting at the senior center when they started getting more orders than the two of them could fill on their own.

"Hullo-oh" Gloria began speaking at the kitchen door before entering but stopped short in the doorway with the screen door bouncing against her backside. The story of her exciting lunch hour and the following rather tame office birthday party died unspoken.

Aggie sat at her usual spot at the table, but a man clad in a button-down plaid shirt and jeans, his grey hair pulled back in a neat ponytail, stood in front of her, his back to Gloria.

"Gloria." Aggie peered around the man, speaking with her accustomed brightness, muted by a hesitant note. "I'd like you to meet Hank Luddell. He's Susie Luddell's brother. You know my friend who collects our orders from the Center. She couldn't make it today and Hank said he'd drop them off."

Gloria managed to insert a nod and a smile to Hank during Aggie's flustered speech. The other woman sounded not at all like her usual laid-back self. Had she interrupted something?

Gloria shook Hank's warm, firm hand. Kind of a fox for someone who must be at least fifty.

"Nice to meet you." Hank smiled briefly, turning back to Aggie. "Guess I'd better get going. I'll tell Sue you got the lot." He nodded at a cardboard box sitting on one of the kitchen chairs.

"Thanks again," Aggie spoke after him as Hank and Gloria maneuvered around each other. He headed out the door she'd just entered, while she went toward Aggie and the worktable. "You stop by any time."

"Sure will." Hank called, closing the door behind him.

"Wow." Gloria dropped into the chair across from Aggie, next to the one holding the box. Finding Aggie with a gentleman caller constituted a major disruption to the natural order of things--at least as much as seeing a man fly. "He's a cutie. What were you two talking about before I came in?"

Aggie blushed. Blushed! Gloria looked at her as if she'd never seen her before. She'd gotten used to Aggie just being Aggie--older yes, but a friend, someone who listened to her and cared about her, got her engaged in their various projects and took her dreams seriously. But now... Aggie didn't actually look old, not as old as she must be to be Greg's mom. She had a few gray threads in her headful of light brown curls and a few lines around her eyes and mouth, but mostly laugh lines. The figure in her wheeled chair might be a bit plump, but on Aggie, it looked good, like ripe fruit looks better plump. She was pretty--and blushing like a schoolgirl.

"Nothing much," she answered, even as Gloria took in the totally new concept of Aggie as someone with a romantic life of her own. "We just got to chatting. He's a nice man. Sue's having foot surgery and he's helping her out with all her errands."

"That is nice of him." Gloria turned to the box beside her, concealing her smile. "Not every man would take the time away from his wife and kids to help out his sister." She started pulling out the blank holsters and setting them out on the table.

"Oh, Hank's not married." Aggie pulled a few of the blanks across to her side of the table. "He spent too much time on the road as a backup musician for a country rock band to settle down."

"You learned a lot about him for such a short chat," Gloria teased.

"Well, maybe." Aggie's blush deepened. She cleared her throat. "I finished a couple of prototypes for our windowed holsters today." She handed one across to Gloria. "What do you think?"

"I think I'm not done talking about Hank." Gloria grinned with intent to tease and took the prototype.

"Oh now. You stop. I just met the man--and don't say anything about him to Greg either."

"Why not? Greg's a big boy now."

"Yes. He is." Aggie's tone sobered, "But I'm still all the family he's got. I want him to feel secure where I'm concerned. I'll always be here for him, bar death or disaster."

"Sure." Gloria fiddled with the prototype, tugging at the stitching that secured the clear pocket to the main body of the holster. "If you suppose Greg would feel threatened by your flirting with a cute guy your own age."

A business card--one of their own--filled the clear pocket of the holster. Gloria pulled it out and pushed it in again. It would be easy enough to change out the pocket's contents. She'd have to come up with a set of sample mottos to insert. Would there be copyright issues if she used some common t-shirt slogans?

"It's hard to know how Greg feels," Aggie continued. "He's such a man, keeps everything under his hat."

"Huh." Gloria hadn't pictured him that way at all. Greg was Greg, like Aggie was Aggie. She liked teasing him because it was so hard to get a reaction, him being all Rational Reasonable Man. If he didn't have a sense of humor and easy-going manner, she'd accuse him of being Mr. Spock.

"I can sound him out on the idea before it goes any further than innocent flirtation." Gloria shot Aggie an arch look.

"Don't you dare," Aggie scolded. "Maybe it's time we discuss your love life." She sat back, crossing her arms over her breasts with mock severity.

"My love life is great." Gloria lost her smile, and suddenly, returning to business matters-at-hand seemed by far the safest course. She held up the prototype. "This is perfect, and using them to display business cards is another great idea. I'll make up some sample slogans to display in them."

"You can't fool me, young lady." Aggie lifted a brow, but a hint of her smile remained. "But if you want to talk business, we'll talk business. I like the ones saying, 'I'm up and dressed, what more do you want?'"

Chapter 8

Greg flew back to the lab, hardly noticing the wonder of it. Recent events still preyed on his mind. What if the kid, Howie died? The possibility ate at him. He'd put the young thug in the path of the bullet, but he wasn't the one who'd brought guns into play. Howie had fired the first shot.

Maybe they had expected to find the place empty, but they'd come with guns, come prepared to do violence. The 'kid' might not be more than seventeen, but he'd clubbed down the older man, terrorized the wife. Greg hadn't meant him harm. If the kid had been hurt, he'd been hoisted by his own petard.

Arriving back at the Computer Science building, Greg made an effort to land lightly. The small crater of his original lift-off still dented the tar and gravel rooftop. Crap. He'd better drop an anonymous note in the custodian's office before it rained again.

He'd expected the hero business to be cleaner than this. Even after *The Dark Knight*. Even after *Watchmen*. Comic book stories were pure fiction. Leaking roofs and potholes were real. Feeling responsible for injuries he'd inadvertently inflicted. That was real.

Greg finished out the afternoon at the lab with no more heroics than helping direct a student with a late paper to her professor's office.

By the time he headed home, he felt glad to do it the good old-fashioned way, taking the bike lanes along Lyndale, legs pumping hard, the cooling breeze in his face.

His mind stayed on overload, trying to digest it all. Not just the hero business, but where to start uncovering a few clues to Professor Stevens' scheme. He needed something to bring to Morrissey as a basis for asking questions. Referring to a conversation he should never have heard would only embarrass the man.

How had Morrissey discovered the situation? Had Stevens left some trail? Research projects were still ongoing. Stevens wouldn't have completed his plans for them, whatever it was he planned.

☆☆★☆☆

"I have to see the news tonight." Gloria paused in the act of attaching rhinestones to one of ten assorted-color "Disco Sue" models. They'd probably have footage of her rescuer. If not otherwise, she'd see him again on the news reports. She turned up the TV volume as Greg entered the kitchen.

He gave her an odd look, like he meant to say something, but he turned instead to Aggie.

"Any leftovers tonight, Mom?"

"Oh, hon, you know I always make enough for an army." Across the table from Gloria, Aggie looked up from her project.

"Yet you claim to be a pacifist."

"Nothing like a good meal to convert an enemy to a friend." Aggie gestured to the stovetop. "Swedish meatballs in the pot and a lefse experiment in the skillet."

"Should I be afraid?" Greg teased, turning toward the stove.

"Only if pizza-style lefse violates your sense of cultural propriety."

The dish must have passed muster because Greg didn't answer and there followed only the sounds he made as he fixed himself a plate.

Gloria paid no mind to the usual mother-son banter, but kept an eye on the TV. Just the weather report now, a bit cool for June, but nothing remarkable. Until they turned to the local news.

"You've got to see this, Aggie." Gloria gestured at the screen, waving her hand like a flag in a high wind. "That crazy business I mentioned, what happened over lunch. It's on the news."

"Crazy how?" Greg looked over at the small TV occupying a shelf above the worktable.

"Just watch." Gloria turned up the sound another notch.

"Spectators caught this footage in Uptown earlier today as a masked hero actually flew down to save a woman and two children from an elephant gone wild."

"That can't be right, Ken," commented the stiffly coifed anchorwoman. "Men don't fly."

"Some claim the incident was staged as a publicity stunt for the Renaissance Festival. People on the scene say it was real. You folks at home can judge for yourselves."

The screen showed a shaky amateur video clip as it turned its focus from some belly dancers to capture a shot of a costumed hero in green and gold descending out of the clear sky to place himself between the cowering figures Gloria recognized as herself and the children she'd tried to protect.

The camera zoomed in, showing the elephant as it slid backward, propelled by the man braced like a buttress against its huge leg. Before the news broke for a commercial, a close-up revealed the bunching of strong muscles, caught the clenched jaw and zoomed in on those somehow-familiar eyes behind the mask.

She sighed aloud. "Isn't he amazing?"

Aggie chuckled. "Does Pete have a new rival?"

Gloria laughed. "In my dreams. Wonder Guy is a hero. He could have any woman in the world. What would he want with a nobody like me?"

"You know I don't like that kind of talk," Aggie scolded.

"I know, I know. I'm a very special snowflake." Gloria rolled her eyes. It was nice of Aggie to encourage her self-esteem, and maybe she was special to those who knew her, but how would anybody else ever notice her among all the zillions of other special snowflakes in the blizzard?

"There's no one in the world exactly like you, and your friends know it. Greg will back me up on this. Won't you, dear?"

"Of course. There isn't anyone like you. I bet he'd count himself the luckiest superhero in the world if he had you."

Gloria had no response. She wasn't going to argue with someone who said something so nice. She ignored the heat on her face and turned back to face the television.

The news team returned to their topic.

"A costumed hero is also reported to have stepped in to stop a home invasion this afternoon."

"It sounds like quite an influx of these costumed men, Ken. Weren't there reports of a hero in red yesterday?"

Gloria's hands fell idle while she followed the talking heads. Greg munched a rolled section of pizza-style lefse, but his gaze stayed intent on the screen.

"That's right, Linda. Someone caught footage of that fellow too." The clip reran behind them. "Police want to speak with both these masked men. Authorities ask them to come forward."

"Why's that, Ken?"

"In two of these incidents men were injured."

"The criminals were injured, Ken?" Linda wore her most earnest expression and an amber necklace Gloria admired for the way it brought out the red highlights in the newswoman's blond coif.

Ken leaned straight toward the camera. "That's right, Linda. Allegedly, these heroes injured the alleged criminals in the act of preventing the crimes. One purported house-breaker is reported in serious condition."

"So the police need to interview the costumed men as witnesses?"

"That's right. There's no intention of charging them with anything at this time."

"I should hope not, Ken. These men are heroes. Possibly superheroes. The world needs men like them." A starry look shone in her eyes.

"Well, Linda, even superheroes are not above the law."

"Outrageous." Gloria muted the TV. "The man who stopped that elephant is a hero. The police can't treat him like some criminal." She should send an angry message to the news station for even implying he'd done anything wrong

"What, no more 'dorky' for dressing in costume?" Greg paused with a forkful of Swedish meatball halfway to his mouth.

"Well," Gloria hesitated to admit she'd been off base. "At first I thought the guy in the red costume was just after attention, but he did stop a couple of crimes and the guy today saved my life. I was there. That elephant would be wiping me off its feet if Wonder Guy hadn't jumped in. He saved those kids, too. I'd like to kiss him right on the mouth."

Aggie spoke up. "The police can't treat a man differently because he's a hero. They have their jobs to do, and if people were injured they have to talk to everyone involved."

☆☆★☆☆

Greg said nothing, sitting silently in place while Gloria and Aggie turned to other subjects. What should he do? He was a witness, in not one but several crimes. Didn't he have a duty to step up and testify? But that would throw the whole 'secret identity' thing out the window. His career as a crime fighter would be over. What then? What if some of the criminals or their connections wanted to take their grievances out on his family? On Aggie? Maybe even on Gloria if they guessed how he felt about her. Wasn't this exactly why Superman, Spiderman and the other superheroes maintained their secret identities? To protect their loved ones?

One possibility would be to send the police a message, videotape himself in costume, do something super to prove it was him and agree to give a deposition if they agreed to protect his anonymity. They did as much for criminal informants. They could do it for a crime fighter, right?

☆☆★☆☆

Elysha paced along the edge of a pool among the trees making this plaza one of the few places tolerable for her kind in a city laced with the burning aura of iron.

"How dare she keep me waiting?"

She addressed the question to the air, but Minik, one of the feral goblins who served her, answered. "Humans don't know their place." He groveled nicely, bending his gnarled limbs into a hunkering crouch.

Elysha allowed him a small smile, for the sake of having her superiority acknowledged.

"Too true," she said, again to the air. It wouldn't do to encourage familiarity by actually addressing the creature, except in command.

"Go," she told him, flinging an imperious hand toward the streets. "Hurry her."

"At once, Mistress." Minik cringed, backing away. The diminutive creature turned tail and scurried off in the direction she'd indicated.

Consorting with humans truly was beneath her, but they had their uses. If not for those meddling 'fairy godmothers' she wouldn't need stoop so low just to assure a plentiful flow of the invigorating dark energies that made humans tolerable.

Her minions were able to taunt and provoke and tease humankind into foul moods, but they couldn't be trusted with more complex business. It took deeper machinations to produce the kinds of pervading misery and despair constituting Elysha's true meat and drink.

It took her own superior wit and her capacity to cast a glamour and pass among humans as one of their own, albeit a superior specimen, appearing thinner, taller, younger and richer than any of them.

She smiled to herself at the way the creatures squirmed in her presence, knowing themselves inferior to her. How sweet, the way they judged themselves, given only the image she showed them. Foolish things. They were inferior, of course, but not based merely on appearances.

The bones of the building behind her stood out in silhouette against the lighted windows. The night hummed with the music of water flowing over ledges into the pools surrounding her, and with the whine of a few insects. Amazing things, to have survived the most determined efforts of humanity to eradicate the little bloodsuckers.

Elysha's smile widened. It would amuse her to blast the tiny pests in mid-air for target practice, igniting tiny explosions of blood like macabre fireworks. Although…any annoyance to men constituted a friend to her.

She ought to help her little friends in their good work, like those meddling biddies had been helping the humans lately. This had gone beyond uniting a pair of lovers here and there in order to generate a bit of sweetness and light into the world. You win some you lose some. Two people's happiness scarcely lessened the sea of troubles assailing the rest of their species.

Something seemed askew lately. She smelled less trouble in the air, fewer of the energies she craved and those interfering old busybodies had done something to cause it. She didn't know what as yet, but she'd find out.

☆☆★☆☆

Kathleen Pedersen cursed the need to hasten alone through the city streets so late at night, even in as tame a neighborhood as Nicollet Mall outside Orchestra Hall. With no events scheduled, the plaza seemed eerily deserted despite the glow from the glass-walled building. The shadows seemed alive. Probably only the shifting leaves of the trees in planters among the pools and fountains.

She shuddered at a prickling sensation in her calves and hurried her steps. She clutched a canister of pepper spray in her jacket pocket, though no one was near to threaten her.

Why did Ms. Ellis insist on these midnight meetings? Yes, their business of brokering the sale of stolen research was illegal, but it would look a lot less suspicious if anyone she knew saw them having coffee during regular business hours at a downtown café.

When she spotted Ms. Ellis seated on a ledge beside one of the shadowed, half-hidden inner pools of the garden plaza, Kathleen drew a relieved breath.

"There you are." She tried to inject a bright, casual tone to her voice, but the effort only bared her relief.

Ms. Ellis smiled the close-lipped smile that always struck Kathleen as too satisfied, the kind of smile giving rise to clichés like 'the cat who ate the canary.'

"Good evening," Miss Ellis greeted her, and without any other preliminaries proceeded to business. "Why did you request this meeting?" Her smile widened, as if she drank in the waves of anxiety Kathleen must surely radiate as the unavoidable byproduct of her mission.

"There's been an... accident," Kathleen admitted, then went on to explain.

☆☆★☆☆

Another day, another $116.60, after deductions.
Gloria stowed her patchwork suede and leather
bag in her drawer, turned on the computer and
pulled her chair up to the desk. Seven twenty-
nine, according to the computer's task bar. Early.
Of course, Jo usually started at six and left at three
to avoid the worst of rush hour traffic.

Gloria picked up her phone and punched in Jo's
extension, wanting to compare notes on the news
coverage of yesterday's lunchtime adventure. The
phone rang unanswered until Jo's voicemail message kicked in. Rats.

"Hi, it's Gloria. Call me when you get this."
Darn. Guess she'd have to concentrate on work for
a while. First, get the coffee started.

By ten o'clock Gloria had squared away Mr.
Carlson's scheduling and correspondence and
written up the changes to the procedures docu-
ment he'd given her over coffee at their morning
check-in meeting. As she turned to check her own
messages, it struck her she'd not yet heard back
from Jo. She frowned, finger tapping the back of
her mouse. This wasn't like Jo. Maybe her friend
was having one of those mornings, driving other
things from her mind. Gloria turned to her phone
and punched in Jo's extension only to get voicemail again.

Her uneasiness deepened. Maybe Jo was too
swamped with work to check her messages.
Things were quiet here in R&D today. She'd

126

caught up with her own tasks. Maybe Jo needed some help, a friend to lighten her workload somehow. Gloria certainly knew how to file papers and input data with the best of them. Time to visit HR.

"Hi." Gloria greeted Mary when she reached HR's reception desk. "I'd like to go back and see Jo." She waved at the door dividing the reception area from the main block of offices and workstations.

Mary, a pleasantly plump woman with wavy brown hair, kind eyes and a ready smile, turned to her with an uncharacteristically furrowed brow. "I'm sorry. I got a call from Jo this morning, saying she won't be in. She sounded bad. Said she's sick."

"Well, dang." Gloria bit her lower lip. She'd seemed fine yesterday. Whatever it was had hit awfully fast. Maybe some twenty-four hour bug. "I'm sorry to hear it. Did she say what it was?"

Mary leaned over the barrier of the reception desk. "No, but it sounded like a bad cold. Her voice was so hoarse you'd hardly recognize it. I told her to drink some hot tea with honey. That's just the thing for a bad throat."

Gloria tsked. "Well I hope it's not too bad. I'll have to give her a call at home." She smiled to Mary. "Thanks for letting me know."

"You betcha." Mary brightened visibly. "You say 'hi' to her from me too."

"You got it." Gloria spoke over her shoulder, already heading back to the elevators.

☆☆★☆☆

After a restless night, Greg pulled on slacks and his favorite t-shirt reading, *There are 10 kinds of people in the world: those who understand binary and those who don't.* As soon as he'd finished in the bathroom and had a mug of coffee in hand, he booted up his computer.

If he walked into some precinct police station, he'd be certain to waste hours talking to underlings without the authority to make the kind of decision he needed in order to work with the police. They might even try to detain him, unmask him. He couldn't have that. It would spoil everything before he'd barely gotten started.

No. He'd go straight to the top. Greg found the city's website and hesitated with the cursor hovering between directory headings. The top. Hmm. Mayor or chief of police? This involved police business, but the mayor would have the clout to apply the kind of outside-the-box solution the situation demanded.

Wonder Guy acted in a special capacity. If he let the police treat him like plain old Greg Roberts, it would reduce his effectiveness. Who would be most likely to recognize the fact and back him up on it?

For the first time in his life, he regretted not paying more attention to local politics. At least, to politics outside the Computing Department and his online games. The internal battles to control the direction of Multi User Dungeon campaigns involved all the mudslinging and backbiting of a presidential election. Point being, he knew nothing about either of these men. Time for some Google-fu.

An hour later, he'd learned the mayor and chief of police were both new to office as of last fall. Mayor Jennings had been elected by a close margin on his promise to restore social services slashed by a budget-obsessed predecessor. But, in office for only half a year, Jennings had yet to establish a record of consistent follow-through on his promises.

Police Chief Levinson, while new to his title, had a long record with the Minneapolis police force, starting thirty years ago as a patrolman. He'd spent five years between traffic, vice and narcotics before making detective, and steadily worked his way up the ranks through positions of increasing authority and responsibility. From what Greg had found, his record looked good. No citations for discipline problems or use of excessive force, anyhow.

Growing up with Aggie, Greg had heard her stories of police raids on the commune. She still spoke disdainfully of their ignorance in mistaking a pee pot for a component intended to make bombs. She also spoke bitterly about a cop who'd shoved her twelve-year old self around and smashed a beloved guitar in the--vain--search for drugs.

Levinson's bio, however, made him a family man with two grown children, listed no political affiliations, but several awards and commendations earned early in his career.

Greg pushed away from the computer desk sharing what space in his tiny bedroom wasn't taken up by his queen-sized bed. The sound of somebody's lawn mower growled through the open window from a few houses down the block.

Logically, he saw no reason to prefer one man over the other. Except, Levinson's background must have given him experience dealing in practical ways with unpredictable situations. A politician might be better at negotiating the human element, but Levinson must have some political acumen too, to have achieved his position. Heck, he might have to deal with both men before this was over.

Greg rubbed his eyes, turning back to the computer screen. So, where would he find Chief Levinson this morning? City Hall? He started searching for a blueprint.

☆☆★☆☆

Back at her desk, Gloria used her cell phone to speed dial Jo's home number. She leaned back in her chair, gently swiveling side-to-side, fiddling with a pen as Jo's phone rang, two, three, four times. When the answering machine kicked in, Gloria opened her mouth to leave a sympathetic message and offer to visit after work.

"Hello. Who's calling please?" A man answered, voice brusque and deep.

"Is Jo there?" Gloria asked, hesitant. Jo hadn't mentioned seeing anyone lately. "Tell her it's Gloria."

"I'm sorry, ma'am. I'm Detective Algerson, Minneapolis P.D. May I ask when you last saw Ms. Willard?"

What the hell? "What? Where's Jo?" Gloria stilled her chair and dropped her pen. "What's going on? Is this some kind of joke? How do I know you're who you say you are?"

"No, ma'am. I am not joking. If you've seen Joanne Willard in the past twenty-four hours, we'll need to interview you. May I ask where you're calling from?"

"Why do you need to talk to me? Where's Jo?" She had an awful feeling.

"I'm sorry, ma'am. Ms. Willard's body was recovered early this morning."

Gloria missed whatever he said next. Her heart dropped, plummeting below foot level and into a pit, as if a chasm opened suddenly below her. Her mouth went dry. The office around her faded into invisibility. *Oh God.*

The detective continued speaking. "We're trying to establish her whereabouts over the past day. When did you see her last?"

"No. She can't be dead. I just saw her yesterday. We were supposed to have lunch today." This wasn't real. It wasn't possible. It had to be some ghastly mistake they'd laugh about later. When everything was all right again.

"At what time did you see her yesterday?" The man's tone conveyed a kind of bored patience.

Gloria felt numb, as if broken loose from the world around her and floating at a distance, but she heard herself answer, "We got lunch together in Uptown. At the parade, on the news, where an elephant went out of control. Maybe they caught her in some of the footage. I drove us back to the office and didn't see her again before I left for the day."

"Thank you, ma'am. I or somebody on my team will come speak to you later for a more complete statement and ask you to answer a few more questions."

"Wait." Gloria's thoughts caught up to her. "What happened to her? Where did you find her? She's--she was my friend."

"I'm sorry. We can't discuss any details yet. This is an ongoing investigation." The line cut off.

Investigation? Did this mean they suspected foul play? They wouldn't ask her when she'd last seen Jo if she'd been killed in an auto collision, or died of a brain aneurysm or heart attack would they? Gloria clutched the arms of her chair until her fingers ached, fighting against the sucking pit of emptiness in her gut. Her head spun. She shook it, trying to think clearly. This just couldn't be happening.

☆☆★☆☆

"Miss Willard dead?" Mr. Carlson's raised brows furrowed his forehead right up to where his hairline had once begun. "Why. I've met her, haven't I? Young lady from HR?" He scowled down at his desk. "Dreadful business. The police suspect some foul play?"

Gloria nodded, not trusting herself to speak again. She supposed her eyes had to be red-rimmed and puffy. She hated to impart the news to the older man whose air of gentle abstraction made him seem oddly out of place in his position as the department head. Luckily, he had the acumen to delegate most practical matters to department sub-heads Kathleen Pederson and Don Blake.

"You'd better take the afternoon to tell the police whatever they need to know--and take some time for yourself." He gave her a smile clearly intended to convey comfort and understanding, but clearly also saying, don't involve me in this. "I know she was a friend of yours."

"Thank you," Gloria managed a shaky return smile. Turning away, she headed back to her desk to collect her bag and sweater. She'd talk to the police all right. She'd answer their questions and dig for answers to a few questions of her own.

Chapter 9

Minneapolis Police Chief Paul Levinson had ascribed recent reports of costumed superheroes in town to publicity stunts. Until he looked up from his desk at a sound--not the usual coos or rustlings of the pigeons--in time to observe a human figure fly up to his window. He peered closely. No sign of wires, harness, any kind of mechanical support. Making a conscious effort to keep his jaw from dropping, Levinson reassessed the news reports, and his previous beliefs concerning the workings of physical reality. The flying man maneuvered in mid-air, pried open the sash and stepped over the broad red sandstone blocks of the sill into the office.

Levinson scowled at the intruder. "You're supposed to call first, make an appointment with my secretary."

The man in the golden mask quirked one corner of his mouth as he grinned, glancing around the office. "I anticipated trouble getting anyone to put me through." The man's tone revealed wry good humor.

Levinson removed his hand from the button meant to summon his--armed--secretary to the office.

"You're the one on the news last night." He leaned across his desk, the only thing keeping him from grabbing the intruder by the collar, making his words an accusation.

"Right." The costumed man crossed his arms over the large 'W' on his chest. "They said you folks, the police, wanted to talk to me."

"Happens we do, or you'd be in even more trouble right now. I don't care who you are, Joe Schmo or Wonder Guy--that's what they're calling you? You don't come busting into the office of the chief of police without an appointment."

"No sir." The masked man dropped his arms to his sides. "I don't mean any disrespect. It just happened I was in a position to help out with a few situations over the past couple days."

"It just happened?" Levinson snapped, rising to his feet, bracing his hands on the desk. "Things don't 'just happen,' Mr. Whoever-you-are. I believe in choices and responsibility, cause and effect."

"Sir, normally I'd be the first to agree with you, but--"

"You think because you can fly, you've got the right to crash into somebody's office, crash your way into somebody's house?" Levinson pressed on. *Keep the other guy off balance, accept no excuses.*

"No sir. And I didn't crash. I opened the window first this time. I crashed into that house over by--"

"You think superpowers give you the right to ignore good manners? Maybe you think you're above the law?" *No way superpowers exceed my authority.*

"No, I--"

"So, why didn't you stick around to give a witness statement?"

"I need to protect my identity. I want to use these powers to help the people of Minneapolis. If we can come to an understanding--"

"An understanding, eh?" Levinson eased back into his chair, steepling his hands before him. *And now to the point.* "What sort of understanding do you have in mind?"

"You've heard of Batman, right?"

"Right." No need to mention the size of the comic book collection he'd amassed as a teen and still preserved in plastic slipcovers on shelves in the attic. "So you'd like to keep your identity a secret, is that right?" It fit the costume, and if this guy was the real deal, he'd be a fool not to take advantage, but how would it play with City Hall?

"Yes sir. Unless you want to hear the story of my origins on another planet in another plane of existence." The lips below the mask quirked again.

"Why should the Minneapolis Police Department make an exception for you? Why shouldn't you follow the same rules everybody else has to follow?" *Give me something I can take to the councilmen.*

"Sir, I believe in doing the right thing and that usually means following the law."

Levinson had a few reactions to that 'usually' but let it ride.

"But I can be a lot more helpful to the police and the people of Minneapolis if I can keep my identity a secret. I wouldn't want to endanger my--the people I care about if, in the course of fighting crime, I were to make enemies who might make them targets for revenge."

"That's understandable, and I don't want innocent civilians endangered. But I can't have anonymous vigilantes accountable to no one running rampant in my town either."

"Batman got to keep his secret identity as far as the police of Gotham City were concerned, and they even had the bat signal to call him. And sir, would you rather have criminals get away with crimes I might be able to prevent?"

"Are you suggesting the Minneapolis Police Department can't do its job in protecting the people of Minneapolis? No." He held up a hand. "I know. It's only too often the damage is done before we're even called. If we had twice the manpower and there'd still be more than we could do." In fact, his predecessor had lost the position of police chief because of the steady rise in crime rates in recent years. Not that anyone wanted to increase the department budget.

Levinson wasn't a man to doubt his senses. He'd seen this guy flying, soaring unsupported up to the window. If there'd been any kind of wires or harnesses, he'd have seen them when the man came through the casement. "Would it satisfy you to reveal your identity to a couple of select individuals as your contacts on the force?"

Wonder Guy stepped back toward the window. "I'm sorry. No one can know. If I didn't keep the secret I wouldn't trust anyone else to keep it, and too much depends on it."

Levinson reached out before the costumed man exited the same way he'd come. "Wait. I'll tell you what." The chief leaned further across the desk, "Save your stories about alien origins. I'll instruct the officers handling your cases to list you as Wonder Guy and you can wear your mask and costume and a Viking helmet for all I care, while they take your witness statements. But," his tone deepened to a warning growl, "if there's any evidence you're misusing the privilege we'll revisit the whole issue."

"Thank you, sir. I don't know how I got these powers or how long they'll last but I want to make them count while they do." Wonder Guy extended a gloved hand and they shook.

Levinson's had a vise-like grip, and had caused many a man to wince, but he might as well shake hands with a marble statue for all the give in this character's clasp.

"Right, then." The police chief pressed the intercom on his desk phone, "Betty, call over to the precincts handling the "superhero" cases. Tell them to send the detectives in charge up here."

☆☆★☆☆

Detective Algerson, a tall, middle-aged man with slightly balding dark hair, greeted Gloria in the lobby at ABM. He flashed his badge and gave her a nod and the door look of a basset hound.

"I'll want to interview Ms. Willard's other co-workers," he said as Gloria escorted him to the security desk to check in. As they waited their turn, she told him the same thing she'd told him earlier over the phone. She hadn't seen Jo again after they'd returned from lunch yesterday.

"I confirmed her presence at the parade yesterday. We did find her image in some of the footage. What time did you arrive back at this location?"

"It was nearly 1:30. We were late. I'll bet security can confirm the time we used our passes."

"Good." He spoke to her over his shoulder as he presented his badge at the security desk and turned to sign the register. "I might have more questions for you later, after we've checked that out."

Gloria wouldn't let go of him that easily. She had questions of her own. She turned toward the elevators, leading the way. "I can bring you up to HR and introduce you there. Then I'll head home. The boss gave me the afternoon off."

"Men have died for less." He spoke dryly enough to confuse her.

"I beg your pardon?" She hit the call button for the elevators.

"Sorry, Ma'am. Police humor." The lines of his face drooped, in no way suggesting anything related to what she'd call humor.

"That's not very funny."

His tone turned apologetic. "This has been confirmed as a murder investigation, and we have to consider every possible motive."

Gloria gaped at him as they stood waiting for the elevator doors to open. Was he suggesting she might kill Jo for an afternoon off? Why would anyone want to murder Jo? It must have been some random thing, a mugging gone awry. "It couldn't be murder. Everyone loves Jo."

"Apparently someone felt otherwise," the detective said as they entered the elevator.

"It must have been some stranger." Gloria used undue force to punch the button for the fourth floor. "No one who knew her would do it. Where did you find her?"

"We're not disclosing that information at this time. The body was moved from the scene of the killing, so we can't discount the possibility the attack occurred here at her workplace, or anywhere else she many have been since she was last seen alive."

Leading the way from the elevator to the HR reception desk, Gloria tried to digest this latest disclosure. None of it seemed real. Jo couldn't be dead.

She waited until Mary finished a call and turned to them with a smile, then introduced the detective.

Gloria lingered nearby while the detective tersely explained his business.

"That's not possible," Mary exclaimed on hearing the news. "Jo called in this morning, said she was sick."

"We believe the person you spoke with was the murderer, hoping to delay discovery of the crime."

"Oh no." Mary looked stricken, her eyes wide and face pale. "Oh, this is horrible."

"I'm sorry, ma'am, but we'll need your help to see that the killer is brought to justice. Please think back and tell me anything you can remember."

"Of course." Mary dabbed at her eyes. "But I don't remember anything out of the ordinary."

The detective pulled out a notepad and pencil. "Would you describe the voice of the caller for me?"

"She said she had a cold. She sounded so hoarse I'm not even sure it was a 'she.' It might have been a man, disguising his voice, talking a bit high, you know?"

"Yes, ma'am." He scratched beside his ear with the pencil. "I don't suppose you folks record incoming calls?"

Mary paused, pursing her lips. "Why, I don't know. You'd have to talk to someone in security about that."

"I'll take him back and introduce him, show him Jo's cubicle after he's done here." Gloria led Algerson through the security door, past the break room and back to the payroll section where Jo worked. Had worked. Jo's cubicle stood between Patty and Anne's and the alcove housing the fax, printers and the mail station. Now the two women from neighboring cubicles hovered at the edge of Jo's empty space, talking in low voices. Mary must have called them from the front desk.

"You heard?" Gloria asked as she drew near.

"It's awful." Anne choked on the words. Her eyes shone damp. Reddened eyes and nose did little good for her pale redhead's complexion. The evidence of tears threatened Gloria's grasp on her own. They pressed heavily behind her face. She had to hold herself together. At least until she got home. First, find out everything possible about what had happened to Jo.

"I can't believe it." Patty looked stunned, as dazed as if she'd run smack into a wall. The whites of her dark eyes showed stark against her chocolate skin.

"I know." Gloria shared a commiserating look with the two before turning to present the detective waiting behind her. "This is Detective Algerson. He's investigating Jo's death and wants to ask some questions."

"That's right." Algerson stepped forward and Gloria made herself inconspicuous, taking a step back and to the side, near the fax machine. "Just a few basic questions. We want to establish Ms. Willard's whereabouts prior to the time of her death." He pulled out his notepad. "First, would you spell out your full names for me?"

Gloria looked into Jo's cubicle. Not empty, really. Printouts lay splayed across the work area beside her keyboard. Her collection of calendars decked the bland gray walls like garlands of kittens and nosegays of Far Side cartoons. Jo's favorite Dilbert mug sat to one side, still holding a couple inches of yesterday's coffee. Odd, Jo never left the office without washing her coffee mug. Gloria frowned.

"When did you last see Ms. Willard?" Algerson went on.

"She was still here when I left for the day," Patty said.

"Yeah. She usually comes in early and leaves early, but yesterday she said she wanted to finish up her project." Anne stood with her arms crossed, holding tightly to her elbows. "She was so responsible."

Yes and tidy.

"Do you know anything about the project she was working on?" Algerson pursued. "Or what time she left?"

"She was wrapping up reports on last year's payroll taxes," Patty answered. "She said she had a couple items to follow up on. I don't know how late she stayed."

"I don't think she left at all, not on her own. Look." Gloria pointed to the mug on Jo's desk. "Jo always washed her mug out at the end of the day. Always. She liked having it clean and ready for coffee first thing when she came in."

Patty gasped. "That's right."

"Oh my God." Anne shuddered visibly. "Do you think something happened to her here?"

"No," Algerson said, scanning the area. "I don't see any signs of violence here, presuming your desks are always this cluttered."

Gloria swallowed hard against a sour surge in her gut. She felt light-headed.

"The clutter's normal." Anne's pale complexion flushed. "We get a lot of paperwork."

"What's going on here?"

Gloria had missed the approach of the stout, gray-haired woman in a gray suit-dress, and so had Patty and Anne, judging by their guilty starts.

Patty recovered first. "Oh, Ms. Dexter. This is Detective Algerson. He's here about Jo." She turned to the detective. "Ms. Dexter supervises HR."

"Yes, and you should have come to me first before disturbing my workers." The older woman's eyes narrowed at the detective as if pinpointing strike zones.

The detective turned to Ms. Dexter. "Of course. Perhaps you'll tell me more about the projects Ms. Willard was working on before her death?"

"Certainly. Why don't we step into my office so these two can get back to work." Ms. Dexter cast a significant look at Patty and Anne, and a questioning one at Gloria as if to ask what business she had being there. All business. As if the woman hadn't known and worked with Jo on a daily basis for a couple years.

"I guess I'd better be going." Gloria turned toward the elevators. She wouldn't learn any more while the detective stayed closeted with Ms. Dexter.

She had to get away. Away from the reminders of Jo's death. She still couldn't digest it, or accept it as real. From the look of things, Jo might return to her empty cubicle at any moment, turn on the computer and take her usual seat. It seemed impossible for the world to have changed so completely in one short day.

☆☆★☆☆

For the next half hour, Levinson fired off a seemingly endless stream of questions about Wonder Guy's powers, under the claim of anticipating cases in which the hero might be of particular use to the police.

"X-Ray vision?" The chief leaned across his desk as though he might lunge at his visitor on the least provocation.

Greg, still standing, uneasy in the man's presence, focused hard on the outer wall of the office, and sure enough, the shadowy form of the neighboring Government Center building emerged, like a giant, elongated stone toaster.

"Yep."

"Hmm. What do you think of taking a look through the walls of suspect meth houses to verify whether there's drug dealing in progress?"

"I wouldn't be comfortable with that unless you had a search warrant, and if you did, you wouldn't need me."

The police chief grunted, eased back in his padded chair. "Thought you'd say something like that."

The representatives from the precincts arrived, and Levinson turned to them.

"Wonder Guy, I'd like you to meet Sergeant Rognby, Precinct 5 and Detective Sergeant Diaz, Precinct 3. Gentlemen, meet Wonder Guy."

Greg nodded to the two men, taking courage from the clinging fabric of the mask concealing his features. "Hello."

"We'll be treating Mr. Wonder Guy here as a special case. Think of him as a cross between an informant and someone in witness protection. We protect his identity and he helps us out where he can." The chief leaned across his desk, extending his hand to Greg. "It's been good to meet you."

"Likewise." They shook, Greg careful not to exert any pressure at all. Wonder Guy's strength took some getting used to, and crushing the chief's hand would get things off to a bad start.

Before turning back to the papers on his desk, Levinson addressed Rognby and Diaz. "Gentlemen, take his statements and send him back out where he can do some good."

Greg followed the two detectives from the chief's office to the elevators. The secretary, a woman wearing a conservatively styled dark suit dress and severely cut gray hair, stared as he passed. Greg gave her a smile and nod.

"So." Diaz, tall and dark, in an impeccable suit, looking like a younger Ricardo Montalban, turned to him when the elevator doors had closed behind them. "You know that other guy, the one in red, who ran across the lake the other day?"

"Oh yeah. That was me too."

146

"How many costumes you got?" Rognby, tall, blond, and built like a linebacker, tossed the question straight and hard as a football.

"Do you wear the same suit every day?" Greg flung one back at him.

"No," Rognby admitted. "But I'm showing my face so people know who I am."

"Good point," Greg said.

"Makes me wonder." Diaz spoke as they reached a marble-tiled hallway on the basement level and conducted Greg to an interview room. "Did Batman, Superman and Spiderman have a whole set of identical costumes so they weren't wearing the same one every day?"

"Think of the laundry they'd have to do every night if they only had the one costume," Rognby said, wincing.

"Superman could walk through fire, completely sterilizing his costume anytime he wanted," Greg mused aloud. "Bruce Wayne was a millionaire with the money to afford a lot of backup costumes. Poor Peter Parker'd have had a lot of laundry, though."

☆☆★☆☆

Later, his witness statements complete, Greg couldn't fly directly out of City Hall from the basement without destroying parts of the building and surrounding streets and sidewalk. Instead, he walked to the Government Center through the wide, well-lit, tiled tunnel under Fourth Street.

Everyone around him wore either business dress or everyday jeans and slacks. Well, some Somali immigrants wore long robes and head coverings, and the policemen wore uniforms, but all the stares at his costumed form made him self-conscious. Weren't business suits, uniforms, robes, jeans and everything else some kind of costume too? Why should he feel weird? His costume made at least as much sense as the guy wearing his leather jacket on such a warm spring day.

What good did it do him being a superhero if he only felt like more of an oddball than ever? Maybe that was his real problem. One thing to be said for Gloria's fiancé, Pete fit in. No one would stare at Pete while he did nothing stranger than walk between City Hall and the Government Center.

Greg paused at the glass wall shielding the sheets of water falling from the reflecting pool in the Government Center Plaza above. The fountain seemed as wonderful as any of the magical events he'd encountered these past few days. Water flowed like skeins of glass and silver over the stone lip above, catching the sunshine as it fell into the basin a level below the plaza. Tempting, to break through the glass, take flight up and out, through the pool's well and into the open air. But witnesses surrounded him and, most importantly, he had no desire to face Chief Levinson if he damaged public property.

Greg took the escalator up to ground level and exited the building before giving in to the urge to take flight. He made a running leap to the high blue yonder and people who'd been only staring before gasped and cried out in astonishment below him. He twisted in midair to wave to the crowd of school children clustered around the circular reflecting pool.

He positioned himself above the center of the pool, where he'd earlier seen water flowing to the well from below. He understood why people threw coins into a fountain. Especially now. In a world where fairy godmothers wielded magical powers, why not make wishes? He might not know what underpinnings of quantum connectivity or super strings, what sub-atomic manipulations made such magic real, but he knew more to be possible in the world than allowed for in any of his previous philosophies.

He flew high above the pool before he dropped as if falling, to cries of alarm, diving to the bottom of the well. Entering the well surrounded him in the water's magic of silver and song. There, in the enlivening mists, Greg caught himself and leapt high again, careful not to damage the tiled flooring on liftoff. He arrowed up and out, meeting the cheers of children.

What a rush! Even as the air burned his bare jaw with acceleration, Greg's heart lifted. Maybe drawing stares could be some fun after all. Greg turned and waved again before heading home.

☆☆★☆☆

Zzzz. The buzz in his ear grew shrill, turning to a high-pitched squeal. Greg slapped his head, and then shook off the effects of the mighty blow.

"Agh! What the--what was that?" A feedback signal?

The squeal sounded again like a nail through his ear. Greg banked to a hasty landing on the flat rooftop of a red brick apartment building in South Minneapolis.

"Serafina," he called.

"Yes, dear?" The tidy, white-haired figure stood beside him. "I'm sorry about that. There seems to be some interference with our signal. I don't know much regarding these technologies with the metal bits and electricity. I plugged one of those radio devices into the costume."

She circled Greg as she spoke, peering closely at the costume. She seemed almost to sniff at it.

"Ah, yes. It seems someone gave you a gift." She reached up, plucked at his shoulder and handed him what looked like a pin, for very broad definitions of pin. It had a bulging over-large head trailing a length of long fine wire.

He'd watched enough TV to know a tracking device when he saw one. Detective Diaz had clapped him there on the shoulder as they'd parted earlier.

"Someone wants to know where Wonder Guy goes, where I live." So much for establishing trust with the police department. He sighed, envying Batman's relationship with Commissioner Gordon.

Serafina tsked. "Well, I'm afraid we must disappoint them."

Greg held up the tiny device before his eyes and turned on the heat vision. Without ever having tried to apply it before, he knew how to activate it. He turned the heat of his anger on the object before his eyes. Heat shimmered around the tiny device until the filament slumped into the head, and the head collapse into a shiny bead of metal. He flicked the bead to the gravel underfoot.

Serafina smiled a prim smile. "I attempted to call you just now in order to draw your attention to a pair of young men who are presently breaking into cars in the parking ramps at the large market complex to the south of us."

"The Mall of America?"

"Yes, dear. Once there you can follow the sound of breaking glass."

Chapter 10

Gloria made it home in half the usual time. Amazing what a difference driving home at noon made, compared to rush hour. When she approached it, she balked at going into her own house. She got enough of Dad during her regular schedule. She couldn't deal with him now, not with her world reeling and strange around her. She headed straight for Aggie's, opened the back screen door, and stopped short, finding the inner door closed and unaccountably locked. It took a moment to digest the fact of this barrier between her and her goal.

In the shade of the huge maple dominating the yard, she stood with the slight spring breeze blowing around her, carrying the scent of freshly mown grass. Had she come to the wrong door of the wrong house? No, her own house stood right next door, like always. She registered the note taped to the window in Aggie's kitchen door.

Out for coffee, back before dinner. Don't worry.
- *Aggie.*

What a day for disruptions of the sacred order of the universe. Once, long ago, she'd liked surprises. Today's events reminded her exactly why that had changed. Gloria sat down on the top step of the cement stoop, heedless of her nice linen skirt. She wanted to talk to Aggie, but Aggie had gone. She'd counted on talking to Aggie, needed to talk to someone. Gloria gulped in a deep breath. She would not cry. Despite the evident lush life of familiar lawns and houses and trees, the world had become an empty desert.

A couple more deep breaths steadied her. She dug in her bag, found her cell phone and punched Pete's work number. He didn't like her calling him there, but under the circumstances, there ought to be an exception. Right?

"Hello? This is Pete in accounts receivable."

"Pete. It's me, Gloria." Her voice sounded shaky to her own ears.

"What is it?" He spoke in a hushed tone. "You know I'm not supposed to take personal calls here."

"I know. Just. I need you. My friend at work, Jo? She's gone. Dead. She was killed last night. Oh, Pete." She gulped, struggling past the constriction of her throat, dragging in the air like hauling up an anchor.

"Hey, I'm sorry, sweetheart. That's terrible. I want to be there for you, but I can't talk right now. What say we get together as soon as I'm off work?"

Gloria spoke past the rushing in her ears, the sinking of her heart. "Sure. I guess."

"That's my girl. We'll talk then. I'll take you out. Later." He cut the connection.

Gloria lowered her head to her knees. The rushing in her ears resolved into the whoosh of the breeze through the leaves above her. Birds chirped and called, a car door slammed somewhere down the block. More distantly, a lawnmower growled. It all seemed part of some other world. Here she trembled alone in the darkness behind her eyes, where the flood came sweeping past all restraints.

"Hey, Glo-worm, what's wrong?"

Gloria started upright, wiping at her eyes.

"Greg. What are you doing home in the middle of the day?" She managed to speak, but her voice sounded wrong: weak, false.

"I thought I'd make myself a sandwich for lunch--what about you? Don't you have work today?"

☆☆★☆☆

Greg stood with a hand on the rail of Aggie's ramp beside the back steps. Something had to be very wrong. Gloria hadn't snapped at him when he called her 'Glo-worm,' the nickname he'd come up with when he was ten, for the sole purpose of getting her goat. Over the years, it had produced reactions from shrieks when she was ten, to growls, to a roll of her eyes in her teens, to her current dismissive snort. But always something.

He'd used it now unthinkingly, from fond habit. With her head bowed across her knees, she might have been only resting, but when she looked up the bleakness in her eyes struck him like a fist to

154

his chest. No sign of the usual gamut from sunshine to storms that made her face a continual fascination to him, but signs of her tears wrenched his gut.

"Aggie's gone," she said, tilting her head toward the door behind her.

He read the note taped to the glass. She wouldn't cry over that, would she?

"You get off work early?" He took a seat beside her on the stoop. "Is it some kind of holiday?" He could never remember the holidays. He'd gone to campus more than once to find buildings locked and closed. "Did you want to get into the house to work on your project?"

"No. No," she repeated with more force. "I wanted Aggie. I wanted to talk to her. And, no it's not a holiday." She looked at him with some exasperation breaking through the dullness of her expression. "You'd know that if you paid any attention to the rest of the world." She broke off. "I'm sorry. I'm just so upset."

"What is it?"

She folded over again, resting her face in her hands. His high IQ didn't help him here. Was she crying again? Should he give her a hug? Aggie would give her a hug. He moved an inch or two closer, enough so she'd be able to feel someone beside her, know she wasn't alone.

"I'm not my mother," he said. "But I'm here. You can talk to me."

"Thanks," she mumbled into her hands. She lifted her head, shifting to face him. Her knees brushed his legs. "It's so awful. I still can't believe it." She shook her head. "My friend, you know, Jo. She's dead." She reached out, clutched his hand.

He held her hand between both of his. Her slender fingers looked so fragile. He had to find a way to comfort to her, to steady her. He couldn't stand seeing her this shaken.

"Dead? How?" he asked. "Was she ill?"

"No." Her tone turned angry, then softened as she said, "No. That might have been better, not such a shock, not so scary." She paused as she drew in a long ragged breath. "Someone killed her."

Her hand clenched in his and her shoulders shook. The tremors ran through her like waves through water. He didn't hesitate to put an arm around her shoulders. If nothing else, he'd be steady for her. A rock. In their whole lifetime as friends and neighbors, he'd never once thought Gloria frail or weak. She seemed so small now, trembling, leaning against him into the shelter of his arm. Sitting this close to her, he breathed in the roses and musk of her perfume and caught the hint of citrus in her hair.

"Hey." He had to say something. "Hey, are you crying?" Her face stayed hidden against his chest. She made a snuffling sound.

"Just," she hiccuped, "a little."

"It's okay," he said. "I've heard you cry before. Remember when Tommy Lindahl beheaded your Barbie doll?

Was that next sound a sob or a chuckle? She snuffled, and he released her as she straightened, pulling away, wiping her eyes. "I'll be okay. It's such a shock, so awful. Jo. Someone killed Jo. Who'd do something like that?"

"Killed? Murder?" Really? Hard to get his mind around that. Murders happened on TV all the time. Not in real life, not around here.

"Yes. It must have been yesterday evening after Patty and Anne left for the day. It might even have happened in our building." Her voice choked on the words. "The police wouldn't tell me where. It's worse not knowing. I imagine all sorts of things." Gloria huddled against him again, not bothering to hide her tears. She sobbed into his shirt.

He sat stunned, too concerned for Gloria to fully appreciate the miracle of holding her close. Where had he been? Where had Wonder Guy been when this happened? Why hadn't Serafina alerted him? He'd spent yesterday evening back at the computer lab. Not only working on his thesis project, but investigating ways Professor Stevens might have gained access to student work. Maybe Serafina would only contact him when he was in superhero mode, in costume. He had a life. He couldn't play superhero every hour of every day. Yet, he might have been able to save Gloria's friend. Gloria hadn't been this hurt or lost since the day her mother died.

☆☆★☆☆

Gloria's tears subsided soon enough, leaving her drained and hollow. She still couldn't grasp the finality of losing her friend. A gash ripped the fabric of her life, leaving her to feel small and vulnerable before a looming darkness. She'd been here before. Back when her mother died, more than ten years ago now. She shivered despite the warmth of Greg's arm around her.

"Why don't we wait inside?" Greg suggested. "Aggie probably won't be out long."

Gloria took a deep breath, looking up and around at the quiet, shaded yard, the sunlit neighborhood, all too aware now of the shadows in the familiar scene. Greg's presence steadied her, a long-familiar part of everything right and normal, a rock in the turmoil shaking her now.

"Sure. Aggie won't mind if we go in and grab something to drink." She rose to her feet, calmer now for having let the flood of tears escape. "Have you got a key?"

"Yeah." He stood, keys jangling as he dug in the pocket of his slacks. "Don't you know where she keeps the spare?"

"Oh, yeah. I guess I do. I've never needed it. She's always here." Gloria frowned at the plaintive tone of her own voice and eyed the note on the door. "Since when does Aggie go out for coffee in the middle of the day?"

"It's a mystery to me." Greg fit his key to the lock and led the way into the kitchen.

She went straight to the table and dropped onto a chair.

He leaned into the fridge and pulled out a couple of sodas. "Don't tell me..." He put his hand to his temple like a mind reader. "Anything diet for you, 'who needs the extra sugar' right?"

"You know me too well." Gloria grimaced as an unwilling smile collided with her inner gloom. She took the can of Diet Coke he proffered and popped the top. "And I don't need to hear about the evils of aspartame yet again."

"I think you do," Greg teased. A pop and fizz announced the opening of his Mountain Dew. "You're still drinking the stuff."

"Like sugar is any better." Gloria rolled her eyes. This was good. Normal old Greg took her mind off things she didn't want to consider. She clenched her fist against further tears. She needed to understand this, and clearly. Something dangerous loomed. "I'm afraid I've got worse trouble than sugar or aspartame right now."

"The police don't have Jo's killer?"

"They don't even know who the killer is--not last I heard." She took a swig from her can. The bubbles and caffeine seemed to help clear her head. Now she almost regretted coming home. She might have learned more if she'd stuck around the office, but not while Algerson stayed locked behind Ms. Dexter's door. She'd had no excuse for accompanying the detective downstairs to talk with people in the security office. Tears had overwhelmed her not five minutes ago. She'd never have held out against them if she'd stayed. She sighed, tapping the side of her can with a fingernail. With tears past, anger set in.

"You know the worst part?" she asked.

He sat across from her sipping from his soda, relaxed, aside from the hint of worry when he looked at her. "What's that?"

"Ordinarily I'd talk to Jo about something that upset me this much. I'd go to my desk and dial her extension. I caught myself starting to do it a couple times before I left the office today. I needed her and she wasn't there. Someone took her away from me. It's not right. It's not fair. I want to hurt whoever did this."

"Hey." Greg set his can down. "You're right. It's not fair."

"'Life isn't fair.' People always say that, but I want it fair. If life isn't fair, people should be. This wasn't life being unfair. Somebody, some person did this. Some creepy a-hole took Jo's life and should pay for it." She set her jaw. Someone would pay before Gloria finished with them.

"Go, Gloria." Greg gave her a round of applause.

His encouragement warmed her.

"You're not the only one who wants things fair. The whole justice system exists because people, most people, anyway, want things fair. Most of us want good people protected and bad guys punished." The look he gave her turned grim. He looked like a stranger for a moment. Someone with more depths and shadows than she'd ever imagined Greg to have. "I hate that someone did this to you."

"They did it to Jo, not to me." Sweet of him to think first how it affected her, but Jo was the one who had lost her life.

"They took away your friend. They've got you scared."

No denying that.

He glowered, a dark, implacable look, almost frightening in its intensity--though comforting how it arose on her behalf.

"Did anyone have something against Jo?" He'd returned to his usual practical, logical self.

"No. We all loved her. She listened. She kept the coffee pot full in her section. She always remembered everyone's birthday. She brought donuts to the office. She made me laugh." Gloria strained to get the words out as her throat tightened again. "On my last birthday she got me this miniature stone bear. It symbolized strength."

"There must have been something, some reason. Was she seeing anyone?" He had the determined look he got whenever he sank his teeth into a particularly challenging puzzle.

"No." She took a deep breath. Greg always helped keep her focused. "Jo wasn't seeing anyone. She broke up with a guy, Kevin, last month because he moved to Pittsburgh. He had a good job offer and Jo didn't want to leave her life here and spend the rest of her life with him, especially not in Pittsburgh."

"What's wrong with Pittsburgh? It ranks high on livability."

"Jo's from Denver. She's--she was--a big Broncos fan. She hated the Steelers."

"Oh. That lets Kevin off the hook." He frowned, and his mouth tightened reminding her of the

161

thousand times she'd seen him bent over some puzzle or homework problem. "What makes one person kill another? It seems so stupid to destroy something you can't replace."

"We've both seen plenty of detective shows and cop shows in our lives." Watching movies while doing crafts or playing computer games had been a favorite activity in Aggie's house all through their school years. "It always seems to come down to some sort of passion like love, hate, jealousy--or money. Love triangles weren't Jo's style and I can't imagine her making anyone hate her enough to kill her. She wasn't rich so nobody stands to inherit anything from her." Nothing but paperbacks and knick-knacks.

"Maybe someone saw her as a threat?" His long-boned fingers tapped a slow tattoo on the tabletop. "Maybe not physically, but might she have learned something damaging about someone?"

"She did work on payroll." Gloria considered the matter. "Maybe she caught someone falsifying time cards or something?" That seemed too much of a stretch. Supervisors had to approve time cards.

"People who know too much, like blackmailers, always end up as murder victims on TV, killed by people trying to protect their money or their secrets."

"Jo wouldn't blackmail anyone." Gloria scowled at him. "She'd take a payroll issue straight to management. It's hard to imagine anyone falsifying timecards on a large enough scale to be noticeable."

"Maybe not blackmail then. Maybe not even related to payroll. Maybe she stumbled onto something somebody wanted to keep secret?"

"We're not likely to figure this out. We don't have access to the witnesses the way the police do. I feel so...jumpy, thinking someone might have killed her at work. Someone I know. Who should I suspect? Who can I trust?"

"You can trust almost everybody, and the police will figure it out. At least you'll know for sure what happened, all the people who aren't murderers."

She did have a few people she trusted. Greg. Aggie. They'd never met Jo. Also Pete, of course. He'd only met Jo once when he'd picked Gloria up from work as Jo was leaving the building. Ages ago. It all seemed ages ago. Time lay broken into two distinct pieces: *The Before and After of Jo.* Just as there'd been *The Before and After of Mom.*

☆☆★☆☆

"Before we open the meeting, Serafina will present her progress report." Philomena stood, regal with her erect posture and perfectly arranged silver hair, at the head of the age-darkened walnut table dominating the library conference room in the chapter's headquarters. Today the room accommodated the members of other area chapters as well as those local to Minneapolis. Some twenty ladies-of-age sat around the table.

"Good morning, ladies." Serafina spoke in bright, bird-song tones, rising from her seat at Philomena's left while the chapter president resumed her place. "I'd like to thank you again for authorizing the public display of magic and contributing energy to the cause. We've not yet flushed the opposition into overt action, but if you'll look to the bar graph on screen." She indicated the PowerPoint display projected on a screen lowered across the library windows.

"You can see the fluctuations of various energies over the past few days as compared to the averages for the past ten years.

"Note how Anger and Despair have dipped well below the current norms." The display advanced with a soft click. "This next graph shows the steady rise in those same energies as seen over the past decade. You'll recall, of course, this troubling trend is what prompted our present course of action.

"Undoubtedly, those of our kin addicted to the dark energies are responsible for the spike of unhappiness. The ordinary unseelie sprites would be incapable of such an organized effort as our analysis suggests. There is some higher intelligence at play here. If our countermeasures continue, I have every faith this force will soon expose itself by attempting to interfere with our appointed hero."

The ladies gathered around the table murmured and nodded in agreement.

Chapter 11

"Thanks for staying here with me," Gloria told Greg. "I'm sure you had other plans."

"Nothing that can't wait." Greg rose. "Except a sandwich. Aggie won't mind if I fix us a couple. You still like peanut butter?" He moved around the counter dividing the worktable and crafts area from the stove, refrigerator and kitchen cupboards and withdrew a loaf of bread from the box.

Food didn't appeal to her, but it had been a long time since the bagel she'd grabbed on her way to the office this morning. Maybe she wouldn't feel so light-headed if she ate something. Gloria glanced at the clock over the fridge. During their clock-making phase, she and Aggie had made it look like the cross-section of an orange. Past one o'clock already. If there was ever a time for comfort food, this was it. "Sure. Peanut butter with raisins and honey sounds good."

"Sure you wouldn't like one of my 'specials'?" He grinned.

She grimaced. His peanut butter, pickle and cheese sandwiches actually tasted better than they sounded, but it wouldn't do to tell him. "Not on your life."

"Why didn't you go home?" Greg laid out pieces of bread on the cutting board and then spread them with peanut butter, dipping his knife deftly into the jar and out again.

"What?" She followed his motions as he applied raisins and honey to one sandwich-in-the-making and then, with smooth efficiency, laid slices of cheese and pickles on the other. She'd sure rather watch the efficient dance of his sandwich-making process than think about the subject at hand.

"When you got here and Aggie was gone, when I found you sitting alone out on the back stoop? You looked like some homeless waif. Why not go home?"

The question annoyed her. "I didn't want to go home," she snapped at him. "Why do you come to your mother's house for lunch? Why do you still live over her garage instead of on campus like a normal grad student?"

"There's no such thing as a normal grad student," he responded as if by rote, but flinched from the unwarranted attack. He set her sandwich before her and settled back at the table with his own.

"I'm sorry." She put a hand on his. "That's not fair of me. Money's tight while you're in school."

"It's not just that." His tone grew thoughtful. "I feel better knowing I can check in on Aggie every day. Mom likes everyone to think she's totally independent, and she even fools herself most of the time, but she can't always do what needs doing."

He took a bite from his three-tiered sandwich and chewed.

"She can't?" Aggie was fooling people? If so, she'd had Gloria fooled too. She bit thoughtfully into her own sandwich.

"There are things she can't reach, things she can't lift." He took a swig from his soda.

Well Aggie needed a hand with reaching and lifting, but that had never seemed any big deal.

"She dropped her cell phone between the bookshelves the other morning and wouldn't have been able to call for help--except I stopped by that morning and pulled it out for her."

"Oh no." Aggie always had her cell phone.

"Yes, and that wheelchair of hers has gotten stuck more than once. The left wheel has jammed--"

"She's going to get it checked out. It happened last week when we went to Michael's together."

Gloria paused. She'd lost Jo. What would she do without Aggie? How had she never noticed what a fine line Aggie kept between coping with the practicalities of her illness and maintaining her independence? Why didn't Aggie ever say anything to her? Weren't they friends?

Greg noticed. He was right there, taking up the slack without ever mentioning it. Even now, here he was when she needed him, needed someone. Was he neglecting his work, the research project vital to his whole future, for the sake of sitting here with her right now?

"Anyhow," she said, "I'm glad you're here. For Aggie and now for me. Thanks."

He made a gruff, throat clearing noise. "It's okay. I'm sorry about your friend."

"I wonder if the police have been able to contact Jo's family. She doesn't have anyone locally, just some cousins in Colorado."

"The police should have access to her information." He set his half-eaten sandwich back on the plate. "Why don't you call them to make sure?"

"Yes. If they don't, I've still got the number on my phone for her cousin, Jenny, who she stayed with on vacation last year." Gloria dug in her shoulder bag, "That detective gave me his card in case I thought of anything relevant."

She found the card and her phone, stared at both for a moment before summoning the courage to punch in the number. Greg sat silently across from her, sipping his soda.

It was only a moment before the call picked up.

"Detective Algerson?" she asked.

"Yes, ma'am?"

"It's Gloria Torkenson. We met earlier. I thought of something. A couple things. Have you checked on Jo's ex yet?"

"We've been unable to contact him as yet."

"He moved to Pittsburg a while back. The split was friendly. I wanted to let you know, if you were looking, he probably had nothing to do with it."

"That's good of you, but we've already ruled him out. Others have confirmed he no longer lives locally.

"Oh, I have contact info for Jo's family in Denver. She doesn't have anyone locally."

"Good. We can use that. Your HR department's info, what Ms. Dexter gave us, proved to be outdated. Just let me write down what you've got."

She read off the number from her phone's contact list.

"Good. We'll contact her people," the detective assured her.

"Detective Algerson," Gloria softened her tone, pleading. "I have to admit I'm almost afraid to go back to the office, thinking there might be a murderer there. Can you tell me anything on how the investigation is going?"

Greg rolled his eyes. She frowned at him. She felt silly playing for sympathy with the detective, but that wouldn't stop her. "Please?"

The detective cleared his throat. "Well, ma'am, I don't think you need to worry. We now believe this to be a stranger killing. Your security people found the door beside your loading bay propped open and the traces of blood we found at the scene were identified as Ms. Willard's."

"Oh. Oh no. So, Jo surprised someone breaking in?"

Greg straightened in his chair, raising a brow. She held up her hand for him to wait.

"I'm told employees sometimes leave that door propped open when they go out for a smoke," the detective said.

"Yes. Sometimes." All the dang time. Still, it wasn't as if anyone would see it from the street or like the neighborhood had a noticeable crime rate.

"Your security people found some equipment, new computers, still in their shipping crates, missing. We believe thieves took advantage of an open door and Ms. Willard surprised them in the act."

"Oh no. Poor Jo." Gloria bit her lip. Jo nearly always took the back exit. She loved to park under the flowering crab apples at the end of the parking lot. Especially this time of year, while they bloomed pink, and white, and red and fragrant. "Oh, that's awful."

Gloria ended the call in a daze, thanking the detective for sharing what they'd learned. It was all so terrible. Some stranger, probably some hardened criminal had killed Jo.

At least the detective's conclusion cleared her co-workers. The people she worked with had their quirks, but they all seemed like decent sorts.

"Are you going to be okay?" Greg asked, reminding her of his presence.

She shrugged, gathering strength to speak. "At least I don't have to worry about a murderer in the office. That's kind of a relief."

☆☆★☆☆

Greg listened as Gloria filled him in on what the detective had told her. He'd had half a mind to ask Serafina for a superpower to help him to solve the case. Only what sort of power would do the job? The ability to view past events claimed by some psychics? The ability to force people to tell the truth, like Wonder Woman's lasso gave her? All moot now.

Looked like the police had this one covered. He should stick to dealing with situations beyond them, where Wonder Guy could make a real difference.

"I said," Gloria spoke forcefully, "I'll be okay now. Where were you?"

"Just thinking." Murder lurking behind some familiar face, the possibility chilled him. He'd always taken people at face value, but a person, like a lake, might show only the reflected sky rather than what lay hidden below the surface. "I'm glad the police have ruled out your co-workers as murderers."

"Amen to that." Gloria shuddered. "I didn't want to go back to the office suspecting someone there of murder." The crusts of her sandwich lay abandoned before her. She stood, gathering up her plate along with his. "But, like I was saying as your mind wandered." She gave his shoulder a light cuff as she passed behind him to deposit their dishes in the sink. She gathered the utensils from the cutting board. "I'm okay now, or at least a lot better. I'm sure you didn't plan on spending your whole afternoon babysitting me."

"I don't mind." He twisted in his chair, watching her graceful, sure movements as she turned on the faucet and grabbed a sponge to wash up.

"And I love you for it." She spoke over her shoulder and the sound of running water. "But I'll be okay here until Aggie gets back and I don't want you neglecting your research project on my account."

"I don't like leaving you by yourself when you've been so upset." He hesitated. He did have work to do at the computer lab, not to mention being concerned now over what trouble he might be able to prevent while on duty as Wonder Guy. "Isn't your dad home? You could hang out with him..."

Gloria's scowl killed the rest of his thought, leaving it to shrivel unspoken. She put the last plate in the drainer and rejoined him.

"Greg. I hate to break it to you, but watching my dad drown himself in alcohol is no way to get my mind off bad stuff. I'll do better to put together a few orders of cell shells. I like working with my hands. It soothes me."

She looked tired. He hadn't realized before the effort it took for her to keep a bright face on life, to keep up the stance of cheerful optimism she usually wore. Gloria didn't feel at home in her own house. She seemed more at home here with him and his mother than at her place with her father.

Even here, she never seemed to relax, as if she believed no one would accept her if she didn't put up her usual brave front and give them her patented engaging smile. How long had it been now since he'd last seen her lose it?

Her twelfth birthday party. When her parents had thrown a backyard barbecue to celebrate. He'd been there when she'd learned of the traffic accident that caused her mother's death. He'd never seen her cry so wretchedly before, or since, until today. Now, as then, it left him longing for some way to make her world right again.

It all came back to him now. Gloria's aunt Cecily had approached the weeping girl when she sank to the lawn beside him at the picnic table. Her aunt knelt beside her and put an arm around her shoulder. She gave Gloria's slim, huddled shoulders a shake. "Stop it right now. All these people are here to help you celebrate your birthday. It's your duty to be the hostess, to make sure everyone has a good time. It's selfish to curl up and cry this way."

Only then had someone told Cecily the news, and she left Gloria behind while she went to comfort her husband for the loss of his sister.

"C'mon, Gloria." Greg had bent to take one of his friend's limp hands. "Let's go over to my house for a while. My mom will know what to do."

"We haven't cut the cake yet." Gloria looked up, her expression blank.

"Someone else can cut it."

"It's my job."

"Your Aunt Cissy didn't know." He'd fallen silent, unwilling to say what he thought of her aunt, or to speak of the terrible thing that made nothing else matter.

"Being hostess is still my job." Some spirit returned to her voice and eyes. The party continued, kids yelling over by the Slip n' Slide, adults chattering around the grill and along the picnic tables.

Hardly anyone seemed aware of what had happened.

"The party can wait," he'd insisted and tugged on her hand. "People are still eating their burgers and hot dogs. You should get away from here for a while anyhow."

"Okay." She gave in so readily he'd been afraid she was broken.

When they got to Greg's place, the instant she saw their faces, Aggie left off mixing a fresh batch of lemonade for the party. She rolled over, pulled Gloria up on her lap, and rested the girl's head on her shoulder while Greg explained what had happened.

Gloria never did get to cut her birthday cake. One of the mothers who'd come to help out with festivities took over the task, making up plastic-wrapped plates of cake to send home with the guests as they left, as most did, very soon after the news broke.

Today came as an echo of the past. At least this time Gloria seemed to be over her tears, for now. If she wanted to be alone, and doing her craftwork gave her comfort, he'd leave her to it.

☆☆★☆☆

Gloria loved this part of it. Maybe not the smell of the hot glue, but she loved transforming a plain bit of leatherette by affixing rhinestones arrayed like a scattering of stars, or making it punk with steel grommets and chains, or steam punk with bits of clockwork and brass. She loved the variety of textures, materials and styles her imagination conceived.

She and Aggie had standing orders for popular items too repetitive to be much fun--like those featuring gold, silver or rhinestone capital initials. Gloria rewarded herself for completing a job-lot of these by taking time to work on one of their high-end pieces. Like now, as she tweezed tiny orange and white Swarovski foil-backed crystals into place on the butterfly-shaped flap of a black cell shell.

With old episodes of *The Gilmore Girls* playing on the shelf behind the worktable and her attention focused on filling in the pattern of a Monarch butterfly's wings, she wouldn't have to worry about what had happened to Jo. She'd move on with her life. In theory.

Jo's family would come, dispose of Jo's stuff and her apartment. Jo's coworkers in HR would pack up her desk and take over her workload until the company hired someone new. If they decided to hire anyone at all, and didn't dump the extra work on Anne and Patty.

In any case, after a while, the waters of daily life would flow back in, smoothing over the impression Jo's life had made in the world, like waves filling in footprints left along a beach. It would be as if she had never been there at all.

Gloria blinked away fresh tears. Dwelling on the past would set her off again. Maybe she should have stayed at the office, commiserating with Anne and Patty--if Ms. Dexter had the heart to let them.

She'd come home hoping to find Aggie, only to wind up alone. She'd expected the work, if not *The Gilmore Girls*, would be enough to take her mind off things, but she'd seen this episode before and her mind kept wandering. Situations she'd ordinarily find amusing seemed trivial in the face of Jo's senseless murder.

Gloria turned back to her work. The droplet of glue meant to secure the crystal in her tweezers had set while her attention wandered. It hit her, how much of the pleasure in the work she did here with Aggie was the pleasure of their camaraderie. Even when they had nothing particular to say and only shared their reactions to whatever show played or passed tools and supplies across the table.

With Aggie and Greg gone, it seemed too much like she sat at somebody else's table, in somebody else's house. She couldn't go home. She had no real home. She had the small refuge of her bedroom in the face of her father's zone of chaos and she bided her time there until her escape--until she moved in with Pete.

People chattered rapid-fire at each other on-screen. Gloria set aside her tweezers, reaching for the glue gun to set another droplet of hot glue in place. She paused, hand in the air. How much of her attraction to Pete lay in the prospect of leaving her father's house for his? If she had an apartment of her own, would she be quite this eager to get married to Pete?

How long had she felt this way? It had been almost as if she'd lost both her parents when Mom died. Dad had continued to work and support her, to pay the bills for years afterward, until he lost his arm. Afterward he'd withdrawn into himself, as if going through the motions of living. He hadn't been someone she could turn to for comfort. He'd never been what she'd call sociable. Mom had been the one to make friends in the neighborhood, to listen to Gloria, to reassure her when she felt sad or frightened. Dad just didn't know how. His way of being social was to share his beers in front of the television.

She'd been fifteen when he started offering her a beer now and then. She imagined all too easily what she might have become if she'd ever accepted.

No wonder she'd been attracted to Pete. Pete was The Anti-Dad, the polar opposite of what her father had become. Pete talked to her. He listened to her. At least, he did when he wasn't working. He didn't drink, or if he did, it was like an afterthought. "Oh, there's wine with dinner? Sure, I'll have a glass." Was that the substance of her relationship with Pete? Was it based entirely on his not-dadness?

Chapter 12

Greg hated leaving Gloria alone, but when he looked back before letting the door close behind him, she already had the hot glue gun in hand and a bead tray open before her. She'd said she was okay. He had to take her at her word.

She might be okay, but could he say the same for himself? An innocent woman had been murdered and he might have prevented it. Greg glanced around the yard, making sure no one would see and said, "Super-ize Me."

At least Wonder Guy might have prevented it. If he'd been around instead of living Greg Roberts' life. What did Greg Roberts do that was more important than saving innocent lives?

Greg, now as Wonder Guy, leapt into the air at an angle to avoid entangling himself in the branches of the trees shading the yard. Good one. He looked back to verify if he'd managed the leap without leaving a pit in the patio tiles. It seemed to be as much a matter of intent as thrust. Lucky Newton hadn't known about this. It might have set physics back a hundred years.

The cool wind of his flight, the freedom of the surrounding blue expanse, lifted his heart as ever, but his thoughts dragged. He couldn't spend every minute of the day and night as Wonder Guy. The world needed Greg Roberts too, didn't it? What if his technology research helped save lives someday? Light-speed computing might be invaluable in medicine and a thousand other applications. Not everything worth doing could be done in a flash or drew the kind of attention Wonder Guy got. Who knew what might be built on the few bricks of knowledge he would lay in his lifetime? Now it seemed like Wonder Guy was his competition.

BZZZ. He clapped a hand to his ear. "Ow!"

"OOPS. VOLUme control seems to be off." Serafina's voice diminished from a roar to a normal speaking tone before the words were out. "Hurry, dear. Something quite disturbing is happening at one of your lakes."

"Which one?" He twisted in midair, high enough to see the city spread below him, the lakes a shining chain to the west.

"The one in the middle."

He plummeted toward Calhoun even as she spoke.

In seconds he'd made it close enough that screams drew him to the north end of the lake. People scattered, running, scrambling out of the water and away across the beach.

Wonder Guy hovered far above the scene.

Two monstrous shapes, locked in combat, roiled the waters of the lake. At first sight, he thought one must be Minne--the dinosaur sculpture, which made its rounds of the city lakes every summer--come to life. Except, the scale was wrong. This creature must be nearly a hundred feet long. He blinked in amazement. Apatosaurus. What his mother still insisted on calling a Brontosaurus.

Impossible. The other, only slightly smaller creature in the melee stood upright, lifting tiny forearms and a massive, toothy jaw toward the Apatosaurus while the gargantuan tails of both creatures whipped the water around them to froth. Tyrannosaurus Rex. This couldn't be happening. *Thinks the man soaring unassisted in midair.*

A boat bobbed too close to the monsters, over-turned in the churning water. Two swimmers swam frantically away from the bloodstained wa-ter where the two impossible shapes clashed. He scanned the water, but spotted no injured people. The blood must belong to the dinosaurs, but that might change any second.

Greg dove, plummeting like a missile, maneu-vering through the high-flung spray, past the Tyrannosaur's flank to grab a middle-aged man by the straps of his Day-Glo orange life vest and lift him free of the water. He held the man suspended from one hand as he dove to save the woman, visi-ble only by the bobbing appearances of her orange life vest among the waves. Greg dodged a lashing tail, diving beneath it, dunking himself and the man to grab the straps of the woman's vest with his free hand. He turned in the same instant to lift both his passengers up and away from the churning water.

Greg swooped high to avoid the waves and the battling monsters. The woman screamed, dangling from her vest. She looked young enough to be the man's daughter. Maybe she was, despite lacking any family resemblance. Not his concern, especially now.

"Don't worry, ma'am," Greg shouted over the wind of his passage, already soaring back toward the beach. He deposited them on the beach and turned in midair, soaring high again, to return to the battle from above.

The Apatosaurus bled from several gashes across its long neck. Its battle strategy consisted of swinging its massive neck from side to side, knocking into and deflecting the tyrannosaur's lunges. T-rex's low center of gravity, combined with the support of the surrounding water, assured that it couldn't be knocked off its feet to give Apatosaurus a chance to escape.

These creatures shouldn't exist. Not in this time and place. He had no idea how to send them back wherever they came from. A concern for later. He had to stop this battle now. If T-rex killed Apatosaurus it wouldn't be long before the enormous predator menaced the rest of the city.

Poised above the battle, Greg put a hand to the radio connection in his mask. "Serafina? Are you responsible for this? Are you manufacturing monsters so Wonder Guy can play hero?"

"Oh no, dear." Her voice sounded tiny in his ear. "I'd never do such a thing. I have an idea as to where this trouble came from and will explain later, but something must be done now."

"All right then." First things first. Separate the combatants.

Greg took a deep breath and plunged toward the water, aiming to come down behind T-rex. The huge beast staggered, thigh-deep in the lake, when a lash of Apatosaurus's neck caught it broadside along its jaw. He spotted the huge predator's tail through the murky green water and dove beneath the rough waves. He grabbed the end of its tail where it narrowed enough to get his arms fully around it and hauled it across his shoulder. The pebbly hide gave him a good grip. Straining against the great weight, he battled his way above the water's surface in time to gasp in another breath.

With the tail slung over his shoulder, Greg rose higher and higher, dragging the massive beast behind him. It took him a tremendous effort, as few things had since he'd gained Wonder Guy's powers.

Below him, T-rex squalled an ear-piercing shriek when it found itself upended, falling forward, face first into the water and dragged up backward by its tail. The cries ended when the beast's head hit the water and submerged. Soon the head trailed the neck upward, spilling a long stream of water. The ferocious jaws dangled high above the lake's surface, high above the bewildered Apatosaurus, weaving its own head side to side, apparently seeking some sign of its recent attacker.

Now what? Dropping the T-rex from a great enough height would kill it. The only living tyrannosaurus in the world. With Wonder Guy's strength, he could haul it away somewhere safe. But where? He did a hasty mental shuffle through the possibilities. Set T-rex atop one of the city's skyscrapers--where it might fall on people? Trap it between the locks on the Mississippi--where it would disrupt shipping? He had to get it entirely away from human habitation. Maybe somewhere in the Black Hills of Dakota, or the Badlands. The tyrannosaurus should be safe enough wandering around those maze-like canyons until a properly equipped scientific team came to take charge of it. It shouldn't take more than an hour to get there if he climbed high enough and angled his descent.

Greg continued his climb. The gargantuan beast slung dangling over his shoulder twisted and squalled. It made a valiant effort to twist high enough to reach him against the pull of gravity. He felt sorry for the creature so out of its element, despite knowing, given the chance, it would swallow him in a single bite. However the dinosaur had gotten here, he doubted it had been the poor beast's own idea.

"It's a drag, big fella," he spoke to the length of tail in his arms, a body part as capable of understanding him as the beast's tiny brain. "You'll be safe on your feet soon enough."

☆☆★☆☆

The wash of the hero's sympathy overwhelmed Elysha. She lost the thread of the spell that displaced the great lizards from their proper epoch. It broke in her face, stinging like a whip as the monsters snapped back to their proper places in space-time. What had she been thinking, bringing two of the beasts here?

She'd gotten the idea from that foolish statue the humans set out in the lake. She'd thought bringing a real creature forward would wipe the grins from their faces and generate a proper bit of horror and panic. Not until its appearance did she realize the first thing was more interested in chomping on trees than on people.

Live and learn. In retrospect, she should have sent that one back before summoning the predator. Of course the monster with the huge jaw full of teeth totally ignored the scuttling humans in favor of prey more its size. Even so, she'd hoped for at least a few fatalities.

The experiment hadn't been a total waste despite her huge expenditure of energy. Hundreds of humans had been deliciously terrified, scared out of their wits, scrambling for safety. Many had been ready to trample their fellows into the ground to save their own skins. Unfortunately, the surge of tasty self-interest had been offset by many small acts of heroism. Strangers acted as one to get children to safety and rescue swimmers and sailors caught in the confusion. How disappointing. Sometimes she wondered why she even tried to engineer disasters anymore.

But, of course, she hadn't expected to get more from this exercise than she had.

His appearance justified the whole thing. Just as she'd suspected. The old biddies had created a Hero. That sort of thing went out of fashion centuries ago. What were they thinking?

Still, she now had a bead on the fellow. She'd soon find a way to get rid of him.

☆☆★☆☆

When T-rex vanished from his grip Greg shot abruptly a thousand feet higher before catching himself, as if he and the earth had been playing tug of war and the earth had suddenly released its hold on the rope.

What the hell? Where had a several-ton dinosaur disappeared to? Not to forget asking where it had come from in the first place. What in heck was going on here?

He did a flyby over Lake Calhoun, verifying the Apatosaurus, too, had disappeared. As if he weren't already sure magic lay at the root of the whole incident.

The crowds milled below, agitated as a disturbed anthill, some people venturing out to the beach again, but warily. Others gathered in small knots at some distance. A television crew moved among them. The KARE 11 News van parked on a sidewalk nearby.

Great. No chance of landing here without drawing a crowd. He angled his flight path into a long curve, heading back to the University.

☆☆★☆☆

"No, dear. I didn't know there would be dino-saurs." Serafina stood with Greg on the roof of the Computer Science building. "There's no telling what Elysha might do, after all. But I recognized her power signature. She must have noticed the good work you've been doing and made this ef-fort to draw you into the open. But now we know she's the one who's been aggravating the general levels of misery in this area in recent years."

Given the diminutive woman's matter-of-fact manner, it took Greg a long moment before the outrageous import of what she said hit him.

"So, I'm what? Some kind of goat you staked out to lure a tiger into the open?" He'd never been this outraged. He imagined himself as a cartoon char-acter, steam shooting out his ears.

"Not at all, dear. Not unless the goat has bullet proof armor and heavy artillery." Serafina tsked. "There's no call to get worked up. You're making a real difference for the people of this city."

"Would they ever have been in danger from dinosaurs if I hadn't gotten sucked into this hero gig?"

Speaking of which, he muttered, "Back to me," and shed the flashy costume and mask for his familiar slacks and math t-shirt. He might be safer standing up to a little old lady while he had super-powers to call on, but as she gave him those pow-ers in the first place, any sense of safety had to be pure illusion.

"The threats they faced would have been sub-tler," Serafina said in a soothing tone. "But we certainly don't expect you to deal with Elysha directly. You may encounter a few challenges she throws your way, but now that we know who's obstructing us, the FGU will address the problem of Elysha."

"FGU?" Greg tried to make sense of her words. Somehow, with Serafina, he always found himself feeling like he sat in the advanced version of a class, having missed the whole introductory course.

"The Union, the Fairy Godmother's Union, of course." She frowned, a slight moue of her usually smiling mouth. "Didn't I give you my card?"

"Yes. Yes you did. But who exactly is this Elysha? And how did she manage to put a couple of dinosaurs in Lake Calhoun?"

Serafina gave him a speculative look as if gauging how much she should tell him, or how much he'd be able to understand. He bristled under the scrutiny.

"She is certainly not a fairy godmother, or a member of our Union." Serafina's disapproving look mellowed as she went on. "But she is somewhat akin to us. She does not share our goals, but she has powers of a similar nature, if the power of rose essence to please can be compared to the power of skunk musk to repel."

"I get the idea." Greg crossed his arms. The gesture felt much the same whether he wore his superhero costume or his math T-shirt, though in the latter case, it probably wouldn't seem as impressive. "So, she can defy the known rules of physics too?"

Today Serafina's hat included a bunched swath of gauze around the edge, forming a tidy brim shielding her eyes from the sun. The same sunshine beat down hot and heavy on his unprotected head. He gestured to the stairwell, and Serafina continued talking as they moved off the roof and started down the stairs.

"Precisely, but she does not have a cooperative nature." The fairy godmother's nose wrinkled. "And so acts alone, or with the help of a few minions, and usually in secret because she cannot contend with the combined efforts of the Union."

"But now she knows about me? What does she want? What can I expect from her?" He hadn't signed up for this. He'd signed up to impress Gloria and do some good in the process. "What if she goes after Gloria?"

"There, there. Elysha knows about you now, but only in your guise as Wonder Guy. She has no way of knowing who your loved ones are.

"As to what you can expect from her: nothing direct. She thrives on what you would call negative emotions. Though all emotion is necessary to being human, Elysha does not respect the balance of energies. She's addicted to fear, anger and misery. What you can expect from her is trouble. You can foil her by minimizing the trouble around you."

"I'm supposed to go along with this program?" Greg ground his teeth. If he refused, gave up the powers, and went back to normal, how could he sit studiously at his computer while people around him suffered from trouble he might prevent?

Serafina turned on the stair above him as he paused on the landing, putting her eyes at the same level as his. "Will you give up your hero's powers when a hero is needed?"

Her eyes, while kindly, looked as sharp as any hawk or eagle's.

"What's the use of it?" he asked her. "There's more trouble than the whole police department or Wonder Guy can prevent."

"I can tell you Gloria is already impressed with Wonder Guy."

"She is?" If Wonder Guy impressed her, it might still mean something when the mask came off. "Hmm. Well, is there anything else I can do to make sure Elysha stays away from Gloria and my mom?"

"She's averse to cold iron and steel." Serafina faded around the edges as she spoke. "And to laughter and good fellowship." The tiny lady vanished.

☆☆★☆☆

In a patch of woodland in the park along Minnehaha Creek, Elysha lounged on a mossy bank shaded by trees and soothed by the sounds of running water.

"How fares the swarm?" she asked Minik who crouched at her feet.

"They grow," he reported.

"Tell me when they reach a size and strength to lift children from their mothers' sides."

"Yes. They near such size, but can only seize a small dog or a cat as yet."

"Then feed them more. Remember to use herds scattered widely through space and time so the mutilations will be dismissed."

The gnarled creature scuttled away and another, a will-o-the-wisp figure only visible to such knowing eyes as hers, drifted near when Elysha beckoned it.

"What have you learned?" she demanded.

"He flew swift, but I as swift as he." The reply came as a whisper to be heard only by her ears, attuned to mysteries. "To a rooftop I shall reveal if you follow. There he spoke with an ancient one. They spoke of thee."

☆☆★☆☆

Gloria completed the last section of the Monarch's wings. What next? She looked through the book of butterflies. Mmm. This one, with the iridescent blues, a Blue Morpho. She looked through the drawers of beads on one of the shelves behind the worktable, selecting containers with colors ranging from robin's egg to deep indigo.

What did she love about Pete, aside from the promise of security and escape from her father's house? He listened to her as she chatted about her day at work, her projects, the movies they saw together and YouTube clips she posted on Facebook. Being a good listener was a great quality in a guy. Of course, Greg had been the one listening to her today.

She put a drop of glue on the wingtip of a sky-blue, butterfly-cut blank and picked up a mirror-backed iridescent crystal with the tweezers.

Lots of her friends were good listeners. Aggie listened. Jo had listened. That didn't mean she should marry them. What did it mean to share your whole life with someone? To create a common destiny, good times and bad? Would she see Pete the same way if something happened to him and he couldn't work, like her dad? She loved her dad, but she didn't love sharing a household with him. He was a chore. What if Pete hung around the house all day and let himself go? He'd be miserable if he couldn't work. She'd probably have to entertain him 24/7. He wasn't exactly self-directed.

The more she pictured Pete left to his own devices, without the bulwark of his job, the more he lost substance and luster in her eyes. What they shared seemed increasingly superficial.

Tweezing one tiny crystal after another into place to form her butterfly wings, she lost track of time. Her heart lifted when Aggie's wheels rolled up the ramp to the back stoop. She glanced at the clock to find it already after four. On an ordinary day, she'd be getting off work now. Gloria muted the DVD player. Keys jingled, but the expected sound of their turning in the lock failed to follow. Instead, she heard a low murmur of voices.

She set down the glue gun and went to the door. Maybe Aggie needed a hand if she'd been shopping.

Gloria opened the door and gaped at the man standing on the steps beside her friend.

"You remember Hank, don't you?" Aggie looked up and blushed as she gestured to her companion.

191

"He was kind enough to invite me out for a cup of coffee."

"Kindness had nothing to do with it." Hank grinned in a smile she'd think rascally if not accompanied by a just-kidding wink.

Gloria had to grin in response.

"Oh, you." Aggie's blush deepened as she swatted the air in his direction. "But what are you doing home from work this early?" she asked.

Gloria lost her grin. "Something happened."

☆☆★☆☆

Back in the computer lab, Greg set up another batch of simulations and let them run. He had the lab to himself. Judging by the junk food wrappers and abandoned soda cans remaining at a pair of workstations in the back of the room, Eric and Will had been here earlier. Their computers were processing. They must have gone off somewhere to tend to other business during the run time.

Having the lab to himself made this a perfect opportunity to call Tech Support. While students and graduate TAs handled a fair amount of daily upkeep and troubleshooting for the computer labs, the permanent staff set up the servers, managed the networking, maintenance and software installations and security. Ted Amundson, a junior member of the IT team, did most of the grunt work. Just the person Greg wanted.

"Hey, Ted," he said when the familiar voice answered his call.

"Yeah. Who's this?"

"Greg Roberts, up in the Grad Lab."

"Right. Hey, Greg. What can I do for you?"

"I came across something the other day when I did a check of the computer I'm using for my simulations."

"Right." His voice held a question mark.

"Looks like this system's being monitored with a keystroke-capture setup and the data's being sent off campus."

"Yeah, right. Prof Stevens asked me to set up the added data backup precaution. Said he was afraid some new virus would make it past our firewalls and wipe out all the research projects."

"Huh. I was just wondering." Greg shifted the receiver to his other ear, leaning back in his chair. "So where's he sending the backup data? Might save me some time in finding my data if there is a problem."

"He gave me an IP address for a secure server. Don't have its physical locale."

"What's the IP address?" Greg jotted down the info. "Well thanks, Ted. Guess I'll check on it with the Prof." *Eventually.*

What now? Too soon to confront Professor Stevens. Professor Morrissey must have followed the trail further than this before talking to Stevens. How had he found out Stevens was selling off the research data? He must have tracked the IP address. Greg sighed. Dammit, Jim. *I'm a computer engineer, not a hacker.* Still, he'd learned enough to get started. He had a feeling Eric could show him a few tricks.

☆☆★☆☆

Hank wheeled Aggie into the kitchen with a promise to call her again soon and left the two women alone together. Aggie could perfectly well have wheeled herself in and would have bristled at anyone else who'd offered, but she thanked Hank in dulcet tones before telling him she could have handled it herself. Not until he'd left did Gloria pour out the whole story of Jo's death and the police investigation.

Aggie caught Gloria's hand, squeezing it as she wound up her account of Jo's death, her voice choking at the last. The older woman's grip conveyed warmth and a surprising strength. "Oh, Gloria, honey."

"I still can't believe she's gone." Gloria leaned back in her chair at the table, the half-finished Blue Morpho cell shell on the table before her. Having lost one friend, she kept casting glances across the table to reassure herself of Aggie's continued presence. Life now seemed ephemeral as a soap bubble. "I thought I'd take my mind off it by focusing on one of the more complicated beading projects, but that trick never works." She tried for a joking tone but it came out as a sigh.

"You've been here by yourself all afternoon? I'm so sorry I picked today to go out." Aggie matched Gloria's sigh with one of her own.

"Oh, don't be sorry. How would you know? If anyone deserves to get out more, it's you. Besides, I wasn't alone the whole time. Greg stopped over and sat with me for a while. It helped a lot." He'd made an amazing difference in fact. She didn't know what she'd have done otherwise. Maybe just sat on the stoop weeping until Aggie returned. She'd needed an understanding ear, the comfort of a friend.

"I'm glad to hear my son made himself useful." Aggie smiled fondly. "He does come in handy once in a while."

"Yeah," Gloria admitted half reluctantly. It was more fun to tease Greg than to stop and consider his virtues. "Pete was at work, but he said he'd come by afterward and we'll talk over supper. Except now I don't feel much like going out. Or much like eating. I'm just tired. Exhausted."

"I know. Grief takes it out of you." Aggie bit her lower lip. "I've lost a few people over the years. Your mother, Evie for one. We were good friends. It surprised me how close we got. You never know who you're going to get for a neighbor but it turned out we had a few things in common, and she was great: kind, funny, smart. With her around, Ike was a whole different person. I don't think he ever got over losing her."

Weird to think of her mother being someone's friend the way she and Jo had been friends, but of course there'd been more to her mother's life than being Gloria's mother or her father's wife. Now she'd never have the chance to know her mother as one adult with another. All she had were her childhood impressions of the woman who'd cared for her, hugged her, scolded her, fed her, read her bedtime stories and tucked her in at night. She remembered the lilac scent of her mother's bath powder, her way of doing all the voices in the stories she read aloud and the feel of the soft cotton t-shirts she'd worn with jeans around the house.

Did she remember her mother's face? She might remember only the images from old photographs. It seemed hard to believe at this moment, but eventually her memories of Jo would dim too. How long would it take for her friend to become no more than a few faded memories?

"I'm sorry." Gloria recalled the topic at hand. "I am tired. Maybe I'll call Pete to cancel, get to bed early tonight so I can make a fresh start tomorrow. Just..."

"What?" Aggie had picked up the piece Gloria had been beading and turned it from side to side, absently studying the glitter and shine of the iridescent blue crystals as if she too were lost in memories.

"I hate to have to deal with Dad tonight." Maybe he'd been a different person for her mother, but the person he'd become represented too much work, weary as she was with shock and grief. He'd find a way to make her loss about him and his needs. She couldn't handle it right now. Ike had never been good at offering comfort. Even Pete might listen and make sympathetic noises, but he'd never lost anyone close to him and right now she needed to be with someone who actually understood.

"Well, when you call Pete, you can call Ike too and tell him we decided to make it a sleepover," Aggie offered. "He'll understand when you explain what happened. It's hard to tell sometimes, the way he's been, but your father does love you.

Maybe he just needs you too much to loosen his hold and admit it."

"Thanks." Gloria felt suddenly shy, like Aggie had read her mind. "I'll make the calls."

"And I'll make some popcorn and we can watch a movie, or work on projects--or both--until you're ready to sleep."

☆☆★☆☆

Long past his usual suppertime, Greg finished coding a new set of simulations to run overnight. Even then, the thought of eating held no appeal. All afternoon, he'd had trouble concentrating. Someone's life might be in danger while he focused on testing potential variables in a photonic CPU. It seemed impossible to gauge the relative value of his work in computing against what he might do as a superhero. Maybe he should ask for the power to be in two places at once.

He clicked a few keys to start the simulation, gathered his scrawled notes into his backpack, collected his water bottle, helmet and bike's front wheel. He'd leave his things on the roof of the building for now and make a sweep as Wonder Guy. He'd feel better about going home for supper if he'd first done everything in his power to safeguard the city.

It might be June, but in Minnesota the evening breeze still got plenty cool, at least up on the roof, and cooler still when Wonder Guy leapt high into the air. There must be some insulating property in his costume considering how little the cold bothered him. Or maybe that was part of being Wonder Guy--like Superman, as impervious to the cold as to bullets, comfortable even in an arctic fortress of solitude.

Greg soon forgot the evening's chill as he cut higher through the evening sky. The subdued twilight colors of the heavens stretching around him created a dreamlike ambience. He might be flying in a dream, the world melting into shadows and watercolor pools around him, if not for the cold breeze slapping his face. The lights of houses and cars appeared like stars below him, only adding to the effect. Highway 35 became a chain of sparkling gems, crossed by the blazing diamonds and rubies of I-94. Everything looked peaceful and perfect from this height.

The transmitter blasted a sharp buzz in his ear.

"Ow!" He clapped a hand to his head. "What?" He modulated his tone. "I mean, what?"

"That's better, dear. There's a robbery in progress over on the West Bank of the University," Serafina said, tart and brief.

Greg turned his flight path even as she spoke. He'd already strayed nearer to St Paul than he'd intended. He'd have to follow Riverside Avenue back toward the University to reach the west bank.

"It's a bar on Riverside, near the intersection with Cedar Avenue," she continued. "But remember what I told you--"

He lost the rest of her words as he found himself abruptly flailing, hurtling uncontrolled through the air, arcing downward along the path he'd begun, like a thrown ball losing its impetus. He yelled, "Holy fucking shit. What the hell?"

"Language, dear."

St. Mary's Hospital loomed before him. He tried to gauge whether his path would smash him into the top floor of the building or not. With a rush of air, the brick façade slid too quickly by. Descending at a shallow angle past the building, he missed it by inches. Luckily, no other tall structures stood in its neighborhood.

Or not so luckily, nothing remained to stop him from smashing to earth at high speed when he reached the end of his descent. Coming in at this angle, it looked like he'd smack into the road in front of the very bar he'd been aiming for. It said good things about his sense of direction, but nothing else about the situation looked good. He'd lost Wonder Guy's power of flight and had no reason to expect he still had Wonder Guy's impervious-to-bullets ability to withstand the impact.

This was it. So much for Greg Roberts and his stupid dreams of winning Gloria's love.

Chapter 13

When Gloria told him she was too tired to go out, Pete said he understood perfectly. "You should get your rest," he told her. "I'm glad you're doing better now than when you called before."

"I'll be even better after a good night's sleep." She said her goodbyes. If she was doing better, it was no thanks to him, but she could hardly blame the man for wanting to keep his job.

She tucked her cell phone back in her bag then joined Aggie at the kitchen worktable.

"It's fine with Pete," Gloria reported, resuming her chair. The Blue Morpho cell shell sat completed. She started collecting the containers of tiny crystals, returning them to their proper places on the shelves. "He even seemed relieved." More relieved than sympathetic to her loss, but maybe she wasn't being fair. "He doesn't usually like going out on week nights when he has to be up early for work and we already went out to dinner with his parents the other night."

"Well, that's for the best then." Aggie backed from the table. "Why don't I fix us something to eat?"

"I'm not very hungry." Gloria slumped back in her chair.

"Some soup will do you good." Aggie wheeled toward the fridge. "I'll heat up some of that chicken, wild rice and veggie soup I made Sunday. I bet if you try a taste, you'll want some more."

"Fine." Gloria found the remote. "Mind if I check out the news?" They'd been tuned to some ancient sitcom with the sound turned low while they chatted over their projects. She hadn't even registered which show.

"Go ahead." Aggie moved between fridge and stovetop. The stove had been customized to be accessible for her. She did a lot of cooking. Gloria loved her chicken wild rice soup. Aggie actually used wild rice, unlike some restaurants she'd visited where they used a mix including a few grains of the wild, but mainly consisting of white rice. She flicked to a news report and turned up the sound.

Dinosaurs? What the heck?

"There, you see it, Ken," the newswoman said. "Footage captured on a cell phone this afternoon at Lake Calhoun, where hundreds of people reported seeing real dinosaurs battling in the waters of the lake."

"But by the time our cameras arrived on the scene, any dinosaurs had disappeared. Isn't that right, Linda?"

"That's right, Ken. People at the scene say the local hero known as Wonder Guy carried a T-rex above the clouds, as seen in this clip, and a minute or two later the other dinosaur--"

"The Apatosaurus I believe, Linda."

"That's right, Ken. The Apatosaurus vanished from the lake a couple minutes after Wonder Guy carried the T-rex away."

Gloria watched the footage, fascinated. Wonder Guy slung the tail of the gargantuan beast over his shoulder, hefting it like a bag of potatoes, dragging it from the lake, up to the heavens. Wow. Even as strong as he was, it seemed incredibly brave to tangle with a vicious monster many times his own size. Wet from his dip in the lake, his costume did even more to show off the lean musculature of his powerful form. If only she'd spoken to him when he'd come to her rescue just yesterday. She could kick herself for missing the chance. She'd probably never get as close to him again.

"Unbelievable, Linda," Ken continued the commentary. "Authorities have declined to comment on where the dinosaurs came from or where they went. A spokesman from the mayor's office suggests it was some sort of trickery, a hoax perpetrated with hi-tech holographic imagery."

"No one can say for sure, Ken, but Wonder Guy has been in the news before. The police have confirmed that he has prevented several crimes around town, and yesterday cameras caught him in action restraining an elephant that went out of control during a parade in Uptown."

"That's right, Linda. We're all grateful to this masked hero who has been doing so much to keep Minneapolis safe for it citizens. Now here's Ted Ewing with the weather."

Gloria turned down the sound. "Did you hear that, Aggie?" She lifted her voice over the clatter Aggie made in pulling bowls and spoons from their places.

"Something about Wonder Guy and dinosaurs?"

"Yes, and they showed video clips. But dinosaurs, live ones anyway, in Minneapolis? It's crazy. Whoever said it must be some kind of hoax is probably right. Maybe it's a promotion for some new dinosaur movie."

"I suppose." Aggie's tone allowed for doubt.

"I saw Wonder Guy up close. He's real. What he did with the elephants seemed real. Only, how could there possibly be live dinosaurs in this day and age?"

"Sometimes the answers aren't as simple as we'd like. Not black or white, real or hoax. A dream is a real experience. While dreaming, you feel real feelings and see real visions, even if it isn't real in the same way this table and chairs are real, or the soup is real." Aggie tapped her ladle against the steel saucepan.

Gloria stared at her friend. "When did you get to be such a philosopher?"

"It was my minor in college," Aggie reminded her. "I must have mentioned it before."

"Maybe. I've always been more impressed that you majored in art." She grinned. "When I was a kid, I thought I'd won the lottery, having you for a neighbor, with all the arts and crafts projects you shared with me."

Aggie wheeled slowly back with a couple bowls on the tray across her lap, steaming with scents of chicken broth, marjoram and sage. "I was glad to. My only son showed no interest. I'm only sorry you never got to go to art school yourself. You have such an aptitude for it."

She set a bowl before Gloria and brought the other to her own place at the table. The scent of the thick, creamy soup tempted Gloria into taking a sip. The flavor filled her mouth with warmth and comfort. She tried a bit more. "Mmm. This is good, Aggie." She paused to swallow. "Oh yeah, real good, and thanks. I'll get to school someday. In the meantime, I love our projects together. I'm doing something artistic here." She smiled at the shelf where they displayed what they counted as their finer 'art' pieces.

They fell into a companionable silence as they ate. Gloria turned up the TV, now reporting the national news.

☆☆★☆☆

"Do you read me, dear?" Serafina must have been calling him all along, with her voice drowned out by the rush of air and the pounding of his pulse in his ears as he hurtled helplessly toward impact with the road below. Only moments had passed, though it seemed a lifetime.

"Yes." His voice sounded higher pitched than usual. "I read you."

"Good. Don't worry, dear. You'll regain your power before you hit ground. Just get further past St. Mary's."

Gee, that's swell. The road rushed under him. What did St. Mary's have to do with it? He skimmed above someone's SUV, envisioned himself hitting the road, bouncing, hitting again, scraping his hide off all the way down Riverside and onto the highway. But no. If Serafina had it right, he had to focus on lifting back into flight when his power kicked in again.

He strained upward as the road rushed to meet him. Inches from impact, he gained some height. He strained harder, reaching, arching upward, gaining enough height to avoid smashing into a bus passing down the intersecting Cedar Avenue. *Hot damn!*

Greg angled around and brought himself to a controlled, careful landing outside the bar. He put his hand on the brick wall and leaned there for a moment, just outside the door, as his racing pulse steadied.

"Serafina?" he inquired. "What was all that?"

"Later, dear. Robbery in progress."

"But--"

A gunshot cut through his thoughts. Greg dashed through the bar's door. Bullets slammed into his chest, no more a deterrent than moths against the windshield of a speeding car.

The bar occupied a long, narrow space where half a dozen patrons, a waitress and bartender sat or stood frozen. Two men in ski masks. The one furthest from the door held a gun on the patrons. No one appeared injured. The first shot must have been a warning.

The gunman nearest the door faced him, gun aimed at the big W on Wonder Guy's chest, staring expectantly, as if still waiting for his target to fall.

Greg stepped forward and plucked the gun from the robber's hand. "I'll take that."

The other gunman, guarding the rear exit, swung toward him. Before the man blinked, Greg hurled the confiscated weapon straight at his chest. He had to gauge his strength carefully, afraid of killing the man if he threw too hard. The impact sent the gunman flying to the end of the hallway and crashing against the steel fire door, where he slid to the floor and lay gasping, all the wind knocked out of him.

Greg reached the side of the fallen gunman in an instant and scooped the weapons from the floor. He turned to face the bar full of wide-eyed patrons. "Has anyone called the police?"

The bartender, his blond hair in dreads, answered, "Didn't get the chance."

"I got it." The waitress raised her cell phone, on which a video played, showing Wonder Guy's arrival in miniature, robbers, patrons and all.

A couple of the burlier patrons stepped forward and grabbed the first robber by his arms.

Greg waved the bartender over and handed him both guns. "Keep these two covered until the police get here, will you? I can't stick around."

"Sure thing." The man took one of the weapons and handed the other to one of the guys detaining the first robber. "Here, Lenny. You cover this guy. Say," he said before Greg made his exit, "you're that guy who was on the news?"

"Yes, sir." Greg nodded his acknowledgment before he ducked out through the fire door.

He paused in the alley where shadows had deepened from twilight to full night.

"Serafina?" He spoke into his mask's radio.

"Yes, dear?"

"What happened back there? When I lost power and almost crashed to a grisly death against Riverside Avenue?" The reminder of his near miss prickled across his skin.

"Oh, that. Yes. You remember what I told you concerning Superman's powers, dear? How you're also subject to his vulnerabilities?"

"Um. Yes?" It came vaguely back to him, but Superman didn't have many vulnerabilities. "So, I ran into some kryptonite?" He leaned back against a brick wall. Sirens sounded in the distance, nearing the bar.

"Don't be silly, dear. There's no such thing as kryptonite. The planet Krypton was imaginary."

"Forgive me if the distinction seems a bit fine coming from my fairy godmother."

"No need for that tone, dear. Krypton was Superman's birthplace. St. Mary's hospital was your birthplace. Do you see?"

"Oh. Right." Aggie had mentioned he'd been born right here on the west bank. She'd been a student at the University at the time. Serafina had said something about sharing Superman's limitations. He supposed it made an odd kind of logic to equate Wonder Guy's birth hospital to Superman's birth planet, though he'd never quite understood why chunks of Superman's home planet should be dangerous to him.

"Do you understand the limitations now, young man?"

"I think so. Thank you, ma'am."

The connection fell silent.

St. Mary's, huh? He'd have to avoid the place. At least there wouldn't be pieces of it scattered around town the way chunks of kryptonite had been scattered over Earth in Superman's universe... unlikely as it seemed to Greg that pieces from a planet in a whole different star system would make it so far. The infant Kal-El's ship's propulsion would have carried him much further than the initial impetus of the planet-destroying blast would carry Krypton's fragments across light-years.

☆☆★☆☆

"You again." Elysha greeted the sylph she'd sent to keep track of the costumed hero who'd spoiled her fun with the dinosaurs. "What are you doing back so soon?"

"Please, mistress," pleaded the being, gossamer as animated cobwebs, in the rambling way that never ceased to try Elysha's patience. "You said to return if I did learn something of use against the man who flies."

Elysha did not actually smile, but eased her forbidding glower. "True," she said. "What have you learned, then?"

"I returned to the place where I did leave him before," the sylph began. "I waited long and long but he did not appear again, and I did languish near the bitter steel."

"Yes, yes. He did appear again finally, did he not?"

"Yes, mistress. At long last, when the harsh glare of day did flee into the soft shadows he returned and I did follow him."

"Spare me the details. Did you learn naught of use to me?"

The sylph drew itself together, becoming a bit more opaque in the deep shadows of Elysha's glade.

"He flew above a place and then he began to fall," the sylph said in a rush. "His power fled him near this place and he came near to being dashed to the earth, until he passed too far from the place and did regain his power."

"Ah," Elysha sighed. "It pleases me to know of this. Now you must show me this place of which you speak."

☆☆★☆☆

By the time Greg returned to the University for his bike, he'd stopped an arsonist, two break-in attempts and a kid he'd caught tagging garages down the back alleys of South Minneapolis. He'd delivered the captured perpetrators to the appropriate precincts and given brief statements to the police all the while making sure to avoid passing anywhere near St. Mary's.

Returning to the University, he picked up his bike, helmet and backpack. He flew with them back to his own neighborhood, not wanting to bike all the way home again. He ducked into the alley, changed from Wonder Guy back to plain old Greg Roberts, and walked his bike the last short stretch to the back gate leading to his own apartment over the garage.

It seemed later, but all Aggie's lights still shone warm through the buttercup yellow kitchen curtains.

Only as he thought of checking in with his mother did he recall Gloria's state when he'd left her. Had Aggie found her when she'd returned? 'Out for coffee?' What was with that?

☆☆★☆☆

Aggie looked up from her laptop when Greg stepped in through the kitchen door.

"You should keep this locked, Mom," he said in greeting.

"Why's that exactly? Do you need practice using your key?" She saved the database file in which she tracked orders for the Cell Shells.

"I'm not the only one who might want to come in." He locked the door behind him and leaned across the counter dividing the worktable area from the kitchen appliances and cupboards.

"No, there's Gloria too, and Susie Luddell when she stops by and a few other people around the neighborhood. Should I give everybody their own key?" She found herself poised between annoyance at his assumption of command in her life and being glad he felt concerned for her.

"I'll bet you already have given them their own keys."

"What's behind this sudden solicitude?" she asked him. "I've always kept an open door."

"Did you talk to Gloria today?"

"Yes." Ah. That was it. Gloria had mentioned he'd been there earlier. "Poor thing, losing her friend so suddenly."

"Right." Greg leaned further across the counter, speaking in such earnest tones she hardly recognized him. "You never know when the wrong person will be in the wrong place. I want you to take care of yourself."

"Well." She'd gotten used to an abstracted Greg and a Greg enthusiastic about matters of physics and computing far beyond her, but how did she address this new, quietly confident Greg? "I appreciate your concern. I'll try to pay some attention to the locks, maybe adopt a Doberman or a Pit Bull. Now that I think of it, a moat would be nice, but of course, crocodiles would never survive a Minnesota winter. I'd have to stock it with something else."

"In this climate, we'll probably have to settle for leeches." He cracked a grin.

"Have you had supper yet?"

"No supper. I wanted to check in on you before I go back to my apartment."

She'd tired of telling him he didn't need to check up on her every night. It wasn't like she didn't have a cell phone with her at all times. She'd call for help if she needed it. Still, she could do worse than a son who cared enough make sure she was okay.

"There's plenty of leftover soup." She nodded toward the fridge. "Help yourself."

"Sure." He started to turn to the cupboard, but turned back. "Is Gloria okay? It hit her pretty hard, one of her best friends being killed."

"She's asleep in the guest room at this very moment," Aggie assured him. "Totally exhausted, poor thing. So much emotion takes it out of a body." She turned back to her laptop. An old episode of 'Frasier' played on the TV, with the sound turned low.

"She didn't go home?" Greg pulled a bowl from the cupboard.

"Her home isn't the best place for her when she's already hurting." Aggie glanced toward the back bedroom, hoping Gloria was actually getting the sleep she needed.

As smart as he was, Greg sometimes missed a lot. He seemed to take the people around him for granted, as if they'd always be there. But now... so much would change soon, with Gloria getting married and moving away. It was early to say, but with the way things looked between her and Hank--from the moment they met--there might be some more big changes coming along. No telling how Greg might handle the shifting of the emotional landscape in which he'd lived so long. Time to have a talk with him.

He produced various clacking and sloshing sounds as he ladled some soup for himself and stuck the bowl in the microwave.

"Say son." She met his eye as he turned back to face her across the counter while the soup heated. "How are you doing these days?"

"What do you mean?" He shrugged. He'd never been good at deception, though, and she could swear he wore his hand-caught-in-the-cookie-jar expression--too bland--and his gaze shifted from meeting hers.

"You know what I mean. Things are changing around here."

He still looked confused. The inquiring look he turned her way stayed in place, his eyebrows only lifting a fraction higher.

"Gloria's getting married. She'll move away. I know how you feel about her."

"What's with all you women who think you know how I feel better than I know it for myself?" His voice held a growling note, like a frustrated wolf or bear might make.

Aggie fell silent for a moment just as the microwave beeped and Greg turned to retrieve the soup. He'd never spoken to her in such annoyance before. She'd struck a nerve for sure.

"Who else has been telling you how you feel?"

"Never mind that." He put the bowl of soup on a plate and came around the counter to join her at the table. "Why do you have to talk to me about Gloria?"

Well, that was direct. Greg had never been even this confrontational before. She wasn't sure whether to count it as a good thing. She'd generally count an accommodating, reasonable-minded son as a blessing, so she might not be completely happy about it, but a man needed to stand up for himself.

"You've obviously been sweet on Gloria for years now, and it can't be easy for you to watch her planning to marry someone else."

"Mom, I want Gloria to be happy. If she's happy with someone else, so be it."

"I want Gloria to be happy too. We're not talking about Gloria now. We're talking about you. I'm your mother. I also want you to be happy."

Greg reached across the table, placed a hand--how large and strong it had become from the little boy's hand she remembered--on hers.

"I appreciate that, Mom. I'm doing okay. I'm old enough to know things won't always go my way. I can handle it."

"Of course you can." She patted his hand as she drew hers away. "I want you to know I understand. Gloria's making a big mistake. If Pete would make her happy I'd be happy for her--even if I didn't like her choice--but my gut tells me she'll wind up feeling trapped and bored out of her mind with Pete."

Greg looked up from a spoonful of soup, eyebrows lifting above widened eyes. "You may be right." He frowned. "It's still her choice."

"I suspect Gloria doesn't believe she's got a better choice." Aggie leaned toward Greg. "You've heard how her father talks to her. He wants to keep her right where she is. He won't let her get the idea she deserves anything better."

"Ike's attitude's not stopping her from marrying Pete." Greg smiled, as if admiring Gloria's spirit, even while his heart suffered by her actions.

"She's settling for Pete." Aggie pressed on, noting how brave a son she had. "She could do better."

"Why do you say she's settling for Pete?" Greg's spirit of scientific curiosity came to the fore.

"She deserves someone who'll bring stars to her eyes," Aggie said. "Pete doesn't do that for her. She seems pleased with having the relationship. She likes the attention, likes being romanced."

She couldn't say for sure what was in Gloria's heart, but she'd known the girl for her whole life. She knew when Gloria was passionate about something, be it a challenging project or a new dress. Gloria had never had stars in her eyes over Pete. Not the way she had stars in her eyes over every new design she came up with for the Cell Shells, or like the stars she'd had in her eyes while watching the clips of Wonder Guy on the news tonight.

"She's not even as excited about Pete as she was to see that superhero on the news again tonight."

"She was excited over him, huh?" Greg wore a cagey, trying-too-hard-to-be-nonchalant look.

"Yes. I'm just saying, I've been in love, and Gloria doesn't show the symptoms where Pete is concerned."

"I don't see what we can do about it." Greg wiped his mouth, holding his spoon poised above the bowl. "It's still her choice to marry him."

Aggie sighed. The conversation had gone way off track. She'd just wanted to make sure her son was prepared to handle the changes coming his way. How had it come around to questioning Gloria's relationship? But she did question it. She wasn't going to stand--or sit--by and watch Gloria make what might be the biggest mistake of her life.

"I know you're right." Aggie frowned. She flicked the touch pad of her laptop to chase away the screen-saver before it went into sleep mode. She'd left the machine idle too long. "It's her choice. We have to respect it. But, as her friends, if we think she's making a mistake we should do or say something. I'm not sure what. She's never seemed willing to talk about her relationship with Pete. She'll talk about anything else, but she gets defensive when I bring him up, as if she already knows there's a problem and doesn't want to face it." Aggie fell silent.

"Don't worry, Mom." Greg set his empty bowl aside. "Gloria's got a lot of heart and a lot of sense. Things will work out."

Aggie grinned at her boy. "You know me," she said. "I want to make them work out."

"This time, we have to trust in something besides ourselves to make things work out." He stood and gathered his dishes. "Some things are bigger than we are."

"When did you get to be such a grown up?" she teased him. It came as a bit of a shock, her boy genius showing a new maturity and confidence.

"Just this week," he replied, grinning. "I'm still getting used to it."

Chapter 14

Gloria's workstation held too many reminders. Her desk phone reminded her of countless mid-morning calls, staying connected with Jo in the midst of a workday. Her own coffee mug reminded her of the unwashed mug left behind on Jo's desk. One of her Outlook folders was still full of messages from Jo--forwarded jokes and links. Some of the subject lines still made her smile, but tears came to her eyes as well. She'd never get any work done if she let herself dwell on what had happened. She finally turned to the queue of new messages.

Things were slow in the R&D department, as usual for a Friday. Half the researchers and Mr. Carlson found reasons not to come in at all, giving themselves a long weekend. Even so, talk from the support staff buzzed with yesterday's events. Word went around that Jo had been killed exiting through the loading bay door. A memo from management forbade anyone--meaning the smokers--from propping any company door open in the future. Security sent out a memo advising employees who worked late to call for an escort to their cars and included a long list of safety tips.

Gloria noted people's comments, read the memos and focused as best she could on her work. By ten o'clock, she'd caught up with everything on her desk. Mr. Carlson wasn't there to give her any more work. Maybe Patty and Anne would appreciate help with some of Jo's remaining workload. Gloria headed to the HR offices, as much to see how Jo's co-workers were doing as to offer what meager help she was equipped to do.

Mary let her straight through. The receptionist's usual good cheer seemed barely touched by events, except for a sobered note in her voice. "Anne didn't sound very happy about the extra work when I talked to her this morning."

Gloria found both women at their desks. Jo's cubicle looked untouched, but someone had removed the unwashed coffee mug, leaving it to seem much emptier than the absence of a simple ceramic mug should account for.

"How are you doing today?" Gloria asked.

Patty mumbled something unintelligible.

"What?" Gloria leaned into her cubby, sized up the piles of paper. "Got time for a coffee break?"

"No." Patty's tone lacked its usual spark of good humor. She sounded a lot like someone who'd just lost a good friend. "Ms. Dexter expects us to do all Jo's work and our own in the same time it would take us to do just our own work."

"A realistic woman, Ms. Dexter." Gloria made a wry face.

Patty and Anne both snorted humorless laughs.

"Well, that's why I came." Gloria leaned against the divider between Jo's cubicle and the fax-printer station. "Things are slow up in R&D and I thought I might be able to help with the extra work here. Is there anything a non-HR-knowing person like me can do for you?"

"Thanks, Gloria," Anne began, "but I don't think--"

"Wait. Just hold on there." Patty tapped the butt end of a pen against her chin, eyeing Jo's desk like a general considering troop deployments. "I'm sure we can find something." She turned back to her own desk, found a sheet of paper. "Ms. Dexter gave us a list of Jo's projects." She ran her pen down the paper, paused. "Sure. Jo took charge of wrapping up the tax reports for the last quarter. There are some missing documents associated with each report."

"Sure." Gloria followed Patty into Jo's cubicle, standing aside while the petite woman rummaged through a stack of papers until she pulled out a batch of printed spreadsheets.

"Here are the reports she left unfinished. See there." She pointed to a column heading on one page and to a few rows where the column remained empty. "We don't have verification that the tax forms were filed for these particular jobs."

"Right." Gloria took the spreadsheets from Patty. "Jo asked me about one of these the other day." Her eyes welled unexpectedly at the memory.

Anne chimed in, "We'd be happy to get them off our slate. Tracking down the stray documents takes way too much time. Ninety percent of the time for the whole report gets eaten up by ten percent of the items on it."

"The age old story." Gloria gave a crooked smile. "I'm not sure where to look for the missing documents, but I'll do my best."

"It's mostly a matter of tracking people down," Patty assured her. "Wherever there's a form missing, there's a person responsible for getting us a copy. Just use your departmental directory."

☆☆★☆☆

Gloria took Patty's advice to heart and began by bringing the reports back to her desk and sorting them according to which department would have to be contacted to obtain the missing documentation. Unsurprisingly, Custodial Services hired a large number of outside contractors for building maintenance. Whoever handled the documentation didn't meet HR's exacting criteria for record-keeping. It would take her a while to straighten such a mess out. She'd save it for Monday.

Only one report showed items missing from R&D, some 1099 forms for two outside contractors, Inspired Logic and IntelligentDZine. Kathleen Pederson's group. Kathleen, who seemed never to sit still, might be hard to track down, but it shouldn't take long for her to find the few forms needed to close this one report.

In fact, it proved easy enough to contact Kathleen's administrative assistant, Lynn, to ask for a meeting or a chance to catch Kathleen between meetings.

Kathleen's team occupied stations on the opposite side of the floor from Gloria's workstation outside Mr. Carlson's office. The floor plan mirrored itself. Whenever she visited Lynn, she might as well be in a strangely altered universe where different people populated the same cubicles and offices.

"She's out of the office for the morning." Lynn looked up from the Notes calendar on her screen. Lynn's cubicle asserted its individuality with post cards from her Hawaiian dream vacation, a lei of hot pink silk hibiscus flowers and a bobble-head hula dancer atop her monitor. "But I know she's planning to come back to the office after lunch because she still has to sign and file the team time-cards and payroll report before the weekend."

"Good," Gloria said, "I just want a few minutes of her time to square away the tax records on her outside contractors."

"Sorry I can't help. She wanted to handle those herself. She should be in her office around one o'clock."

"I'll try her then."

☆☆★☆☆

Greg biked to the University as usual the next morning. He considered going as Wonder Guy, flying and crime-fighting along the way, but he didn't quite trust this magic stuff after yesterday's power-loss incident. It seemed great when it worked, but he didn't understand its rules. Serafina had suggested there were rules, but they weren't nice and clear-cut like the rules of physics or mathematics. They involved the fuzzy, slippery realms of emotion and imagination.

So he rode his bike, lest the magic suddenly fail him and he be left to make his way home later with neither magic nor wheels.

Fortunately, the morning air filled his breath with June, the sky shone clear and blue, the breeze wafted mild but cool enough to make exertion a pleasure. The Greenway made a nice, semi-secluded route across South Minneapolis, running along the tracks of an old railway. Here it ran under the roads, in a deep cutting with banks overgrown by wild grass and scrawny saplings. Secluded from cars, at least, if not other bikers, the track felt remote from the city--if one ignored the sounds and smells of traffic from above. At this early hour, with the sun just rising, few bikers used the path. He'd go for minutes at a time without seeing anyone at all.

A scream, somewhere ahead of the deserted stretch of trail. Greg skidded to a halt, spraying gravel as he scanned his surroundings. There, the sound of cursing, a woman's voice just beyond a curve rounding the abutment of an overpass.

He quickly rode the few yards around the curve to find a woman sprawled on the path, her bicycle on its side near her with one wheel spinning in the air.

"You okay?" he called.

"No." She winced visibly as she spoke, trying to rise to a seated position. "My damned foot isn't working."

Greg knelt beside her. "It's still attached," he told her, "but the angle looks wrong."

"I can't believe this." The woman, probably Aggie's age, who'd be attractive if not for the lines of pain etching her face, had short, silver-shot red curls emerging from her black helmet. "I have to get downtown for a job interview this morning."

"Looks like you'll have to reschedule." He already had his cell phone out of the brass-studded brown leather Cell Shell Gloria had made him for his birthday and punched in 911 as he spoke. "You can call them as soon as we get some medical help here."

"I'll call them now if you help me sit up."

"We shouldn't move you," Greg turned back to the phone. "Yes, we need medical assistance. A woman's been injured on the Greenway bike path near Cedar, looks like her ankle's broken. What should we do?"

By then another pair of bikers had pulled up beside them.

"Don't move her," Greg told a young woman in a pink helmet who knelt and put her hands under the fallen woman's shoulders, seeming about to lift her. "I've got 911 on the phone. They say not to move her. An emergency medical team is on the way."

"Oh." The kneeling woman turned to the fallen biker. "Sorry. We'll wait here with you."

"I know some first aid." Pink helmet's companion, a lanky young man, removed his blue striped helmet to reveal short, tousled dark hair. He knelt by the injured woman's feet. "What happened?" he asked her.

"Skidded and my bike went one way while I went another, but my foot got caught in the toe hold of the pedal."

Greg stood aside. He'd already done what he could. Not even as Wonder Guy would he have been able to do more. But that was okay. More qualified people had the situation in hand. As it should be. Where did he get the feeling he should be personally responsible for solving every problem to come his way? He hadn't felt that way before taking on the role of a superhero.

☆☆★☆☆

Back at her desk, with her *I Can Has Cheezburger* calendar and her own coffee mug reminding her it was a dirty job and she got to do it, Gloria returned to the spreadsheets Patty had given her, finding the batch pertaining to R&D. The report listed twenty projects associated with Inspired Logic and Intelligent DZine. ABM had paid out nearly three quarters of a million dollars for research projects to the two companies in the last year.

The missing tax forms must be a simple oversight on Kathleen's part. She usually handled such paperwork personally and got it filed promptly. At department meetings, she often touted her ability to seek out the best and the brightest in the computing field and apply their talents to the company's benefit.

At one o'clock, Gloria headed around the floor toward Kathleen's office. As she passed the bank of elevators, she caught sight of the division sub-head emerging onto the floor. Her hair was in a severely cut bob, her gray silk suit impeccable,.

"Ms. Pederson." Gloria quickened her pace to catch up to the department subhead. "Do you have a moment?"

"Just." Kathleen halted, turning to Gloria, with a brow raised. The woman had her suit tailored to reveal only subtle curves. Her honey-blond hair showed not a trace of gray, but the downward lines at the corners of her mouth betrayed a habit-ual frown and a slight pouching when she lowered her chin betrayed years otherwise concealed by a clever use of cosmetics.

"What is it?" Kathleen tapped a finger against the black leather day planner tucked under one arm.

"Just a follow-up HR requested." Gloria rushed to get the words out. She admired the other woman's accomplishment and poise, but often got nervous speaking with her--as if every word must count and she had to convey the most informa-tion in the fewest words in the least time. It took her some effort to avoid stumbling over her own tongue. "You know. Jo Willard, who was...well." Gloria swallowed a wave of sorrow. "They gave me some reports left out on her desk, and I need to verify whether the 1099 forms were filed for a couple of your outside contractors."

Kathleen's eyes narrowed as Gloria spoke. "Of course," she said. "I know the ones you mean.

I'll have to get the files to you on Monday. Today is booked. Now, if you'll excuse me." She turned away without awaiting a response and headed toward her office.

"Monday will be fine," Gloria muttered to herself. No hurry at all. She shrugged and started back to her own cubicle. She'd been through this before. Department subheads had more urgent matters to deal with than helping a lowly administrative assistant square away a report.

☆☆★☆☆

Kathleen Pederson told Lynn to hold any calls and closed her office door behind her.

She leaned back against the slab of dark wood and let herself breathe. *Damn. Damn, damn, damn.* She'd have to do something about those forms--or the HR report on them anyway. She had managed to get access to the report. That HR flunky, Jo Willard, had been willing enough to log in at Kathleen's desk when she'd told the girl, "I have the files here, why don't you go ahead and log in. We can update the database right now." Jo had sat at Kathleen's desk, logged in with her own password as Kathleen watched.

She should have altered the report right away to reflect the non-existent tax forms, but there'd been other, more urgent matters to deal with once she had a dead body on her hands.

Everything had fallen into confusion once she'd struck the girl on the head from behind, using her solid Lucite *Distinguished Service Award*. At least the thing had been easy to clean and set back in its proper place on her shelves. Kathleen could now admit she'd panicked. She hadn't realized she'd need fake tax forms. She wasn't prepared to deal with anyone asking for them.

Jo had said the discrepancy only turned up by accident. They didn't normally include R&D's contractors on the company's Human Resources reports, but once they'd noticed the missing forms, they had to establish their existence. It had looked for a moment as if everything would fall apart around her. Kathleen had seen her plans, her career in ruins. She refused to face the possibility of jail time.

She'd needed to think fast, call on Ms. Ellis for help disposing of the body, for help making it look like criminals broke into the loading bay. She hadn't anticipated that anyone else would show up to ask again about the forms. Now if Kathleen altered the database, Gloria would know there'd been no tax forms for the three quarters of a million dollars in expenses. She'd be the only one who knew.

Ms. Torkenson needed to go away. But it would look odd--too odd--if two employees died within a few days of each other, both of them after working on the same report. No. This called for something less direct than her handling of Ms. Willard.

It wouldn't look quite so strange if Ms. Torkenson died at her own home, by her own hand, despondent over the death of her beloved friend, leaving a note to that effect. If anyone were capable of arranging such an event, it would be Ms. Ellis.

Kathleen shuddered, moving away from the door, to her desk. First, she would alter the database records from which HR had run the troublesome report. Then there'd be no more inquiries concerning her outside contractors. After that, she'd contact Ms. Ellis. Kathleen shuddered again, took her place before the monitor and gripped the mouse.

She had serious doubts about the Ellis woman. Meetings at midnight, and with her strange go-betweens--always some stunted, twisted-looking person in rags. At least Ms. Ellis got things done. She knew people. People motivated to do practically anything.

With all that the woman had on Kathleen, Ms. Ellis could motivate her, too now to do practically anything. At least they were both in this, both equally at risk. But, equally equal?

What did she truly know about the odd Ellis woman with her eerie, almost sickly, beauty and her midnight meetings? The woman had no phone, no email, no street address, but Kathleen also had no other recourse for getting Ms. Torkenson out of the way without creating inconvenient suspicions. Kathleen wasn't letting the inconsequential clerical worker stand in the way of a scheme yielding millions of dollars for her and her partner, with plenty more to come for as long as they kept things under wraps. Not to mention the advancement of her career plans. Soon, ABM's Department Head of Minneapolis R&D. Tomorrow, the New York offices--maybe ABM Worldwide.

☆☆★☆☆

Greg spent the morning in the computer lab, checking the last batch of simulations and setting up the next run. Each run simulated the properties of different components. Finding those optimal for reducing heat when relaying streams of photons constituted his personal treasure hunt. The potential combinations of materials and their properties ran to millions. With his algorithms, he had a reliable means of testing possible solutions--a faster, less costly way than real time tests with actual materials. He'd get to that challenge once he'd figured out his best bets.

After his usual lunchtime, Greg turned to tracking down the IP addresses he'd gotten from Ted in Tech Support.

He hadn't had much luck with them so far. The listings showed up as private registries, like unlisted phone numbers. When Eric came into the lab, still sucking down a McD's large soft drink, Greg hailed him from across the otherwise empty room.

"Hey, Eric. How're your hacking skillz?"

"Why do you want to know?" Eric, grinning like a Cheshire cat, sauntered to Greg's workstation.

"Just trying to get the address of a RL site for this IP address." Greg leaned back in his chair. "It's private registry. Guess I'm out of luck. Nobody could bust their security."

"Think again, *compadre*." Eric leaned in, studying the screen. "Just move aside and let me drive." He pulled up another chair while Greg did as instructed.

Watching Eric in action might have been an education, but the screen switched from one view to the next before Greg got a handle on exactly what Eric did to make the changes. He didn't want to distract the driver while he maneuvered so rapidly around firewalls. Only a few minutes later Eric tapped the screen and announced, "Here it is."

A street address right there in South Minneapolis. Greg quickly jotted down the info. Professor Stevens' name was listed as the contact for the IP address. No surprise, given Stevens had been the one to set up the data transfer. The business name attached to the address was Inspired Logic.

"Hey. I'm impressed." Greg clapped Eric on the shoulder. Maybe he'd skip the mousetrap below the helpful hacker's drawer. It had turned out to be handy knowing someone with Eric's special skills. A bit of pilfering from his drawer wouldn't hurt too much. Not that he wanted to go soft on crime.

"What's with the blank look?" Eric rolled his chair back to its original workstation and started his login procedure.

"Brain stuck in infinite loop." Greg gave his forehead a light whack with the palm of his hand. "Better now. Thanks, Eric."

Eric's attention had already locked on his own computer and he spoke absently, over his shoulder. "Sure man."

Greg left the day's simulations running. He checked out MapQuest for some satellite images of the suspect server address, logged out and gathered his gear. He'd do a round as Wonder Guy, check out this address and see if he might learn anything useful before preparing to confront Professor Stevens.

Chapter 15

Gloria usually only worked until three o'clock on Fridays. Given how many people in her department didn't work at all, she felt no guilt for any missed calls or emails from sticklers who did stay on the job until four o' clock. They'd be answered on Monday. The few urgent projects that might crop up involved people able to reach the decision makers directly.

Sometimes Gloria would stay later because she had a project of her own to work on and liked using the fast internet connections and top grade software applications available at the office. This weekend she'd reserved for wedding planning. She couldn't wait to get home, lock herself in her room with her laptop and research local sources for flowers and music. She and Pete may not have actually set a date yet, but she liked to be on top of things.

During her last half hour at work, she marked time by getting a head start on her Googling. It proved easy enough to find a few local flower shops with websites, but nothing looked right. She loved roses, but either the arrangements looked too formal--boring--or so creative Pete would balk at using them.

She had no interest in the formal arrangements. Formality was not the word for Gloria Torkenson. Staid, classic styles might suit Pete, but didn't work for her. She wasn't into anything too predictable. That struck out country or anything old-fashioned, but she didn't want anything too innovative, either. Did she have a style of her own?

She appreciated a natural kind of beauty, like butterfly wings and woodland glades. She liked playing with the possibilities of many different styles, the way she did with the Cell Shell designs. She liked to draw elements from every possible source, from oriental arabesques, to expressionist modern art, to Pennsylvania Dutch designs, to African and Amerindian geometrics, but she wouldn't say any single style represented Gloria Torkenson. Eclectic was the word. She needed eclecticity.

Staring at the array of floral arrangements on screen before her, she found nothing eclectic enough to fit her style. The more inventive arrangements she loved seemed too wild to suit Pete. Several of the beautiful, formal concoctions of roses, orchids, and lilies looked as if they'd be right at home in his wedding, but not at hers. What did that say about them?

Besides, they were so expensive. She didn't want to spend so much money on a one-time event when it could make day-to-day living so much more manageable. Pete would see eye-to-eye with that line of reasoning. Maybe she should talk him into a simple civil ceremony at City Hall. Their closest friends and family would be there, but they wouldn't need all the expense and foo-foo-raw--one of Aggie's favorite words--of flowers and music and fancy gowns.

☆☆★☆☆

Kathleen left the ABM offices earlier than she'd planned. If she were going to set up a meeting with Ms. Ellis, she'd rather do as much as possible by the light of day.

The gnarly man would be easiest to find. If he didn't actually live in the lot behind the U-Store-It where Inspired Logic had its supposed offices, he at least kept a constant watch on the place and always appeared within minutes of her own arrival there.

At three o'clock the sun still shone high over the half industrial neighborhood, but cast deep shadows between the buildings. Kathleen parked near the end of the row of storage units, at the back of the building, where an alley ran behind the neatly maintained blocky structures, facades blazoned in a broad swath of red and punctuated with rows of garage-style doors.

The breeze struck her as cool for June, but one never knew what to expect in Minnesota. She remembered one May they'd had ninety-degree temperatures one week and snow the next. What on earth possessed her to live in such a place? She should be in New York City. Just a bit more progress on her career plans here and she would be in

New York City, leap-frogging Mr. Carlson to move up the ladder at corporate headquarters.

She walked casually to the alley behind the building, as if loitering while waiting for someone who visited a storage unit. Stepping around the end of the building, she found the usual scrubby growth of saplings lining the neglected tract where the alley cut between the storage facility and the grain elevators further on. The breeze clattered through the leaves and long-limbed brush, sending assorted trash, mostly wrappers from the fast food place down the road, along the rutted way.

Kathleen scanned the scrub growth, peering into its shadows. The gnarly man always seemed to emerge from those shadows. He must have made some kind of nest for himself there, of fallen branches and cardboard boxes, most likely. She wrinkled her nose. Why would a woman like Ms. Ellis, who seemed always to be dressed at the height of fashion, impeccable in her appearance, consort with such shabby creatures?

Perhaps for the same reasons she herself had come here to find him. He would do the job she had for him.

A scuffling noise off to the side drew her attention to the very party she'd come to see. No more than four feet in height, as bent and gnarled as an old tree, wrinkled and clad in rags nearly indistinguishable in color from the dusty surface of the alley, he stood completely still. He stared at her with a look as pointed as if he'd actually said, 'Well, what do you want?'

"I need to speak to Ms. Ellis." Kathleen put some asperity into her tone. Whatever else he might be, he was an underling and should know his place.

"Wait," he growled, fading back into the narrow stand of saplings and brush beside the buildings. Maybe he managed to get into the building through some hole hidden behind the unkempt fringe of growth?

She'd been here before and knew better than to complain of the wait. Through whatever means, the gnarly little man could contact Ms. Ellis and set up a meeting. Probably another of those very uncomfortable midnight meetings the woman seemed to prefer.

Kathleen hugged her suit jacket closer. It seemed both colder and darker here in the shadows behind the blank walls of the storage facility.

☆☆★☆☆

In a fraction of the time it would have taken to bike there as Greg Roberts, Wonder Guy made the flight to the address Eric had helped ferret out. He'd scout out the location, take a look at the place. On the face of it, Professor Stevens had a right to back up student data to a site he deemed secure, but backing it up to an off-campus server smelled fishy. A server registered to a private company? It stank like fish forgotten for weeks in the trunk of the car after summer vacation, a scent he knew from experience.

Having studied MapQuest's satellite images, Greg spotted the site from the air, a set of long low storage buildings in a neighborhood near the grain elevators along Hiawatha Avenue. What kind of research company used a storage unit for its business address?

Greg did another, lower pass. A few vehicles sat in the parking lanes between buildings.

He studied the visitors to the storage units as he circled high above. A couple of college-aged guys loaded boxes off the back of a pickup truck into one unit. An older guy sat on a campstool in the opening of another unit, apparently varnishing the hull of a small motorboat. A woman in business dress stood near the back of one building, a phone pressed to her ear. A late model red Audi sat parked not far from her, beside the last unit in the row.

Nobody looked suspicious, but who'd wear ski masks and trench coats to the site of an illicit operation? He focused Wonder Guy's telescopic vision on the numbers painted above each unit, looking for #248. Bingo, the unit with the Audi parked in front. The woman must have some connection to Professor Stevens. How was she involved?

Greg circled higher lest she glance upward. He wondered how high he'd have to go to be mistaken for some circling bird. Funny how seldom people looked up. Everyone he observed with his super enhanced vision seemed intent on his or her own purposes. Whether they varnished a boat or loaded boxes, drove along the road, stopped at the gas station or McD's, not a single person tilted a head to look at the great blue hemisphere above. Not that he wasn't the same way, intent on the ground below him.

Greg executed a slow roll, surveying the sky above him as well as the land below. Above, only shreds of wispy cloud marked the blue sky. What more did he expect? He rolled his shoulders, trying to shake an uncomfortable sensation of being watched. If anyone did have him under satellite or telescopic observation, he'd just have to live with it.

He should concern himself with the woman below him. Her presence at the professor's storage unit made her a good subject for surveillance. He'd follow her, maybe pick up some clue to her identity and involvement with Professor Stevens' scheme.

Maybe she had nothing to do with it, though. She made no move toward the storage unit. She went instead to the shadows of the alley behind the facility, lingering there for no apparent reason, where a thin line of saplings and brush grew between the narrow alley and the neighboring grain elevators.

He scanned the area from above, the cool air molding itself around his outstretched limbs as if he swam an insubstantial sea. From the woman's stance, she might be speaking to someone hidden in the scraggly growth. Yet, not even his enhanced vision revealed anyone present.

☆☆★☆☆

What now? Gloria wondered, during her evening--if she called three-thirty in the afternoon evening--drive home. She couldn't marry Pete. They didn't fit. Or, she might be able to fit him into

238

her admittedly eclectic life-style, but he belonged with someone more his own style. Someone who'd complement his simple (boring), formal (staid) and unadorned (empty) life-style.

He might claim to love her, even with all the arts and crafts adorning her walls: from her historical t-shirt quilt to her macramé pillow hammock, fruit-section clocks, and experiments in Ukrainian egg-dying that resembled works of Mondrian. But face it, after a while, he'd start wincing inside, turning away, looking for his proper match in some quiet woman of simple tastes.

Gloria drove her usual route, focused on the road and responsive to the traffic, but preoccupied with how little she had in common with Pete, which should upset her far more than it did. She and Pete were over. It left her with a sort of melancholy, as if she looked back at a half-remembered dream, but she was letting go of someone whom, yesterday, she would have said she loved. She did love Pete, in a way. He was as dear as any of her friends and coworkers. Only she ought to feel more for someone she meant to marry.

☆☆★☆☆

Elysha did not sleep as humans did. She let herself slip into a dreamlike state wherein her mind wove itself among the limbs and the roots of the green lives surrounding her to absorb something of the serenity in which they grew. At least, it seemed like serenity to her. Each life ruthlessly striving to extend itself to the heights and depths it could reach, regardless of how one might strangle or overshadow another. All in a season's work. It soothed her to dwell here where such avid life flourished.

Because she did not sleep, the sylph did not wake her when it approached, but it drew her from a restful state and woke her temper.

"Why do you disturb me?" Elysha stirred from her place in a stand of birches, applying the spell that made her eyes shine hard as green flints.

"With news I come." The gossamer thing trembled like cobwebs in a stiff breeze. "The Hero pursues your human tool, she who has met with you at midnight times where the water flows from trap to trap."

"That one." Kathleen, the human woman who craved power above all. Elysha frowned. The threatened scheme still unfolded. Only one of many, it ran deep enough to strike many lives when it finally blew apart like a ripened seedpod. "You were correct to tell me. I cannot allow his interference in this plan."

The sylph steadied in its semblance of a feminine waif made entirely of sheer veils, flickering in and out of visibility in the scant sunshine penetrating the leafy boughs above.

Elysha considered. She bent to retrieve a broken chunk of masonry wedged between the roots of an oak. "Take this."

"It's too heavy, Mistress." The sylph trembled anew.

Elysha scowled. Indeed, the wispy being could no more have lifted one of the monstrosities of steel crowding the city's roads. Ah, a stirring in the brambles alerted her. A gnarled, manlike minion approached.

"The human-who-would-be-queen seeks audience, Mistress."

"Very good." She almost smiled. "Return to her with this." She extended the broken chunk of cement and brick. "Tell her to keep it with her and meet me at moonrise at the usual place."

A set of fingers as gnarled as twigs took the stone, and tucked it in to disappear among the creature's rags.

☆☆★☆☆

Greg maintained his surveillance from such a height he'd seem like a dot in the sky if anyone looked up. A few clouds floated higher still or trailed in such thin wisps, like the veils of an exotic dancer, they obscured nothing of the land below. At least they obscured nothing to Wonder Guy's enhanced vision.

Detective shows and novels--his primary source of instruction on crime-fighting--portrayed surveillance as a boring chore. Maybe they were right when it came to ground-based operations, sitting in a car, waiting for something to happen as minutes turned into hours, but from up here, Greg found it fascinating.

Not only did he have the thrill of flying, of surfing the air currents as if he'd been transformed to some mythic creature like a dragon or Pegasus, but this perspective afforded him views open to no ordinary pilot. Keeping half an eye on the woman

241

who loitered behind the storage facility, he experimented with combining his telescopic and x-ray visions. He zoomed in on his subject to read the license plate on her car and focused the x-ray vision on the contents of its trunk: a rather ordinary spare tire and set of tools. It proved tricky. Overshooting brought him past an object to things on the other side. With practice, he peeked into her briefcase on the back seat of the vehicle. Unfortunately, reading the documents became something different without the spectrum of visible light. He distinguished metal--an iPhone and a manicure set--from the ghost-shapes made by pads and folders, but anything printed on the paper remained unreadable.

Maybe if he had enough time to practice he could learn to use this vision to make such fine spectroscopic distinctions. In the meanwhile, he switched his attention to the object he'd originally planned to investigate, the storage unit beside the car.

Penetrating the roof proved easier than it would have been to see through the metal of the accordion-style garage door. Even with the steel I-beams of the ceiling in the way, he recognized the boxy shapes of a pair of servers and the snaking lines of cables hooked to a ceiling fixture probably meant only to provide light to the unit. The other odd, metallic construct might have been a portable backup generator.

His attention had strayed from the woman, but when she moved, he turned back to her, surveying the scene afresh as she entered her car and maneuvered back toward the main road.

He must have missed something. He scanned the area where she'd loitered, but nothing had changed, only the same scrubby undergrowth and ragged sapling, certainly no living soul.

From this height, he easily tracked her vehicle as it headed north and merged with traffic headed downtown.

As they neared the West Bank area and St. Mary's hospital, Greg flew with renewed caution, attentive to any sign of waning powers. He flew much higher now than he'd been before, when he'd come in too close to his birthplace hospital. Now he figured he flew high enough to be outside the radius of whatever mysterious and illogical influence the edifice had on him. He estimated the distance equaled roughly fifteen hundred feet. If he maintained an altitude of at least three thousand feet relative to St. Mary's he should be okay, right?

His logic seemed good. At least, he passed what he estimated as five thousand feet above the hospital without incident, following his subject's car past the area toward the outskirts of the downtown district, until she pulled into a parking area. What could the suspect woman be doing at ABM's offices? A chill went through him. Gloria worked there.

Though he meant to stay too high to be noticed by casual observers, Greg dropped altitude, drawn to place himself between this questionable woman and anything having to do with Gloria.

Only a sudden queasy feeling of lost control, like brakes going squishy, warned him to pull up again before he plummeted thousands of feet to the un-forgiving streets below.

☆☆★☆☆

Gloria made good time heading home via side streets to avoid the rush hour traffic. It took her longer to get from the front door to her bedroom.

"Where'd you stay last night?" growled her father from his usual seat on the couch, in front of the usual array of empty and half-empty cans on the coffee table as the TV competed with the sound of his voice.

She'd stopped off at the house that morning, showered and dressed while he'd still been asleep in his room. No such luck now.

"I called you, remember?" She kept her tone even. "My friend died. I was too upset to come home and slept over at Aggie's."

"Too upset to walk from one house to the next?"

"Don't start this, Dad." *Don't get sucked in.* Gloria fought the impulse to hunch her shoulders and kept moving, hanging her jacket in the closet. She continued through the living room as she spoke. "What would you have done if I'd started crying? I needed someone to be nice and just listen to me."

"I always listen to you." He wore his aggrieved expression. "You didn't give me the chance. Think I can't be nice to my own daughter?"

She paused at the head of the short hallway leading to the bedrooms. "Maybe you can." Talking to him always came out wrong somehow. Gloria softened her voice. "I was too wrung out to take a chance on it." She bit her tongue. It took so little to set him off.

"Fine thing," he muttered. "It's a good thing your mother isn't here to see how her daughter acts toward her father." He bent to pick up a can still dewy with condensation.

"Now that's too much," Gloria snapped, in more ways than one. "This isn't about you. One of my best friends just died. I was in shock, devastated." She'd had too much of this, too many years of walking on eggshells around this man. "I'm sorry if my grief prevented me from being here for you to poke at, or tell me how I'm not good enough for Pete or his family."

She clenched her jaw. She hated this, hated feeling this angry and hated spewing it at the man she'd come to pity as much as she resented him. It gave her a sick feeling, not in her gut so much as in her heart.

"If it makes you happy," she said as she turned away from him, "I think you're right. I'm not going to fit in with Pete or his family. I'm not going to marry him." She moved to her own room.

Her father muttered, "No, it doesn't make me happy."

She closed the door behind her.

☆☆★☆☆

It took his whole effort to ascend again, fighting with his weakened powers as if struggling up the face of a cliff hand over hand, Finally, Greg gained enough altitude for the sense of weakness to ease, and he no longer felt in danger of winding up flattened against the pavement of the ABM parking lot.

What the hell? St. Mary's was at least a couple miles from here. ABM might have some meaning for him, but represented nothing like his 'planet of origin.'

Greg came in to a careful landing three long blocks away from the ABM building. Best to reconnoiter on foot from here. It would be safer, not risking a fall. It would be even safer to go as plain Greg Roberts, but he couldn't be sure whether he'd be able to detect the influence that had weakened him just now if he switched out of his Wonder Guy guise.

The effect hadn't seemed as strong as around St. Mary's, where he'd been thrown so roughly from the sky before, but this incident had weakened him enough that he felt lucky to have made it safely back to *terra firma*.

At least in this neighborhood, where warehouses and parking lots occupied much of the real estate, he met few pedestrians while striding along the sidewalk in his superhero costume. A few people stopped to stare, but he met nothing worse.

Until he got within a thousand feet of ABM's parking lot.

Chapter 16

She'd have to tell Pete, of course. Gloria sat on the edge of her bed, door closed firmly behind her. She wished she could do it over the phone, but that seemed cowardly, taking the easy way out. Pete deserved better. This evening would be best, on their usual Friday dinner date. As early as possible. Maybe she'd tell him in the car. She had no appetite for supper.

She hated the thought of hurting Pete. He'd been nothing but kind and considerate of her ever since they'd met. Yet, at the same time, she doubted he'd be terribly devastated. No one would describe Pete as a demonstrative man. He'd never displayed what she'd call passionate feelings about anything. Even her.

He always used gifts to show his affection for her. Fairly generic gifts too. She liked roses and chocolates--a pretty safe bet with most women-- and he'd been generous with those. Still, he'd never given her anything as thoughtful as the small multi-tool Greg had given her for her birthday a few years ago. Among its many useful charms, it included an awl to punch holes in leather, and she used it regularly on the Cell Shells.

☆☆★☆☆

At first Greg hardly noticed it. If he hadn't been alert to the possibility of danger, he might have approached a good bit closer to the expanse of parking lot occupied by only a handful of cars this late on a Friday. Only now, on high alert, he noted a slight heaviness in his steps, a sickly tang in the pit of his stomach. A few more steps and the tang grew to queasiness. His steps seemed freighted with lead weights.

Strange. At this rate he'd have to fight every step of the way to make it to the red Audi he'd followed from on high, now parked not far from the main entrance to the ABM building. Time for a strategic withdrawal.

Greg retraced his steps away from the source of his growing weakness, whatever that might be. He scanned his surroundings. Where was a convenient telephone booth when a superhero needed one? Setting his sights on a service station another block up the road, Wonder Guy took to the air.

Moving at a speed no human eye could follow, he landed behind the station next to a dumpster loaded with empty cardboard boxes. Taking refuge behind another large stack of boxes, Wonder Guy changed back to his more comfortable identity as Greg Roberts.

Taking his obvious next step, he set out at a walk back toward the ABM parking lot. This time he drew no stares. Clad in tan slacks, his *You Are Here* galaxy t-shirt and a U of M hooded sweatshirt, he might have been any one of thousands of college-aged men. Comfortable in his anonymity, he relaxed as he walked. He wouldn't want to be 'just another guy' to Gloria, but being just another guy to the rest of the world had its charms.

Greg passed the point where, as Wonder Guy, his steps had grown heavier and slower. This time he encountered nothing out of the ordinary. Okay. Serafina had told him how Wonder Guy, having powers like Superman, shared Superman's vulnerability. She hadn't said anything about keeping his vulnerability as his regular self, an advantage he had over Clark Kent.

Continuing to the very edge of the parking lot, where vibrant flowerbeds made a border between the city sidewalk and the asphalt marked with parking spaces, he still suffered no ill effects.

Debating the need to pull up his hood to block the bright wash of late afternoon sun, Greg strode up to the red Audi.

What would happen if he switched back to Wonder Guy right here? Probably nothing good. Not worth the risk to find out. If whatever-it-might-be had weakened him from a city block away, he didn't want to face what it would do at ground zero. The car looked like a car. Had he learned anything useful? Other than the interesting fact that Wonder Guy's vulnerability didn't extend to Greg Roberts? Not much.

He walked past the suspect car, moving toward the sheltered entrance to the ABM building. Who was this woman and how did she know Professor

Stevens? Her connection to ABM only raised more questions. The odds were astronomical against pure coincidence placing her at the storage unit where the professor directed stolen data. Coincidence didn't connect her to whatever unknown factor had weakened Wonder Guy when he'd followed her too closely. He had a lot of questions for this woman.

She looked like a businesswoman. She probably worked here at ABM. Maybe Gloria would help him get a company directory. Gloria might even know her. That bothered him. This woman might be dangerous, if only judging by her increasingly suspicious involvement in this situation.

Greg sauntered casually past the glass and stone façade of the ABM building, not wanting to attract the attention of company security by loitering too long near the suspect car. Nor did he want to draw his target's attention when she emerged again from the offices, which she might do at any time.

He needed a plan. As if heading toward a car at the far end, in no hurry, simply enjoying the fine weather, he walked along the verge of the parking lot. Consider the options. Maybe he'd back off to a safe distance, resume his guise as Wonder Guy and fly to a height where he could safely resume surveillance, follow the woman wherever she went next. She might be a workaholic and stay here for hours. Or she might lead him all over the landscape without revealing anything useful.

He kicked a large pebble from his path to send it skittering across the asphalt ahead of him. He could confront her. Make up some story, ask her who she was. Maybe he was a student writing a story or essay on the company? He could ask her about her role there. The plan had its appeal, but he'd rather come armed with some real data rather than vague suspicions.

Better something simpler. He turned, facing back toward the building. It still might be hours before she emerged. He needed to hurry her. He'd caught up with the pebble he'd earlier kicked along his path.

Ah, that depended on the kind of car alarm she had. He bent, picked up the stone and tested its heft. He had a fair arm, born of laziness. When he lived at home, going to school, he'd rather chuck his crumpled wads of scratch paper at a wastebasket than get up and walk across the room. Aggie made him get up and retrieve any failed missiles, giving him all the more motivation for improving his aim.

He scanned the area for security cameras, spotted two trained on the entrance to the building, and others monitoring the parking lot. He moved back toward the street. He passed beyond the range of the cameras, checked to make sure no one looked his way, turned and flung his pebble underhand to strike the handle of the Audi's door. He faced smoothly away again, never breaking stride as the car's alarm began to wail.

He reached the sidewalk and looked back, pausing along with a few other passersby, to stare at the car.

The whooping of the alarm cut through all sounds of nearby traffic. In moments, a man in security uniform opened the main door of the ABM entrance, peering out at the disturbance. He disappeared again behind the doors, and shortly re-emerged, accompanying the very subject of Greg's surveillance.

Greg smiled to himself, holding his phone ready with the camera activated. Good thing he'd sprung for the Samsung with the 3x optical zoom. He waited until she'd come as close as she would. As she reached for the driver's side door, he snapped her picture, catching her with her mouth tight, a frown line marring her forehead, wincing at the alarm.

The passersby who'd first stopped had moved along by then, but others had arrived. He lingered only as long as they did. He moved away when the alarm went silent and the rest of the gawkers dispersed. So far, so good, for his plan. Now he must come up with a good excuse to show Gloria the picture and ask if she knew the woman.

☆☆★☆☆

With the moon only a few days past full, moon-rise came early in the evening. Thank God for that. Some event at Orchestra Hall had the plaza crowded with men and women in full evening dress, mostly clustered near the main doors where an outdoor bar stood and a few vendors offered light snacks.

Kathleen smelled the skewers of barbecued chicken from halfway across the plaza, where, in the shadows of an upper level, Ms. Ellis sat like an empress on a ledge among the plaza's multi-tiered pools. Somehow, despite the numbers of people wandering the plaza, none found their way to this particular sheltered corner. Odd how the plaza seemed to grow more hidden nooks and shadowed corners with Ms. Ellis in residence than it owned by daylight among ordinary folk. Odd how the pleasant June evening took on an unexpected chill.

Ms. Ellis might have come for the symphony. Her gown would pass muster with the best of them, silken and flowing with the colors of water and woodland glades at night. Kathleen straightened her shoulders as she faced the other woman's cool regard.

"There's been another complication," she said.

"What sort of complication?" Ms. Ellis managed to scowl without marring the flawless lines of her face. "This is an annoyance. We have more important business than your complications."

Kathleen told Ms. Ellis about Gloria's latest round of questions concerning non-existent tax forms. "I thought the first inquiry was a fluke." She swallowed, keeping her voice barely louder than the flowing of water from pool to pool. "It should never have come up. I've taken steps to make sure it won't come up again, but this girl will know I didn't actually provide the forms."

"And what do you expect of me?" Ms. Ellis raised a brow.

"You know people." Kathleen hesitated. "Nothing can happen to her at the office. It would look too suspicious. Can't you arrange something..." She let her words trail off in a tone suggesting the dark, final nature of the 'something' in question. "...to happen elsewhere?"

Ice glinted in the other woman's gaze. "Such services can be expensive."

"There's enough money in this--"

"Not money." Ms. Ellis shrugged dismissively. "You will owe me. Personally. Some comparable service."

How much did she already owe this woman? Kathleen ignored the sick sensation in her gut. "Of course." She kept her tone cool. "It would be best if it looked like a suicide. The first young woman was this one's friend. Gloria must be distraught over her death, if she gives in to despair..." Again, she let her tone suggest the rest. "Tragic, but understandable."

"Yes." Ms. Ellis' smile showed more teeth than a person should have, but seemed positively gleeful in contrast to her usual imperious manner. "That can be arranged. Perhaps this very evening."

☆☆★☆☆

When Pete called, Gloria told him she had something she'd like to talk about before dinner. He insisted he was starving and asked her to wait until they had their meals in front of them. This meant meeting him at the nearest Perkins family restaurant.

Even though she didn't feel like eating, Gloria went along with the plan. Maybe a good meal would make things easier on Pete.

She still reeled with the sudden changes in her life. Jo's death, her changes of heart and mind.

How much sense did it make to cancel an engagement because her sense of style clashed with Pete's? How superficial. Weren't their feelings for each other the only thing that should matter here?

But that was it. Her feelings expressed themselves in terms of colors and shapes, design and patterns. This aesthetic sensibility said her feelings for Pete weren't what they should be and his feelings for her weren't what she needed from him. She didn't get as much of a thrill from him as she did from a new Cell Shell design coming together in the right materials and colors.

She turned on the MPR news during the short drive. It kept her mind from going through the cycle of guilt and justification over and again. Not much of the news sank in. It all sounded the same to her, more death, more destruction, more threats to national security, more threats to personal liberties, more trouble and strife on every side.

Pete had arrived before her and already sat in a booth, menu opened before him. Gloria ordered hot tea as soon as she'd joined him and told the server she wouldn't be having anything else. Pete raised a brow at her before giving his order for a Bacon Cheeseburger Supreme and handing back his menu.

"Really, nothing to eat?" He smiled his easy smile. "Must be serious. Okay, so what's got you all worked up?"

The waitress had moved far enough from their booth to be out of earshot.

"Pete, I can't marry you." There. It was out. Gloria waited for the words to sink in, for some sign of the impact this news must have on him. Her stomach churned. Maybe she should have ordered toast with her tea. He met her worried gaze with a reassuring smile.

"You have pre-wedding jitters. Nerves," he said. "It's perfectly natural."

"We haven't set a date yet. It can't be pre-wedding jitters," Gloria spoke with growing annoyance. They had planned to spend their whole lives together. She tells him it's off and he responds like she'd mistaken a dust ball for a mouse.

Be patient with him. Maybe he doesn't want to face it. "I've been thinking." She took a deep breath. "Things between us aren't what they should be, not for two people to share the rest of their lives together."

He didn't look up. He had his latest phone out and tapped on its surface, adding up the bill and figuring the tip ahead of time as usual. When he'd taken care of business, he looked across to her, a look she'd always taken as reassuring, but now seemed more than a bit patronizing.

"Gloria, honey, if this is about yesterday, when I wasn't free to talk with you after your friend died, you know I would have if I could. Company policies are strict about calls."

"No, Pete. It's not about that." She took another deep, calming breath. The sick feeling had risen higher in her gut. "But Jo's death made me consider a lot of things. I realized my feelings for you aren't what you deserve. I've been in love with what you can do for me.

"I've been in love with what you represent. I think you deserve better. You deserve someone who's truly in love with you for who you are," she admitted, embarrassed to realize the extent of her selfishness. Pete would take care of her, had the power to rescue her. He'd be the safe, reliable, stable provider she'd never had. So what did that make her? A helpless child?

Please let him understand.

Pete's look had sobered as she spoke. He remained silent as the waitress returned with Gloria's tea and his cola, only speaking when she'd left the table again.

"Gloria. Stop. You're not making sense." He reached across the table and grasped her hand. "Nothing's changed. We're the same two people we were when we decided to get married. Remember how we worked it out? We'll get a little house of our own. We'll have kids in a couple years when I've advanced at the company and you can afford to stay home. Don't you still want our future?"

It made such a nice picture in her mind's eye. She fantasized about children, darling cherubs she loved like the dickens, even if they were imaginary at this point. That was the problem. It was just a pretty picture, like a TV commercial where all one's problems melted in the face of the right laundry detergent. He'd end up disappointed if he expected her to play along with a role based more in her feelings for the picture than her feelings for him.

"Pete," she said, gently disengaging her hand. "It's not about some plan we made for an ideal future. It's about our true feelings, mine and yours, and who we truly are to one another. I've realized I want something more than what we have between us. You're a fine man, but my feelings for you aren't what they should be for the man I marry."

"Gloria, you're not making sense. You've had a shock. Your friend died. I understand. If you need to take a little time..." He made an uncertain wave of his hand, one that seemed to accept the possibility of needing time without necessarily comprehending why it might be required.

He didn't get it. His blank look meant her words had run aground before ever reaching the harbor of his understanding. He didn't see the difference between her acting out the role they'd planned and acting from her heart. She might as well leave a pre-programmed android version of herself sitting here with him. He'd never know the difference. She swallowed the bitter taste of disappointment over her lost dream. Later, she'd deal with her fears of facing the future alone. Pete would only understand if she put words into action.

"I'm sorry, Pete." Gloria got to her feet. "I don't need a little time, I need my whole life. You stay, have your dinner. I'll be going." She slung her bag over her shoulder and walked away.

☆☆★☆☆

Gloria had no trouble making it past her father and back to her room. Ike had passed out on the couch. Lying there, dead to the world, stubbled face slack, a spilled beer staining the carpet beside the couch, he reminded her of her stillborn hopes for her marriage to Pete.

Hell. How would she make it out of here now? If not by marrying Pete, then what? She shook her head. She was being ridiculous. She had a decent job. She could get an apartment on her own. Even some tiny efficiency would give her a refuge, a place to call her own. She might have gotten a place like that years ago. What had stopped her? Dad, something whispered in the back of her mind. Why should it be any easier to deal with him now than it had been then?

Gloria closed her bedroom door behind her, kicked off her shoes. She sat on the edge of the bed and slumped forward, letting the pent up tension drain from her neck and back.

This was her fault. She was a grown woman. She could have insisted from the start that her father go into assisted living if he couldn't manage living alone. She didn't have to stay with him here. Not then. Not now.

It was easier to give in to him. Easier than fighting him about it, fighting the guilt trip, fighting the allegations of selfishness for wanting some freedom. Giving in was easier than figuring out how to manage on her own or finding a place she could afford on her salary. Easier to stay, easier to go along with her father's demands. She'd been taking the easy way too often, in too many ways. It had come to the point where living with things as they stood was no longer easy. Time to make a decision about what she wanted for herself, where she wanted to live, and whether she could do it alone.

☆☆★☆☆

Elysha found her prey readily enough. Kathleen Pederson had given her a slip of paper their target had signed, saying it included the girl's address. She needed no address. Touching the signature gave her a clear sense of the individual behind it, a portrait of her energy, as clear to her as blood scent to a hunting dog. It led her a couple miles south of their meeting place to a neighborhood as pleasant as human habitations came. She found the dwelling in a place surrounded by tall old trees, plentiful among the structures, buffering the annoying tang of metal and the acrid scents of streets and internal combustion exhaust.

The energy trace led her to an open window. Its screen, not the troublesome steel mesh men used many seasons past, did nothing to bar Elysha's influence.

Elysha drew near. The metal used in constructing the house lay mostly shielded beneath layers of stucco and brick and board. She'd grown inured to such trace amounts over her years of dwelling so near to humankind.

The shades of night, shadows of trees, and her glamour combined to make her invisible to the casual eye. She stood at the window and looked in upon her target, the young woman already slumped in misery. This should be easy.

With her voice schooled to tones heard more by the heart than the ear, Elysha whispered her poison to the young woman seated not far from her, on a bed beside the window.

"Your friend has died." Elysha touched her words with the bleak chill of winter. "As everyone you know and love will die. You can hold nothing in this life that will not be taken from you, no one, nothing, no home, no joy, no achievement, nor honor. All shall become dust, until you, too, shall fade to naught."

The girl's shoulders slumped further, her blonde curls tumbling forward unimpeded when she rested her head in her hands.

☆☆★☆☆

A chill breeze from the window raised goose bumps on the back of Gloria's neck, but rising to close the sash seemed too much of an effort. Everything seemed useless, pointless. What was the point of anything when you lost it all in the end? Jo was dead. Gone. It might as easily have been her, or her father, or Aggie--anyone. What good was it to care for anyone when it hurt so much to lose them?

Jo's face arose in her memories. They laughed together over their morning coffee while Jo made wise-ass remarks about Ms. Dexter's management style, or raved over the latest episode of Criminal Minds or a gorgeous scarf she'd spotted as they window-shopped downtown. Jo had wanted to follow the parade to Lake Harriet and ride the elephant. They should have gone, joined in, had fun while they could. Except, what difference did it make now?

What difference if Gloria had been trampled beneath the elephant's feet? What difference if she died now or after years of losing the people and things she loved?

She had no words to fight these questions, but something in her moved determinedly through her bedtime routine. On automatic pilot, Gloria picked up the hairbrush from her bedside table as she did every night before settling down and tucking herself in. She ran the brush through her curls, stopped at each slight tangle until her fingers teased out the knots as if of their own volition. The brush felt soothing against her scalp, but she hardly registered the fact as her thoughts washed around her, compelling as a riptide dragging her out to sea.

"No one loves you." The certainty dragged at her, dragged her from the shores of common sense. It seemed only too true. Pete hadn't loved her. He might have loved a few things about her, but he didn't actually know her. Beyond this face that would turn to wrinkles one day, or this shiny blonde hair that would turn gray and thin, the perky body that would eventually weaken and sag. He loved some idea of her, a fantasy that wasn't her at all.

Her father didn't love her, either. At least, not as much as he loved a cold beer and not having to see the world too clearly. Who could blame him? The world sucked people dry and spat them out. The world waved pretty lures of sunshine and hope in people's faces, only to drag them in, until the bottom fell out and dropped them into darkness and pain. A beer or two didn't sound like such a bad thing about now.

But having brushed her hair made it time to trim her nails. Where were her clippers? Gloria looked around, momentarily distracted. The manicure set usually sat on the lower shelf of the bedside table. Where had it gone? Oh--right. She'd snipped the tags off those new washcloths. She must have left it in the bathroom. Too much work to go get it, but her purse lay at her feet where she'd dropped it.

She bent, rummaging for her multi-tool. It included a mini-scissors and a file. They'd do the job. Habit moved her. It wasn't as if there were any point in trimming her nails. If she were alive, they'd grow back. If she ended this misery, it would hardly matter what condition her nails were in.

Gloria slowed, one hand on the soft leather of her purse. Why bother? Why bother with a minute more of her useless life, with waiting for the next shoe to drop, for the decision to be taken from her and for fate to end her life? Why wait for the next loss? Why wait for the next blow to send her reeling, the next confirmation that she meant nothing to the world, or to anyone in it?

Chapter 17

Elysha whispered, "Why wait? Why let the suffering go on, and on? It would be easy to end this, to end it all..."

The young woman leaned back, pulling something with her, up to her lap. Elysha frowned. Her victim should be too rapt in the spell to notice anything else.

☆☆★☆☆

Gloria's fingers fumbled in her bag, still intent on their mission despite the direction of her thoughts. Good grooming was not a habit easily kicked.

Her fingers found the small tool Greg had given her, there in the inner pocket of her handbag. An electric shock jerked her hand, startling her to alertness.

She looked around as if waking from a dream, her recent preoccupation leaving only a trace of bleak winter on her heart. What had she been thinking?

☆☆★☆☆

Her intended prey fumbled in the bag held on her lap. A jolt, like a lightning strike from a clear sky, struck Elysha. The young woman straightened, pulling forth something blazing and burning in Elysha's magical vision. She shrieked in pain, covering her eyes, falling back a few stumbling steps before she turned to flee.

☆☆★☆☆

A cry sounded, like the shriek of a hawk, somewhere out in the night. Gloria shook her head. She had it all wrong. How unfair, forgetting all the people who cared about her. Like Aggie, who had been there for her practically every day since her mother died, who'd encouraged her and helped her to fulfill her dreams. Her father cared also, even if he got too caught up in his private pain to show it. Greg cared. Mr. Carlson cared. Anne and Patty, and the researchers on her team. Lots of people cared about her.

She turned the multi-tool in her hand, hefted its cool weight. Greg had cared enough to give her something that helped her in small ways every day. She pulled out the mini scissors and began to trim a ragged nail on her left hand. She should probably see a manicurist one of these days, but the way she kept chipping her nails--talk about the futility of life. She smiled at the play on her own recent negativity.

How could she forget all the blessings in her life? She'd discounted not only her relationships, but all the positive experiences she'd ever had, because those experiences didn't last forever. What if life's blessings froze in place like insects trapped in amber? If summer lasted forever, Christmas would never come. If Christmas lasted forever, there'd never be flowers blooming in spring.

Gloria shortened a nail to unify the look of her hand and then trimmed a couple of the uneven ones on her other hand.

Losing Jo was terrible. Not only did the loss leave her feeling hollow as Carlsbad Caverns, but the violence left her with a sense of lingering threat, clenching her stomach and shredding her nerves as if scratching its way across a miles-long blackboard. It would be worse if she'd never had the chance to know her friend, or if she'd never had the chance to know the mother she'd lost. The hurt would fade in time. This hollow ache might always be with her, but a thousand new and better times would intervene, cushioning her from the impact. Time did heal, even while leaving scars.

Lighten up, Gloria. She should get a pad of paper and make a list of her blessings, remember how many she still had. Maybe she could no longer include a fiancé on the list, but she'd done the right thing, in calling it off with Pete. She should count herself blessed for having the sense to recognize as much and the courage to do what she should. If Pete wasn't the right person for her, it left her free to find a better match.

She pulled out the multi-tool's file, tucked away the mini-scissors and buffed where she'd trimmed. There. She held out one hand, then the other, admiring her work. Good job.

Brrr. The breeze seemed awfully chilly for June, but this was Minnesota. Gloria hadn't noticed until now the clouds moving in with the setting of the sun. The cooler air prompted her to rise at last. She closed the sash against the night and her dark thoughts of only moments before, and against the few scattered drops of rain beginning to fall. These gave her a more immediate, if mundane cause for concern. She'd hoped for a bit more dry weather. There were always a lot more mosquitoes after it rained. Gloria shrugged away this worry too. She'd had enough of negativity. She donned a light cotton nightie. Planning to read for a while before sleep, she chose a book promising her a happy ending.

☆☆★☆☆

This meant war. Elysha fumed, nursing her frazzled senses in the cool shadows of her favorite glade. Before, her attack on the girl had simply been business. The human target, Gloria stood in the way of a scheme Elysha had gone to some trouble to set up between Kathleen of the high aspirations and that professor of the rich appetites.

But now the chit had hurt her. How dare she? How dare she hurt Elysha, whose life wove itself through the ages of the world, clad in darkness and beauty beyond the grasp of mortals?

How had she? Elysha's pain, sharp with the tang of metal and technology, still lingered. The blow had been more powerful by far than the usual run of mortal weapons.

☆☆★☆☆

Before returning to the U for his bike, Greg put in some time patrolling as Wonder Guy.

When he dropped a would-be arsonist at the third precinct, Detective Diaz hailed him from his office. "Say, can I ask you to keep an eye out for something?"

"Sure." Greg paused halfway through the door leading back into the deepening twilight. "What do you have in mind?"

"We've been getting a lot of calls about missing pets. I'd suspect a pet-napping ring, but there are no demands for money, and these are ordinary family pets, no special breeds or rich owners."

"I see." Greg frowned. "Not an overactive animal control department?"

"No. I've got reports of dogs taken right out of their collars while chained up in fenced yards."

"I'll keep my eyes open."

"Most of the disappearances have happened around dusk." Diaz slapped him on the shoulder as Greg turned back to the door.

He made a conscious effort not to flinch, reminding himself the slap was a sign of camaraderie. In high school, the jocks who'd used such gestures hadn't been friendly toward him. In fact, he'd taken a lot of flak about being a nerd.

Dusk, he thought, leaving the precinct building. He leapt into the sky. The last light of day lingered, half-hidden beyond gathering masses of clouds touched along their edges with hints of rose and gold. The air smelled of a promise of rain, tempting him to close his eyes and lose himself in the rush of the air's caress, but dutifully he scanned the neighborhood below. In the increasing gloom, telescopic vision alone worked no better than ordinary vision. Greg strained and found an increased range of vision, showing him what must be the same band used by night-vision goggles, picking up differences in heat between the objects below him and their surroundings. Those bright, moving shapes must be the engines of cars passing on the streets. Those softer glowing shapes must be people.

He cruised above the alleyways, looking for signs of pets or people where they shouldn't be, looking for anyone skulking in the backyards, any pet slipping its collar. Hundreds of homes lined the streets of the neighborhood, too many to watch at once. He needed to choose an animal to keep an eye on and do a stake out.

There. A pair of pit bulls shared a yard, their shapes distinctive even as glowing green blobs. Or, maybe not. The pair made an unlikely target for dog-nappers of any sort. There must be easier prey than two full-grown pit bulls.

Greg blinked, adjusting his telescopic vision to identify a cluster of glowing, darting blobs moving between him and the dogs. Ah, mosquitoes, the 'Minnesota state bird.' These must be close to appear so large, and must have fed recently to glow so bright. He looked back to the dogs when the insects moved on, readjusting his sight. Strange.

He blinked again, adjusting his vision from the heat-signature perception to normal vision and back again. No dogs.

Greg flew down and landed in the yard where the animals had been chained not two minutes ago. Two worn leather collars retained some heat from the necks they'd recently circled. Two chains dangled limply from a clothesline spanning the yard.

Somehow, the dogs had vanished in the blink of an eye. In the few seconds he'd been distracted by that swarm of mosquitoes, the dogs had disappeared. It wasn't possible. He'd have seen anyone near enough to take them, or anyone approaching them, and the dogs would've raised a ruckus. He'd have sworn most of the things happening lately must be impossible. Were disappearing dogs more of the same? He made a mental note to ask Serafina when he got the chance. Later. From the house attached to the yard came the sounds of someone moving toward the door. Greg shot skyward again before he'd have to witness the owners' reaction to the loss of their pets, especially since he had no word of explanation or comfort to offer.

☆☆★☆☆

Saturdays had a special magic of their own. A Saturday following a night soothed with the music of the falling rain, dawning on a world washed clean and sparkling with dewdrops did remarkable things for Gloria's spirits. She rose refreshed, eager for a chance to play, create and explore on her day of freedom. Jo's death, yesterday's break up with Pete, her distress, all seemed things of the past. They might have occurred years, rather than days ago. If she didn't think about them too much.

Life went on. Gloria stripped the pale rose cotton sheets from the bed, stuffed them into the hamper with her week's accumulation of other laundry and zipped her bras into their net bags. She pulled on her most comfortable jeans and her favorite over-sized t-shirt, featuring her favorite frog puppet. Maybe it was just the t-shirt, but she found herself humming an old song Aggie had once taught her, "I'm in love with a big blue frog..."

Saturday mornings meant laundry day and catching up with chores for which she had no time during the week. This coincided nicely with Dad's day at the VFW hall, hanging with his old pals. Saturday afternoons generally meant some project time or expedition with Aggie. They'd made a practice of visiting local sites of interest, from the Gibbs Farm to the Swedish Museum to the Minnesota History Museum. Gloria wondered what Aggie might be up for today. So much depended on her energy level. They left it to Aggie to pick their activities, though Gloria had a veto power she seldom used.

On her way to the basement laundry room with the heavy hamper in her arms, she found her father sitting bent over the coffee table, groaning.

"Gloria," he moaned. "If you've ever loved me, will you be a peach and get your old dad some coffee and some of those ibuprofen? I swear my head's gonna fall right off my neck, split in two down the middle."

"Right after I get my laundry started," she said cheerily.

"Have mercy, girl."

"You pick up your empties and clean up around the couch." Where, in addition to his empties, an inexplicable quantity of torn envelopes, used tissues, cutlery and plates bearing half-eaten food had accumulated. "And by the time you're done, I'll have some coffee for you."

"How sharper than a serpent's tooth--"

"That's got to be the only bit of Shakespeare you know." Gloria propped the basement door open with her hip, flipped on the light switch and took the first of the steps. "And you overuse it. Give it a rest." She proceeded downstairs.

A half hour later, she'd gotten Ike his coffee and seen him out the door with his buddy Stu. An hour more, and she'd had her own coffee and breakfast, taken care of the kitchen clean up, vacuumed the living room, taken out the trash, folded and put away her laundry, remade the bed, changed to a cute baby-blue baby doll top and headed next door.

"Oh, Gloria, honey. I was going to call you." Aggie looked up from the morning paper as Gloria entered the kitchen.

Hank Luddell sat across the table from Aggie. Half-full mugs of coffee rested before them, along with a box containing a couple pastries and scattered crumbs.

"Hi." Gloria greeted Hank with an automatic smile, turned back to Aggie and raised her brow in question. What was up here? But the wrenching sensation in her gut told her exactly what was up. She was losing Aggie, too.

Not like she'd lost Jo. Not like she'd lost her mother. But the changes-to-come spread out before her as surely as any array of a gypsy's fortune telling cards or vision in a crystal ball. Aggie wanted this man in her life, wanted to spend time with him. Mentioning her concern about Greg might have been Aggie's subtle way of letting Gloria know, too. Inevitably, there'd be less time for Gloria, less time for their projects and expeditions.

She pushed back the rising urge to fight, to keep Aggie to herself. Aggie, who'd never stood in the way of Gloria's dating Pete, or wished for her young protégée anything but the best life could offer. Aggie deserved whatever her heart desired and Gloria'd be damned if she'd stand in the way of her getting it.

"If you've made other plans for today I can take a project home to work on."

"No, no. I need our outings to keep me inspired," Aggie assured her. "Hank stopped by to surprise me with some donuts for breakfast."

"You said you love the filled ones, and there's a bakery near me." Hank's smile kept a fine balance between humility and self-satisfaction.

"And they're delicious." Aggie gestured Gloria toward the box of remaining pastries. "We got to talking about our expeditions and Hank tells me he's never been to the Sculpture Garden."

"You're kidding." Gloria picked out an apple fritter from the box. "We can't let that stand uncorrected." She turned her biggest smile on Hank. "You have to come with us. We can show you around."

☆☆★☆☆

"Bring them along the path of the winding water. Thereafter, go north along the chain of lakes," Elysha commanded the motley assemblage of her underlings. They gathered, nearly invisible, in the shadows of the dripping undergrowth in the hour before dawn. The rain had ceased, leaving the parklands wet, but not so wet as to keep the swarm from flight.

It took some effort for her minions to hold the legions of whining insects in check, confining them to smaller prey, waiting for the right moment to release them to best effect. Now the moment drew near. The Hero couldn't be in as many places at once as could the members of so large a swarm. He wouldn't be able to save everyone. While he was occupied in the vain attempt, Elysha would strike at her other target.

The undergrowth rustled and stirred as if a gale wind blew there, but no wind stirred in the upper limbs of the surrounding trees. The scales of a thousand insectile wings glistened in the shadows of leaf and branch.

☆☆★☆☆

Maybe he'd stop at the computer lab later. Greg stowed the few groceries he'd bought while out on his morning ride. He hated to let much more of the morning pass without making a patrol as Wonder Guy. He had a bad feeling, which had only grown since the incident with the dinosaurs, and had gone to orange alert status since the incident with the disappearing dogs last night.

Part of the problem lay in the niggling suspicion that he was part of the problem. Men weren't supposed to have superpowers like his, any more than living dinosaurs were supposed to appear in the middle of a twenty-first century city, or any more than pit bulls were supposed to disappear between one moment and the next. The universe didn't work that way. If magic had laws, he didn't understand them and knowing as much made him nervous. Magic was afoot, and while some of it might be beneficent, some of it clearly represented an opposing force, the fairy godmothers' enemy mentioned by Serafina. What had they called her? He had no way of knowing where their enemy would strike next.

He stashed a carton of eggs and a couple of replacement cans of Mountain Dew in his fridge and folded away the empty reusable nylon grocery bags.

Should he contact Serafina? So far he hadn't found her explanations of any of this very illuminating. He needed more to go on. He hadn't known nearly enough about this enemy--only that he was supposed to draw her into the open. Okay, he'd do a patrol, go out there and make himself visible, face whatever trouble reared its misshapen head.

Greg exited the garage and, making sure there were no witnesses, said, "Super-ize me." He took a flying leap in full superhero costume, soared up, among and beyond the leafy branches of neighborhood trees, past a chattering squirrel, and sent a flock of sparrows spiraling up in alarm. He angled back toward the neighborhood where the pit bulls had disappeared. It should be easier by daylight to pick up clues as to how the dogs had managed their disappearing canine act.

His headset beeped. "Young man," Serafina's voice broke through. "Please hurry to the lake called Harriet at once. The situation is dire."

"On my way. What is it?" Greg replied as he veered in midair, turning west to where the lake lay below like an enormous, polished aquamarine, set in its band of deep green woods.

"We can't see the enemy's magics." Serafina's voice sounded thin and faded into the wind whipping past his ears. "But waves of terror and pain have erupted there."

At the lake shore people ran frantically in all directions, taking shelter wherever they could find it, darting behind trees and cars, under picnic tables, diving into the lake and below the water.

What scared them? A droning thrummed through the air. He waved his hand to brush aside some mosquitoes and gaped as the true scale of things sprang into perspective. Not tiny insects near him, but enormous mosquitoes, flying far below, near ground level.

A mosquito the size of a full-grown man darted around a tree and cling with all six legs to a woman crouching behind the trunk.

As the mosquito's proboscis plunged toward the intended victim, Wonder Guy's heat vision lanced the distance, frying the monster's brain in its casing. Dead, the mosquito's six attenuated legs loosened and the woman scrambled free.

Thousands of the giant insects darted everywhere. Greg had to deal with one at a time. He concentrated on individuals in danger and picked off their attackers one by one. True, original bloodsuckers. Talk about vampires.

A sturdily built, gray-haired man ran full tilt along a path winding toward residential streets as a huge mosquito zoomed after him and swooped in from behind, its legs grasping, its proboscis extended.

Greg hit it with his heat vision straight between the bulging eyes, frying the insect's brain, producing a satisfying sound, "Zap." So, that's where the comics got it. A bundle of legs and wings collapsed to the path.

A mosquito flew at a boy and girl in swimsuits. They raced toward a woman beckoning them from the open door of a car. The children's kite trailed by its string, still held in one chubby hand. The insect entangled in the string, ripped it from its owner's hand and dove for the children.

Zap. Another one down. The kite sailed away into the sky.

A young couple huddled under a picnic table on which crawled two monstrous bloodsuckers, while three circled above, droning like dentist drills.

Zap. Zap. Zap, zap, zap. The dry corpses hit table and turf with sounds like the rasping of cornhusks.

People ran in every direction from giant mosquitoes. Zap, zap, zap. The swarm seemed endless. As if caught in an out-of-control video game, Greg lost count of his kills. He soared higher to get more of them in his sights. Zap. Zap, zap, zap. The acrid scent of fried mosquito singed the air as if he'd stuck his nose in a giant bug-zapper. He turned this way and that, blasting one after another with his heat vision. A stream of insects followed victims onto residential streets. Zap. Zappity, zappity, zap, zap, zap. The empty husks hit the road and rolled, inspiring drivers to slam on their brakes.

More winged monstrosities hovered above the water, threatening swimmers who dared to rise for a breath. A swath of heat vision cut them from the air to fall into the placid waters.

Probably only minutes passed before the swarming mosquitoes vanished from the area. Good. Odd. He hadn't killed nearly enough of them to eliminate the threat. He glanced around, and spotted the threatening cloud of the swarm heading north from the lake, toward the heart of the city.

Chapter 18

The widespread terror pleased Elysha. Confronted with their ancient enemy grown to monstrous size, the residents of the city fled in panic. Some fought. Many of the boaters and those near the landing seized paddles, wielding them as weapons, smashing insects out of the air. The ferocity of these defenders pleased her nearly as well as did the fear of those who fled.

She cloaked herself in the shadows of a wooded section of shoreline while she directed her swarming creatures, relishing the waves of horror.

A tall woman, wearing a halter-top with jeans, screamed when a hovering six-foot mosquito grasped the bare flesh of her arm with yards-long legs and struck into her flesh. It drew blood into its proboscis until a young man seized a long wooden paddle from a nearby canoe and used it to crush the fragile exoskeleton of the beast.

No problem for Elysha. She had hundreds, if not thousands more, and the scent of spilled blood maddened her creatures. They darted after the fleeing humans, heedless of a new source of destruction when it fell upon them. When large numbers of her swarm rained from the sky, blasted from above, Elysha scanned the heavens. The pain and deaths of her own creatures produced as much pleasure for her as did that of the human victims, but this came too soon.

Him. She wasn't ready for him. The Pederson woman wasn't here yet with the weapon.

But there, an emanation from the north, the energy signature of her other target. Time to beat a strategic retreat here, but this withdrawal allowed her to go after the young woman who'd eluded her last night. There'd be no easy end for the girl this time. She must be taken. The girl must be punished for the pain she'd inflicted on Elysha. Briefly, she relished the vicious tang evoked simply by imagining how it would feel to wring every possible drop of misery from the troublesome young woman before she died.

☆☆★☆☆

"That'd go with one hell of a sundae," Hank commented, rocking back on his heels. He stared up at the twelve-hundred-pound, bright red aluminum cherry poised above them on its massive spoon.

"I can't believe you've never seen it before." Gloria stood beside Aggie's chair as Hank paced around, getting different angles on the sculpture.

"Not live and in person. I've seen photos. Don't do it justice." He grinned, showing strong, even teeth.

"Now I can't help picturing your giant sundae," Gloria admitted.

"We'd be in the middle of it." Aggie gestured around them, to the surrounding lawn, right at the edge of the pool below the spoon bridge. "And I wouldn't care to be scooped up along with the cherry."

"What's that noise?" Gloria lifted her head, looking around. Not the ordinary noise of traffic from Hennepin Avenue running along the eastern edge of the sculpture garden. "Kind of a high whining, like the world's biggest mosquito." She laughed with her companions. Looking up, she caught sight of what seemed at first a low, fast-moving cloud front. Then it resolved into individual elements and she soon made out their shapes. "Speak of the devil," she whispered, too stunned at first to register the danger.

"Holy crap." *Move now. Gawk later.* She turned to Aggie and Hank, gesturing to the south. "We've got to get out of here!"

"What is it?" Aggie twisted to look. "Good heavens! It can't be."

"We'd better get under cover whether it can be or not." Hank moved behind Aggie, and pushed her chair back toward the Walker Arts Center, which seemed impossibly far away, through the courtyards and across the road fronting the museum building.

"The conservatory would be closer." Gloria moved beside them, but they'd only gone a few paces, not much closer to either destination, when the chair stopped short, causing Aggie to lurch forward and Hank to curse.

"What now?" Gloria bent and looked at the wheels. The right front wheel sat at an angle to the others, an angle she recognized. "Oh crap." The same wheel had gotten stuck before.

The droning sounded louder. Screams and shouts pierced the air and some other patrons of the arts ran for cover, back toward the Walker and the shelter of its solid walls, into the face of the impossible, threatening swarm. Others ran toward the conservatory where palm trees grew even through the harsh Minnesota winters, and a giant, glass-scaled fish reared up on its tail, poised forever in mid-leap. Yet others sought shelter among the many sculptures.

Gloria knelt beside Aggie's chair. She had managed to loosen the wheel before. She just needed to joggle it...

"Leave it," Aggie protested. "Leave me! Get out of here, Gloria. Run for it."

"It's okay." Hank bent over Aggie. "Leave the chair. I've got her. The greenhouse isn't far."

Aggie looked at first as if she'd protest this too, then sighed and lifted her arms to Hank.

The swarm filled the sky directly above them. Gloria looked frantically for something to fend off the monstrous insects diving at them and seized the umbrella hooked over the back of Aggie's chair before she hurried after Hank. Aggie never went out without her trusty bumbershoot. "Rust, just what it takes to make this chair perfect," she'd say.

Gloria wielded the umbrella like a sword and darted forward in time to counter the thrust of a three-foot mosquito proboscis aimed at Aggie, who clung helplessly to Hank. Gloria flanked her companions as Hank moved toward the dubious refuge of the conservatory. Already cracks appeared in the glass panes of its walls, where the giant mosquitoes crashed against them in pursuit of people who fled there for safety. The panes were large enough for the mosquitoes to squeeze through if enough of the glass was broken.

She opened the umbrella in the face of one after another of the determined insects diving at them as she guarded Hank's back. Screams sounded on every side, along with the wailing of small children. Gloria checked the impulse to run to the defense of a six-year old girl who took shelter under a table of sandstone blocks. She couldn't abandon Aggie. The child seemed safe in her refuge. Gloria batted aside another thrusting, needle-sharp proboscis.

☆☆★☆☆

Greg followed the retreating swarm, flying above them, picking off the stragglers and out-fliers with blasts of heat vision. Retreating? No. This swarm hadn't come from downtown. It wasn't returning there. They advanced. Did they have some target in mind? Where? Just how intelligent were they?

He could aim for the center of the swarm, destroy more of the monsters at once in the swaths of heat blasting from his eyes, but then he'd have smaller swarms going off in every direction threatening who-knew-how many people before he could track them down. No, better do it this way. Make sure they stayed together and pick them off from the edges of the swarm.

The man-sized mosquitoes flew lower when they neared Loring Park and the surrounding area. Not until they began a diving run did their target become clear: the sculpture garden north of the Walker Art Center. What the hell? Did the mosquitoes have something against modern three-dimensional art and its patrons?

People ran helter-skelter among the sculptures, seeking shelter from the attack. Screams sounded shrilly from below.

A stout woman on the lawn near the giant spoon sculpture played tug of war with one of the enormous mosquitoes. With its attenuated, stick-like legs, the insect grasped a screaming toddler by the shoulders. The woman clung fiercely to the child's legs, fighting to keep it from being hauled up and away.

Zap. Greg fried the brains of the kidnapper mosquito. The woman fell back, child clasped in her arms. Both scrambled away toward cover.

Zap. Zap. He fried the creature about to attack the woman from behind, striking with a proboscis as long and sharp as a sword.

Most people seemed to be faring pretty well, making it to the conservatory or the museum building ahead of the swarm. Some took refuge in the small Flatpak Visitor Center. Others crawled under or hid behind the sturdiest sculptures.

A man ran headlong at one of the punched steel panels forming part of a hedge and dove aside at the last instant. Three mosquitoes in close pursuit crashed into the panel, trapping their proboscises in the holes piercing the panel, leaving the creatures to struggle to free themselves, as they frantically lashed their long gossamer wings.

A wheelchair sat abandoned on the lawn between the spoon bridge and the conservatory. A man carrying a woman hurried toward refuge, and another woman followed, playing rear-guard, waving an umbrella at dive-bombing mosquitoes. Walking backward, she closed the umbrella to thrust it like a sword, parried a proboscis then opened it suddenly to thwart the forward rush of another attacker.

Greg zoomed in with Wonder Guy's telescopic vision. *My God. Gloria. Aggie. And who the hell is that, carrying Aggie away from her wheelchair?*

He would have stumbled if he'd been afoot. Instead, he faltered in midair as the mosquitoes seemed to notice him for the first time. A phalanx broke from the swarm, rising to rush at him like blood-seeking missiles.

When he turned to face the attacking mosquitoes, he spotted another squadron acting in concert to surround Gloria.

With her attention turned to the enemy before her, others closed on Gloria from behind. Rather than strike for blood, four sets of impossibly long, thin limbs grasped her as others tore the umbrella from her grip.

Carried by the huge insects, like Dorothy in the grip of flying monkeys, Gloria rose helplessly into the air.

☆☆★☆☆

Gloria's senses reeled between vertigo and horror as she struggled frantically against the elongated legs dragging her away in their sticky grip. This couldn't be happening. The repulsive insectile bodies had her shuddering, wincing, and choking back bile. The wriggling mouths and bulging abdominal segments pressed way too close to her cringing flesh. The drone of giant wings drowned all other sound.

Thrashing wildly, Gloria shouted outrage--when not screaming in terror. It had to be a dream. If only. If only she had the refuge of unconsciousness as the bug-eyed monsters lifting her up and the earth fell away below. She had nothing but sympathy for the heroines of old movies who would swoon in the face of danger, but she couldn't give up. She had to fight for all she was worth. She twisted and tore at the clutching limbs until more creatures secured her arms. She kicked against resilient abdominal segments and scaly exoskeletons.

At least, she struggled until she looked down. The lawns and sculptures spread like a map below her. Far, far below. A fresh wave of vertigo dizzied her. Even if she managed to escape the clutches of her captors, she'd only be dashed to death on the tiled paths or the massive curves of the Henry Moore bronze now directly below. The scene shifted and spun, and now it looked like the Calder would be a good bet for impaling her. The whirling of the scene made her stomach swim in sickening waves. She closed her eyes and stiffened, ceasing her struggles, though she still cringed from the huge limbs holding her.

When she grew still, her captors steadied in flight. With steadier movement and the rush of cool wind in her face, her vertigo eased. She dared to open her eyes again. The mosquitoes, flying in unison, leveled out at last and bent their path as if to head south. *Oh, God.* Now would be a good time to faint. Where were they taking her?

A figure in gold and green blazed toward them from below.

Wonder Guy! Gloria's heart leapt in her breast. *Oh, thank heaven. Oh, crap.* Her hair must look like hell, whipping and tangling around her face in the wind.

In the next instant, with a series of sharp popping noises and a smell she remembered from summer evenings near a bug zapper, the giant mosquitoes lost their holds on Gloria's arms. She rejoiced and despaired again immediately, falling free toward the earth below. Her stomach lurched, dropping even faster than she fell through the air. The wind dragged at her hair and clothes, stopping her breath. The pervasive drone of wings fell silent and empty husks of giant mosquitoes filled the air, falling with her. The sharp black point of the Calder sculpture's support rushed to meet them. Gloria screamed.

Strong, gentle arms scooped her up, and she threw her arms around the hero's strong neck, burying her face in the warm crook below his clean-cut jaw, trembling in relief.

"Hey," he said. "It's gonna be okay."

They swooped through the air, but this was totally different than flying in the grasp of the giant insects. She lost all fear of falling. Wonder Guy cradled her gently against his solid chest, one strong arm hooked under her thighs, the other holding her tightly to him. She clung fiercely, arms clutched around his neck. How could she feel so… contented? blissful? happy? in the midst of this craziness? Her face pressed close to the bare flesh where his lower face and jaw emerged from his mask. His scent filled her like the breath of home: human, familiar and safe. She checked the urge to nuzzle him, to nibble her way up to his ear. She relaxed, molding herself to the solid wall of Wonder Guy's body so warm against hers.

They neared the ground, the sound of insect wings growing louder as they descended. The shrill whine, like police sirens on helium, surrounded them.

"Hold on," Wonder Guy told her, transferring her grip from his neck to what proved to be the stalk of the giant cherry on which she now stood. His arms freed, Wonder Guy turned to face the army of horrendous mosquitoes closing in around them.

Gloria shivered without the warmth of her hero's arms around her. Oh. The mist of water spraying from the top of the cherry's stalk might have something to do with her sudden chill. The drone of a thousand insect wings drowned all other thoughts. She clung with a desperate grip to her cherry stem as Wonder Guy flashed from place to place, always between her and the swarming army of mosquitoes.

Like mindless drones, the creatures seemed to have forgotten everything and everyone else to gather their forces and throw themselves against the hero in a determined assault. Their objective seemed to be to get through him, or past him, or around him to reach…her?

This was crazy. Why would these impossible monsters be after her? Gloria trembled in every limb, wet, miserable and frightened out of her wits. If not for the cold of the metal stalk against her cheek or the slick surface beneath the soles of her sandals, she might think it all a dream. This day had become a living nightmare. Only the hero, decimating the onslaught of monsters as she looked on, kept her from giving in to despair.

He moved more swiftly than her eyes could follow. Now in front of her, now above, now to one side, then another. He seemed everywhere at once, and everywhere he turned the mosquitoes died. They fell from the sky like so many giant bags of trash. Luckily, everyone below had already found shelter. She didn't know how he did it and didn't care. He faced them and they died, to fall as dry husks to the earth below. They died, but more kept coming.

So many. Some he only blocked by placing his back directly between Gloria and the mosquitoes' thrusts. Their stabbing proboscises broke against the impenetrable barrier he made of himself.

Her heart stuck in her throat. At least, she assumed the idiom had been coined to cover her present state of breathless, choking anxiety. Her head told her the swarming, bloodthirsty monsters surrounding them couldn't harm Wonder Guy, but how could anyone keep up this dizzying defense against such a seemingly endless barrage of the enemy?

She lost track of time. Her arms ached from clinging to the giant cherry stem. Her legs wobbled, trying to keep her perch on the scanty, slippery footing afforded on the slick aluminum. Her grip slipped and she lurched near falling while struggling to regain her hold. At last, the cloud of whirring wings thinned to reveal stretches of clear, cerulean sky and the incessant drone faded from a thunder in her ears to a thinner whine. Dead mosquitoes littered the lawn below, clogged the pool, draped across sculptures or piled up around them.

As he flashed like lightning from one point to another, Wonder Guy had been drawn further and further from her position. Now a contingent of the mosquitoes moved quietly below, creeping out of hiding from among the corpses of their fellows, moving in coordination as if controlled by a single mind.

Oh God. As they rose in unison, moving arrow-straight for her, Gloria screamed, mind numb with horror. She shuddered at the thought of them touching her again. Worse, this time they might be out for blood. She pressed close to the cherry stem, squirming around to keep its solid steel between her and the approaching monsters, but they came from every side.

Wonder Guy arrived in the instant, put his broad, impervious back to the squadron of mosquitoes stabbing at them and wrapped his arms around her. Standing behind her, holding her pressed into his chest, the whole length of him held tight along her backside, he gave new meaning to guarding her back.

The shock of impact echoed through his flesh to hers as the first wave of assault broke upon his back.

She realized he'd spoken.

"What?"

"Let go." He plucked at her arms, still clenched around the cherry stem. Gladly she released it, turning at the urging of his hands to transfer her hold to him. She clasped her arms around his neck, and in the instant her eyes met his, looking out from behind his mask, she forgot her fear and her weariness. A bolt of exhilaration shot through her, an inexplicable joy.

Gloria grinned, letting the world drop away below them. She hardly registered how they'd shot into the sky, leaving mosquito hordes far below. She might never have this chance again. The belly dancers of the world might surround him as soon as they returned to earth, like when he'd stopped that rogue elephant in Uptown. She'd have to go back to her life and her work and responsibilities. Right now this magnificent man's arms wrapped tightly around her and his gaze stayed locked with hers. For the moment he was hers.

His masked face drew close, his breath warm on her mouth. Gloria leaned in, brushed her lips across his chiseled, slightly parted ones, thrilled as they softened and opened beneath her light touch. She bore down, parting her own lips to kiss him in earnest.

Oh Lord. If they weren't already up among the clouds she'd be flying now. Who knew a kiss had the power to unlock such a rush of sensation, become a whole new dimension of delight? It had never worked that way before. His mouth met hers with equal fervor and with a tenderness melting her from crown to toes. The kiss called every corner of her being to life, from instep to shoulder blades, from forgotten childhood games to impossible aspirations, from the lost and loneliest corners of her soul to the brightest surges of exuberance.

She became a bottomless fountain of joy. The fountain re-doubled in him as if reflected in a mirror. The joy mirrored in him was mirrored in her, reflected in him, reflected in her, multiplied over and over again between them, in infinite regression. The joy became something more than joy, more than hers. Not hers alone, but theirs, a new bliss they created together.

It seemed only natural for her hands to explore the shapes of his shoulders beneath the skintight fabric of his costume. Only natural for his hands to clasp her closer, to feel him grow hard where her thighs pushed close to his. She prayed the moment, the kiss, would go on forever, but each moment only increased her desire to make more of it than a kiss alone.

If the joining of their mouths could thrill so deeply, if it created such joy to touch even with the barriers of their clothing between them, how much better might it be to dispense with all the barriers, to join fully as man and woman?

Gloria groaned, a sound embodying sigh and moan alike, and pulled away. Everything had happened so fast. Too fast. Her world had been tumbled end over end these past few days, leaving her exhausted and overwhelmed, but oddly pleased by the answering groan from Wonder Guy when he released her mouth with one last, tender kiss.

"Are you okay?" he asked.

"Mmm," she said. "I'm wonderful. You're wonderful." She smiled up at his warm, oddly familiar eyes.

"I mean the mosquitoes. They didn't hurt you when they grabbed you earlier?"

"Oh no. I'm good." She glanced to the sculpture garden far, far below, like a patch on the quilt of the city map. Her grip tightened convulsively around Wonder Guy's neck. "Uh, do you think they can follow us this high?"

"No, but I didn't think mosquitoes could grow this big, either." His grin dazzled her. He adjusted his grip, scooped up her legs and carried her into a long, gentle descent.

☆☆★☆☆

Greg approached ground level cautiously, keeping a wary eye out for further mosquito attacks, though none came and the skies stretched clear and empty around them.

He held Gloria in his arms, warm, solid and alive. No one else knew how much those simple facts meant to him. She had kissed him. A dream come true, a miracle defying every hope or expectation. His lips, his whole body still rang like a bell struck resoundingly by her kiss. Nothing had ever felt so right, or so wrong, given she kissed him like that without knowing she kissed *him*.

The sense of something wrong shifted focus when he landed near the conservatory, setting Gloria on her feet. None of the hundreds of dead mosquitoes littering the area a few minutes ago appeared anywhere in sight.

People stood around talking as others ventured forth from their refuges. The lawns looked pristine, but a few of the glass panes walling the conservatory bore huge cracks or were broken out in jagged shards.

Strangers turned to applaud him as soon as he set foot on solid ground. The instant he released her, Gloria ran toward the conservatory. She must be worried about Aggie. He shared her concern, but before he followed, a crowd of people came between them, shouting questions at him.

"What happened up there?"

"Did you see it?"

Other voices chimed in, "They disappeared while you were up out of sight."

"The weirdest thing."

"They shrank!" A little girl's voice piped in. "I was under there." She pointed to a stone table. "I saw one go from big," she held out her arms, "to teeny." She brought her hands together and held something up, pinched between a forefinger and thumb. "See!"

Greg bent to examine her offering, an ordinary mosquito of ordinary size. Dead.

"I see," he said. He addressed the growing crowd. "Is everyone okay?"

☆☆★☆☆

Elysha's smile scarcely faltered when her spell shattered and the pitiful remnants of her swarm shrank away to nothing. Or next to nothing, returning to the size nature had given them to begin with and flying off on their own business, no longer under her command.

She wrapped a glamour around herself and faded back among the trees where she'd stationed herself to oversee the capture of the young woman who'd already eluded her once.

Going after the chit complicated her plans for the Hero, but she'd expected her swarm to keep him occupied while she wrapped up her business with the troublesome girl. She turned to her nearest minion, "Bring the phone."

The small, warty creature muttered, but kept its protests muted enough so Elysha chose to ignore them. The device contained enough cold steel to burn those of her creatures who handled it, but its casing material buffered the effect and the burns would heal.

Without delay, the device was removed from its padded bag and propped for her in the crook between branch and bole. She used a twig to punch in the numbers, not trusting such a precise task to the near-witless underling who'd put the phone in place.

Standing near enough to the dreadful metal to hear and be heard pained her, making her temper short.

"There has been a change of plans," Elysha spoke in tones brittle as the thin layer of new ice over a deceptively deep pond.

"What now?" Kathleen Pederson's voice, even distorted as it was by the phone, still sounded snappish. "I've already wasted an hour waiting for your call."

"Then you'll be pleased to hear you need not bring the weapon today after all."

"Weapon? You mean that chunk of brick and cement? I don't see what good it is for anything."

"It is enough for you to know it will aid our plans in the right place at the right time," Elysha went on. "The young woman who threatens your position must survive for the present. I've discovered a use for her."

"But she knows too much."

"It won't be long. She'll have no time to make use of anything she knows. First, you must help me take her captive."

Yes. The young woman would make an ideal hostage. The energy of loving connection between her and the hero had flamed tremendously strong earlier. The surge of that force overcame all Elysha's spells. But this connection promised an equally powerful anguish should he lose her, fear for her or witness her suffering.

Chapter 19

Gloria hurried to the conservatory where she'd last seen Aggie and Hank headed. She'd kick herself later for failing to say anything to Wonder Guy when he'd had her in his arms. Their kiss had left her speechless. She couldn't believe she'd actually kissed a virtual stranger. It was crazy, impossible, how much she felt for him, given how little she knew him. Maybe he rescued a dozen women a day and kissed every one of them the same way he'd kissed her. The bitches.

She spotted Aggie, still in Hank's arms as he headed back toward the abandoned wheel chair, which looked none the worse for its adventure. Gloria veered to meet them.

"Are you okay?" She and Aggie spoke at the same moment.

"I'm fine," Aggie said, as Hank settled her back into her chair. "I'm not the one carried off by giant mosquitoes. I thought we'd lost you."

The tears in Aggie's eyes triggered a few tears of Gloria's and an ache in her heart. She hadn't realized Aggie might feel as frightened for her as she'd been on her own account.

"I'm okay. Really. I mean, I was scared to death at first, but then Wonder Guy arrived--"

"What happened?" Hank asked. "You two shot into the air and a minute later the mosquitoes disappeared."

Aggie shuddered. "I wanted to stay at the windows, to watch out for you, but a couple of the mosquitoes were trying to crawl in through the broken panes."

"I was about to haul her away from there, whether she liked it or not." Hank shook his head. "When the bugs shriveled away right in front of our eyes. Damnedest thing."

"I missed that part." Gloria bent to the troublesome wheel and, with a few jiggles, had it turning freely again. "There. You know, we don't have to see the rest of the sculptures today. I've had enough of an adventure for one afternoon."

"I have to admit," Aggie patted her chest as if calming a runaway steed, but spoke with her usual gift for understatement. "I've had enough excitement, too."

"I've had enough giant-mosquito excitement to last me a lifetime." Hank followed Aggie's cue, speaking as if he dealt with this sort of thing every day. Or maybe that was his musician's cool. He moved behind the wheelchair, guiding them back towards the Walker's parking lot where police and emergency vehicles now crowded, blocking the way for exiting cars.

"Why don't we go to the museum coffee shop and wait this out?" Gloria suggested, not feeling quite so cool as her companions. It would be nice to take a breather. Who knew how a day that began with giant mosquitoes might end?

☆☆★☆☆

"Today on 'How Do You Do, Minnesota' Professor Pamela Deifenbauer from the University's Department of Psychology is here to talk to us about the phenomenon of mass hallucination." The talk show host, a neatly coifed blonde wearing a double-breasted apricot suit, turned to her guest.

Greg turned up the volume, interested in an academic's take on experiences he still half-wished he could dismiss as hallucinations, if that wouldn't mean losing the kiss from Gloria along with losing the monsters and mayhem.

The professor's gray suit matched her hair. She faced the cameras with the assurance of someone accustomed to speaking to classrooms full of college students.

"What we commonly call mass hallucination is a variety of collective delusion. That is, socially contagious behavior or symptoms occurring within a group of individuals. These can include symptoms of actual physical illness in the cases we call mass hysteria."

"I see." The hostess leaned toward her guest. "Very interesting, Professor. Can you tell us how that might relate to recent reports from people claiming to have seen first dinosaurs and now giant mosquitoes in Minneapolis?" Her incredulous tone suggested that, of course, anyone reporting these things must be delusional.

The professor nodded. "Typically, collective delusion involves small, isolated groups such as found in schools, factories, convents. There were some interesting cases in medieval France, in which whole convents started meowing like cats or biting one another."

The hostess lifted a tentative hand. "Very interesting, but I'm not sure how it relates."

"But I digress. These recent reports were not confined to such isolated communities, but came instead from individuals with no prior connection to one another who happened to be present at the same time and place. This leads me to question whether they are, in fact, cases of collective delusions at all. Of course, one might also point to the rash of flying saucer sightings following an initial report in 1947. The UFO phenomenon is a good example of a collective delusion that's an exception to the pattern of occurrence in confined populations."

"Unless, of course, you believe in alien visitations." The hostess laughed.

Sitting at the kitchen worktable with a cold soda in hand, Greg frowned at the television and flicked it off. He'd made it back to Aggie's kitchen ahead of everyone else. Not surprising, as he'd flown most of the way as Wonder Guy while the others contended with traffic gridlocked in the Walker's parking lot. He waited now, wanting to see how his mother had held up in the wake of the events at the sculpture garden, and wondering what Gloria would have to say concerning her adventures.

That kiss--maybe it hadn't meant as much to her as to him. She was engaged to Pete and had gone out with other guys, giving her a lot more experience with the opposite sex than his few attempts at finding anyone who matched her in his affections. Maybe this kiss was nothing out of the ordinary in comparison to the others she'd experienced.

For him, nothing had ever come close to kissing Gloria, the girl of his dreams. To say the kiss had rocked his world constituted a massive understatement. His world had been rocked, shaken, flipped upside down and turned inside out. His world probably had a whole new topography he'd better re-map at first opportunity.

While eager to hear Gloria's reaction to the kiss, at the same time, it felt wrong to hide from her in plain sight, listening to how she felt without revealing himself as the one who'd held her in his arms, the one who'd shared an amazing kiss with her. It didn't seem a heroic way to handle things and that wasn't the only thing bothering him.

The more he considered it, the less he liked it. Gloria had kissed him, yes. A kiss realizing everything he'd never dared dream. But, as far as she knew, she'd kissed a stranger. A hero, yes, a man who'd saved her from a terrible fate, a man who looked good in tights, but a man in a mask. She didn't know who that man was. She didn't know she'd kissed him, Greg, the guy who'd been here for her all along, someone she'd taken for granted for years.

As much as he'd loved kissing her, it bothered him that as far as she was concerned, she'd kissed someone else, someone not him. It bothered him how much he inwardly quailed at the prospect of unmasking himself to her, facing the risk of her ardor turning to scorn if she found out Wonder Guy was plain old Greg Roberts. He couldn't let fear stop him from taking the next step. Hadn't he learned anything about heroism these past days?

Too, since he'd acquired these superpowers, an elephant had nearly trampled Gloria and giant mosquitoes had carried her away. Her best friend had been killed. Coincidence? Coincidences did happen, but he'd known Gloria his whole life and stuff like this had never happened to her before.

"Serafina?" Greg called. And there she sat, in the chair opposite him, perky, purple velvet pillbox hat on wispy white hair.

"Yes, dear?" Her large, alert eyes turned to him.

"Ma'am." He nodded, collecting his thoughts.

A sinking sense of loss weighted his gut as he leaned forward across the table. He'd only had these powers for a few days, less than a week. It felt good to be a hero, to make a difference. It felt more than good to have Gloria look at him the way she had, eyes shining with admiration and with the kind of interest he'd do practically anything to inspire. He spoke in a rush, before he had a chance to reconsider, "I want you to take these superpowers back. Gloria seems to be in more danger than she's ever been before. It's got to be connected to me, to the superpowers, somehow."

"Tsk. Young man, have you considered you were given these powers specifically to assure you'd be in a position to help when the young lady's need arose? Given her heroic impulses and proximity to unscrupulous persons who have already resorted to murder, danger was inevitable. Danger comes not because you have powers, but quite the opposite. You have powers because danger would arise one way or another."

"Is it true? Is that what's going on?" He'd been leaning forward in his chair, now he leaned back again, reassessing.

"Giving up your powers won't prevent your young lady from being endangered. The forces at play would endanger her regardless of what you do, not least her own impulse to do the right thing."

"Oh," he muttered, deflated. *In that case...* "And I have a better chance to help her this way?" He spread his arms, taking in the whole present situation, superpowers and all. He might be glad for the opportunity to continue to play hero, not so glad to hear Gloria would be in danger even if his world returned to normal. "She needs me."

"Exactly." Serafina nodded, her hands folded neatly before her on the tabletop.

"I don't have a choice then. If Gloria needs a hero, I have to be one." He let his breath escape in a whoosh.

"Well spoken, dear." Serafina's smile twinkled at him.

"Ma'am? I have to ask..."

"Yes, dear?" She tilted her gaze up to meet his.

"I'm a rational man. I believe in the physical laws of the universe. I don't understand how all this can be happening, but it is happening. How?" He ended on a bewildered note.

"I'm sorry to make things confusing for you, dear. You're a bright lad, and I'm sure you understand what you call physical laws aren't actually laws so much as they are patterns your people been able to discern, given the limits of human perception."

"Well, yes, but this magic, what's been happening lately, violates everything we've learned about how the physical universe works."

"Yes, but you have not yet learned everything there is to learn about how these things work." She twinkled again. "When you get to the true roots of creation, you'll find what some of your scientific thinkers dismiss as mere emotion, the connections between caring and perceptive beings, are the very warp and woof and threads with which physical reality is woven."

"But..." Greg faced an empty chair. *How did she do that?* Frustrated, he took a swig from the can solid and cool in his grip. Connections between caring beings? Maybe it would make sense if he understood more about quantum connectivity and string theory...

☆☆★☆☆

Gloria headed directly home after leaving Hank and Aggie next door. Her earlier adventure might have been a half-forgotten nightmare if not for the bruises the giant mosquitoes had left on her arms. She hoped the marks wouldn't itch the way the bites of ordinary mosquitoes did. All she wanted now was a chance to relax in a nice hot bath while she had the house to herself. The quiet neighborhood, where a robin warbled among the trees, had already begun the job of easing her nerves. Just as she raised the key to the lock, a rushing in the afternoon air alerted her and she turned, the sound awakening her memories of recent assault by giant, blood-sucking insects.

Poised for flight, her heart lifted to see Wonder Guy instead of the monsters, alighting beside her. She released a sigh, and her shoulders relaxed as if removed from a hanger. She took a fresh breath and straightened, taking in the lean, long-legged form standing before her. The remembered kiss lit a chain of signal fires along her nerves.

He cleared his throat. "Gloria."

"Yes? How do you know my name?" She flushed, suddenly self-conscious over how familiar she'd been without even introducing herself. "How did you find me? I mean, I meant to introduce myself. I forgot..."

"I'll explain everything." He stepped closer.

The warmth in his gaze reassured her, even from the shadows cast by his golden mask. Everything in her yearned toward him, despite her doubts about kissing a virtual stranger. Had he followed her because he felt as she did?

When he moved nearer still, she surged to meet him. He lifted a gloved hand to her shoulder and leaned in when Gloria lifted her face to meet his lips with hers. Magic.

Her world blossomed into a deeper, richer place. A sensation of rising inner tides sent electricity into every watershed of her limbs, rushing through the tributaries and estuaries until even fingertips and toes tingled with awareness. Desires only sleeping in her before kicked her wide awake, as if she'd slept all her life until now. She moaned and sank into those desires, bringing her arms up around his neck, moving into his arms as if reenacting the moment when he'd carried her flying high above the sculpture garden. He scooped her up, dragging her tightly against a chest as warm and solid as homecoming.

She lost herself in the luxury of silken sensations flowing within and under her hands as she smoothed the silky fabric of his costume across his shoulders. She basked in the golden warmth of the embrace and relished the rare spices tasted where their mouths met. His kiss welcomed her responses, called for more. She might fall into such a kiss and be lost forever, never missing whatever else life might offer.

He moved with exquisite slowness, as if she were his sole focus and there were nowhere he'd rather be than in this moment, in this kiss, melting together with her.

His gloved hands, at first merely drawing her close, wandered lower, cradling, holding, shaping themselves to the landscape of her curves. His touch affirmed the shapes of her back and shoulders, following to the outer swell of her breasts.

She shivered when his fingers climbed onward toward their peaks.

Her hands moved from his shoulders to trace his jaw and face. She found the edges of his mask, the boundary between flesh and mystery. His breath grew harsh when she slipped a finger under the taut fabric shielding his features.

When he pulled away, she moaned a protest. She half stumbled, left colder for the lack of his warmth against her, opening her eyes as he lifted his hands to the golden mask.

He tugged the fabric away, up and over his head, revealing a handsome face under tousled brown hair. It actually took her half a moment to recognize him.

"Greg?"

Her mind reeled. Greg? Not possible. A flying man, okay. Giant mosquitoes, maybe, but this? No way. She took an unsteady step back, shaking off his reaching hand.

"Oh my God, Greg! What's going on here? Since when do you dress up in tights and a cape? What is this?"

"I don't wear a cape." He held both hands up, looking as bewildered and defensive as the time she'd accused him of programming her computer for alien takeover. She hadn't understood *SETI at Home* then, and still wasn't totally clear on how it wasn't a set up for aliens to take control of the internet, but he'd explained it all so earnestly. It was probably okay. But not this, not this time.

"I don't care about any stupid cape. What are you doing dressed up in a costume? What are you doing kissing me?"

"You kissed me too," he pointed out logically enough. "What were you doing, kissing a total stranger?" His tone put her on the defensive.

"You're not a stranger."

"For all you knew, I was a stranger."

"You didn't seem like a stranger. But, good heavens, Greg, you're practically a brother to me! Oh jeeze."

Shaking her head to get rid of the very idea, she turned away. It was too weird, so embarrassing. Greg was part of the landscape of her life. She thought she knew him. She didn't know him. She didn't know him at all. She refused to think of the familiar Greg in the same breath as those kisses.

"But, Gloria--" He put a hand on her shoulder.

She shook it off, spinning to face him again.

"How could you? You lied to me, pretended to be someone else, this superhero. You kissed me under false pretenses!"

"But I am this superhero." His jaw firmed as he pulled the mask back over his face and shot into the air. He did a loop-the-loop, swooped back down, landing in the driveway by the garage. He put his hands under the chassis and lifted Aggie's specially-equipped SUV over his head before setting it gently back in place.

"Oh, stop showing off," Gloria shouted at him. Fumbling with her key, she got the back door to her house open and stepped in. "I'm not talking to you any more, Greg Roberts." She slammed the door between them and leaned back against it, heart pounding in her ears.

Oh my lord. It was true. Greg was Wonder Guy. One and the same. Greg had saved her from the elephant, saved all those people from dinosaurs and giant mosquitoes and stopped all those crimes they'd reported on TV. Had the world gone mad?

She very strongly suspected the world had indeed gone mad. None of the old rules held true and everything she'd ever believed was now subject to doubt. And a good thing. Good because it meant none of this had happened. Jo hadn't really died, she hadn't really kissed Greg and he wasn't really a superhero. There were no such things as superheroes.

If only she could believe none of it was true, but the world remained too real around her. Every familiar object combined to deny the happy theory that she'd imagined everything. The solid slab of the door at her back upheld reality whether she liked it or not. The familiar sight of the kitchen tiles beneath her feet--especially the cracked ones from when she'd dropped the roasting pan--declared the validity of her whole history.

But how could Greg be Wonder Guy? Greg, the nerdy, quiet, boy-next-door, practically-a-brother guy she'd known so long he seemed like part of the furniture. She'd never even suspected he had the potential to become someone like Wonder Guy. Wonder Guy, so handsome, tall, and strong, with his long, sleek-muscled form so well displayed in his skin-tight costume, rescuer of maidens in distress, adored by swarms of belly-dancers. She couldn't get her mind around the two being one. So this is what they meant by cognitive dissonance. She needed an aspirin. She finally moved away from the door, headed to the bathroom medicine cabinet.

All she knew for sure was Greg had deceived her. He'd kissed her under false pretenses. Or just plain pretenses if not false ones. She wouldn't let him get away with it. She couldn't let herself think about the kisses. They'd never happened. She'd kissed the guy she imagined Wonder Guy to be. Not Greg. Never Greg.

☆☆★☆☆

When the door slammed shut behind Gloria, Greg stood frozen in place. For how long, he had no idea. The world might have ended for how little it mattered now. The sun shone from the bare blue sky as the breeze stirred in the heedless trees, but neither sight nor sound touched him.

At last he shook himself, straightened his mask more securely over his face and shot into the sky, straight up and away from the earth. He'd see how high he could climb. Beyond the atmosphere maybe, to some place as sterile and barren as his heart had become. The moon might be nice this time of year. With Wonder Guy's powers, he could probably survive without atmosphere. For a while, anyhow.

He soon crossed above the flight path of an airplane headed out from Minneapolis International Airport.

When he'd passed at least a mile above anyone's earshot he finally let out a pent-up roar, a blast of sound torn from his gut, loosing anguish, frustration and a passion to deny everything that had ever gone wrong on the planet. It wasn't supposed to end this way. It had all been for her. The costume, the heroics, the magic.

The sound of his voice faded away into the blue surround as if it had never been. He was an idiot. He should have known better from the start. If Gloria hadn't loved him to begin with, none of this would change her heart. He'd been a fool to think anything else.

But it hadn't all been in vain. A more sensible part of him fought its way to the surface of his mind. He, Wonder Guy anyhow, had helped a lot of people. One or more of whom would be dead now if not for the heroics. Who knew where Gloria would be if he hadn't been there to save her from those mosquitoes? She might not love him, she might not want ever to see or speak to him again, but at least she remained alive and well, making the world a finer place for the bright spirit she brought to it. He couldn't stand the thought of the world without her in it.

His fairy godmother's scheme to win him Gloria's love had failed. He'd at least take advantage of the powers he'd been given and keep doing what good they made possible for those who needed his help.

His upward flight slowed as the course of his thoughts brought him at last to a sense of resolve. He might feel for the rest of his life as if something inside him had died today, but that didn't mean his hero's work was done. He turned, angling his flight path back toward earth and home.

He still needed to deal with Professor Stevens' scheme and find out the identity of the woman involved, and the fairy godmothers still had their enemy. The one Serafina had told him of must still be out there, dreaming up worse plagues than dinosaurs and flying bloodsuckers.

Chapter 20

The bath helped. Gloria scrubbed herself dry with her oversized Egyptian cotton bath sheet and wrapped herself in its folds. The magical properties of hot water had soothed away the day's stresses and eased the troubles from her mind. She headed to her bedroom, shaking out the damp curls of her hair.

Now she felt sorry to have been rough on Greg. He was a sweet boy who'd always been a good friend. She wasn't as much of a comics fan as Greg, and had never thought much about it, but superheroes probably had good reasons to keep their true identities secret. She'd overreacted to the deception. It wasn't like he'd played superhero just to fool her. She was an idiot if she imagined this was all about her.

Gloria pulled on her favorite, much-worn jeans and a baby blue V-neck t-shirt. Wonder Guy had flown down and landed near her before he'd gone and revealed himself as Greg. It must be true. Greg. She picked up her hairbrush. She couldn't get over it. Greg as Wonder Guy. Greg as the one who'd flown through the sky to rescue her, twice. Greg as the one who'd carried her up into the sky and the one who'd kissed her like a whole new world exploding into being between them.

Her mind skittered away, and the ringing of her phone spared her more time on the subject.

"Ms. Torkenson?" a woman asked.

"Yes?" Gloria answered cautiously, wary of the too-frequent phone solicitations.

"It's Kathleen Pederson."

"Oh. Hi?" Why would Kathleen be calling her at home?

"I'm sorry to disturb you on a weekend, Ms. Torkenson, but I've had some plans change and will be out of town next week, for a conference in Boston. I know you wanted those forms."

"Oh. Yes." It took Gloria a second to recall the mundane matter, entirely forgotten in the wake of giant mosquitoes and superhero neighbor boys.

"Well, I tracked them down, and if you'll meet me this evening before I head to the airport, I can give them to you then."

"Oh, of course. I'd appreciate it. I don't have to be anywhere." It felt pitiful admitting she had no plans for a Saturday night, but she had released Pete from Saturday night date service, and chased away the next contender already. She was pitiful.

"My cousin lives in Boston, and I have to get a couple items I was holding for her from my storage locker. Why don't you meet me there? It's reasonably close to where you live. South Minneapolis, isn't it? Say, in half an hour?"

"Fine," Gloria said. "It's good of you to take time out for this. What's the address?" She jotted it down on the notepad beside her computer.

☆☆★☆☆

"Hey, Mom." Greg entered the kitchen, pleased to find Aggie home safe as usual, no strange men in sight, tracing a design onto a swath of brown ultra-suede. "What's new?"

"You wouldn't believe me if I told you." Aggie had a mug of coffee on the table before her and set aside her work to cup her hands around it, sparing him a smile. She gazed off into space.

"Try me."

"Strangest thing--Oh, do you want some coffee?" She turned back to him, gesturing to the chair opposite her at the table.

He remained standing. "No thanks, but I wanted to borrow your computer."

"What's wrong with yours?"

"You've got a better graphics package. I have some photos I want to format, maybe print one out."

"Oh, sure. The laptop's on that shelf--just lift it down."

Greg got the computer down and sat, placing it on the table before him. "What's so strange you don't think I'll believe it?"

"Have you listened to the news lately?" Aggie nodded to the TV playing at subdued volume on its shelf.

"I caught a bit." Greg turned on the Mac laptop, waited for it to boot up. "Something about giant mosquitoes. Some publicity stunt?" Asking a question for which he already had the answer wasn't exactly lying. Aggie had done it to him all the time when he was a kid, asking whether the elves had been into the cookies or made the mess in the living room when she knew perfectly well he'd done it.

"Giant is putting it mildly." Aggie took a sip from her mug, her gaze wandering off again. "I was there, but I can hardly believe it myself."

"You were there?" He looked up from downloading the photos he'd taken yesterday. "Are you okay?" He'd wanted to ask earlier, but not to admit he'd seen her there.

"I'm just fine." She shook her head. "Just shaken up. I was pretty scared there for a bit, I'll tell you, but luckily a very nice man carried me to shelter."

"A nice man, huh?" A man who'd saved his mother, but a man who'd held her too much like Wonder Guy had held Gloria. Greg studied his mother's face more closely than he had in years. She didn't meet his eyes. Her cheeks seemed pinker than usual. Was she blushing? "Exactly who is this nice man?"

"His name is Hank. You know my friend, Sue Luddell from the Senior Center? He's her younger brother. We've been seeing a bit of each other lately..." she trailed off, apparently catching the look on his face.

Greg closed his gaping mouth. Of course, his mother would go out with a nice guy if she met one. He should be surprised she hadn't met one before this.

"Wow," he said, and managed a smile. "That's great. I mean, I'm glad you've met someone you like, but you can't know this guy very well."

"True, we have only been getting to know each other so far. I'm not saying there's any more to it." Aggie smiled a smile he'd call coy if she weren't his mother.

While they talked, Greg pulled up his photos in Photoshop, found the best one, zoomed in on the face of the mystery woman he'd followed from Professor Stevens' storage unit. He cropped the image. It looked pretty dark. The woman's features were hard to distinguish. "How do I lighten this and sharpen the contrast?" He turned the screen toward Aggie.

"Go under 'Image' to 'Adjustments' to 'Levels.' Say, what are you doing with a photo of Gloria's supervisor?"

"What? Gloria's what?"

"Well, not her direct supervisor, but one of the supervisors in her department. What's her name now?" Aggie cocked her head. "Pearson? Peterson? Something like that. Kind of a high-powered woman. She made an impression on me." She made the same disapproving scrunch of her nose she used on discovering mouse droppings in a cupboard. "I met her a couple years ago when Gloria invited me to be her plus one at their office Christmas party, before she met Pete, when she was still new there and hadn't made friends with people."

Greg went cold, the chill sweeping through him like a winter storm front. This supervisor, involved in a shady deal with a professor intent on stealing research that could be worth big bucks to a business like ABM, and Gloria's co-worker... dead.

It didn't take an understanding of advanced calculus to put these numbers together and he figured long odds on this being coincidence. He had to warn Gloria to stay away from this woman. If she'd listen to him.

Time to confront Professor Stevens. The professor would know how to contact this Pearson or Peterson woman. Greg could connect the man to the data and the server, and connect the server to a contact at ABM. It might not be enough for the police, but it would be enough to get the professor called before the dean, enough to threaten his position at the University.

"What's wrong?" Aggie recalled him to the moment by lobbing a scrap of her brown ultra-suede at him.

"I have to go." He stood, leaving the laptop in place.

"Not before you put away your toy, young man." She nodded to the laptop.

"This is urgent. Gloria may be in trouble." He logged off the computer and set it back on its shelf, speaking in a rush. "You've got to call her." She might not listen to him, but she'd listen to Aggie. "Tell her to steer clear of this supervisor of hers. The woman's mixed up in some dirty business with one of our professors who's stealing student research. It may have something to do with her friend's death."

"What?" The color leeched from Aggie's face like a time-lapse study of the color fading from denim jeans. "It's not possible. How do you know all this?"

Greg already moved to the door. "I can't explain it now. Just call her, Mom. Please."

☆☆★☆☆

Arriving at the address Kathleen had given her, Gloria pulled up beside the last storage locker on the right and spotted the supervisor's sporty car coming up the drive behind her. Great timing, she thought, relieved.

It would've been spooky to wait alone in this deserted spot now the sun had sunk below the horizon and the surrounding shadows of the half-industrial area had deepened. A few security lights kept the drive between rows of lockers from true darkness, but still. The place seemed desolate with no other visitors at this hour, and only the sounds of traffic from nearby Hiawatha Avenue to cut the solitude.

Gloria exited her car when Kathleen's pulled up beside her. She waited as the other woman parked, killed her engine and turned to gather something from the seat beside her before emerging from her vehicle.

"Oh, good. Right on time." Kathleen greeted Gloria with the tight-lipped nod that passed as her version of a smile.

She'd approached close enough that Gloria took an involuntary step, backing up against her car door at the incursion on her personal bubble. What Kathleen withdrew from her Coach bag looked more like a weapon than the expected documents. Weird looking thing. A stun gun?

Shattering pain spasmed through her limbs before everything went dark.

☆☆★☆☆

The voice answering her call to Gloria was not Gloria's voice. Aggie started to apologize for dialing a wrong number, but no, she'd been very careful punching in the keys. The voice might be wrong but the number was right.

"To whom am I speaking?" she asked politely.

"Listen carefully." The woman's voice had a much harder edge to it than Gloria's and she spoke at a rapid clip. "Ms. Torkenson is in danger. She'll die if Wonder Guy doesn't come for her. Tell him to follow the creek."

"What?" What? Gloria in danger? Wonder Guy? This must be some joke. Why would anyone give this message to her? "I don't know Wonder Guy. How can I tell him anything?"

"Find a way."

The phone went dead.

☆☆★☆☆

Gloria woke in a cramped position, bent fetus-like on a hard, lumpy surface. She opened her eyes to a darkness so complete she blinked to make sure they weren't still closed. Her head throbbed.

She strained to swallow against the cloth tied across her mouth, and her limbs protested, aching from the awkward position in which she lay. She tried to sit up and couldn't manage it. The space felt too confined. Even if she succeeded in bringing her legs under her, her hands were secured together behind her back with what felt like duct tape. She groaned, squirming into an arguably less uncomfortable position.

Gasoline hung thick in the stuffy air. Cloth filled her mouth. She forced herself to breathe slowly, dragging the air in through her nose, fighting off panic lest she choke on her gag. She bucked, trying to sit upright, knocked her legs against some obstruction and banged her head, producing a hollow, metallic thunk. Dammit. She was in the trunk of a car.

What on earth? What had happened? How had she gotten here? Last thing she remembered, she'd set out to meet Kathleen to pick up those forms. Things got fuzzy after that. Had she had some sort of accident? No, that didn't fit with being bound hand and foot in the trunk of a car. Someone had done this to her.

She struggled to straighten her cramped legs. None of it made sense. As her pulse quickened, Gloria told herself to take deep breaths. It was hard to get enough of the petroleum-stinking air. She had to think. Were the police wrong about whoever had killed Jo? Had the killer come after her now? If the police were right, Jo had interrupted a robbery and there'd be no reason for robbers who'd taken advantage of a momentary lapse in security to return to the scene of their crime. Besides, she hadn't been at ABM. She'd been meeting Kathleen at a storage facility.

Her head swam from the gasoline fumes. She should have seen it sooner. She'd been too ready to believe the police and their reassuring answers. Jo might have left ABM by the door off the loading bay, but Jo wouldn't have left without cleaning her mug. Someone had made it look like she'd been on her way out. She'd been killed before she'd ever left under her own power.

Kathleen.

Everything clicked into place. Jo had been checking on those same tax forms the day she was killed. Now Gloria had asked about the forms and here she was, after meeting with Kathleen. Too much of a coincidence. Clearly, Kathleen had something to hide concerning the tax records for those independent contractors. Something vital enough to inspire murder and kidnapping.

It would have been nice to think of all this before *falling into the trap.* She should've known better than to accept the conclusions of the police. Not just because of Jo's unwashed coffee mug. There'd been that phone call too. Someone purporting to be Jo, calling in sick. What random killers would bother with that bit of deception?

A scuffling noise outside her prison alerted her. Someone nearby. Gloria twisted and bucked, trying to make some noise. She rocked in place, banging her head again in the process, but it made a thump. Knocking legs against what must be a wheel well made another, feebler thump. The small noise she made got lost in the louder, solid chunk of a car door as it slammed shut, then the sound of the engine kicking on.

As the car rolled, Gloria braced herself against flopping around like an imperfectly stowed bag of groceries.

☆☆★☆☆

Aggie stared speechlessly at her phone for a long moment after the call ended. She refused to tolerate the very idea of any harm coming to Gloria. She thought instead about what to do next. She had no idea how to contact Wonder Guy. This sounded like a kidnapping. She should call the police, the FBI--someone who knew how to deal with such situations. The woman who'd made the threat obviously had Gloria's phone. The authorities could track cell phones somehow, couldn't they?

Aggie dialed 9-1-1.

"Please state the nature of your emergency."

"It's--" she hesitated. Was Gloria a missing person? Maybe someone had stolen her phone and was making some kind of joke to claim they had her too. Why would anyone actually kidnap Gloria? She had no money, no influence. Still, they claimed to have her. "Someone's taken my friend, Gloria Torkenson. They say they'll hurt her unless Wonder Guy comes to them."

She couldn't believe this was happening. The familiar kitchen surrounding her took on a surreal cast. Gloria was almost a daughter to her. Just the idea of losing her was enough to send her heart reeling. Twice in one day, she'd had reason to fear for Gloria's life. She had to stay focused. Numbly, she answered the operator's questions, supplying details about the call, her own identity and relationship to Gloria, the circumstances surrounding the situation.

"I'm sorry." The woman's brisk manner softened at last. "We have to establish that your friend is not acting under her own volition and is absent under duress before we can treat this as a kidnapping."

"I told you." Aggie leaned forward, resting her elbows on the table before her, like her worries had the weight of some solid creature riding on her shoulders. A portly old man maybe, or a baby elephant. She had no strength to shrug it off.

"I told you. Someone else has her phone. A woman. She said Gloria is in danger--she'll die if Wonder Guy doesn't come to her."

"Do you have any idea where Ms. Torkenson intended to go after you last saw her?"

Aggie straightened. "The last I knew she was headed home."

"We'll send someone there to look for signs of trouble, and if you give me the number of her cell phone, I'll start the tracking procedure."

Aggie gave her Gloria's number. "Will you, the police, be able to contact Wonder Guy? Get him to help her?"

"We'll do everything we can, ma'am."

Aggie frowned as the connection cut out. *Not much of an answer.*

☆☆★☆☆

Gloria braced herself against the sides of her prison. She'd grown more or less used to the jouncing after a few initial shocks. The up side of the cramped quarters being she was wedged securely into place.

Given how uncomfortable her position and how terrifying the prospects, it surprised her to find her thoughts turning to Greg instead of dwelling on those discomforts. A more practical person would plot her escape, or at least her next move. Gloria had always admired Kathleen as a role model of the kind of successful businesswoman she wanted to emulate. Kathleen was very practical. She might think of a way out of a fix like this, but Gloria could barely function. Not a single practical move came to mind, and given Kathleen's most recent behavior, Gloria didn't want her as a role model anymore.

She'd been unfair to Greg. He'd been her friend forever, one of the best and truest. She should have been more diplomatic. It was as if she didn't know him at all after all these years. She shouldn't have been so surprised he'd turned out to be a superhero. How shallow was she to dismiss such a constant friend as a hopeless geek all these years?

She couldn't get over it. Even now, she'd start thinking about Greg--old, dependable Greg--and catch herself, remembering how much more he'd revealed hidden behind his golden mask. She'd grown up with him, they'd played together as kids, she'd hung out at his house practically every day, seen him through his gangly teenage years, teased him about his comic books and his other geeky interests. She'd always been fond of him. How had she never noticed he had the potential to be a hero, to look so hot in tights, to kiss like...as if he was made of lightning and thunder and every romantic movie star rolled together?

☆☆★☆☆

While Greg didn't follow Penny Hagestad's Tweets, to her followers it was no secret Professor Stevens of the Computer Sciences department was involved with his grad student to an extent far beyond what the University condoned. Greg had heard about the affair from Eric, who did follow Penny, with an unhealthy degree of interest, and apparently saw no reason not to share what he learned, regardless of how interested his audience might or might not be.

Finding Professor Stevens' present whereabouts, despite it being a weekend evening after end-of-term, required only a stop at the computer lab and some quick social networking. Penny's Twitter page revealed how she planned to spend the weekend with her *amour* at his *pied a terre*. The department directory supplied the professor's home address.

The professor's condo stood on the St. Anthony's Main bank of the Mississippi, where it had a spectacular view of Nicollet Island and downtown Minneapolis. By this hour, city lights made an abstract, downtown-Minneapolis-shaped design against a night sky grown doubly dark with a thick layer of gathering clouds. The scene lay reflected in shimmering duplicate on the dark water below.

Wonder Guy circled the upper stories of the condo building until he spotted the professor standing on his balcony, one arm around a pretty redheaded grad student.

Greg dove down to land beside him and stand, hands fisted on his hips, playing the costumed superhero role to the hilt. Abandoning his companion, Stevens backed away toward the sliding glass doors to his apartment.

Greg moved to intercept him, positioning himself between the professor and his escape route.

"You'll want this to be a private conversation." He locked eyes with the professor, but nodded to Penny who stood backed against the balcony railing. From her admiring gaze, Greg guessed she'd forgotten the professor in favor of the superhero's arrival. "Will you excuse us, miss?"

"Sure," she breathed, moving slowly to the terrace door, never taking her wide-eyed gaze off him.

"What do you think you're doing?" Stevens demanded.

"I think I'm paying a visit to the man responsible for stealing student research and selling it off to the R&D division at ABM."

Stevens sputtered. "What are you talking about?"

"Give it up, Professor. The storage unit housing the stolen data is traceable to you. I've done it. So will the police." The older man's face went pale beneath its fake tan.

"What do you want?"

"Right now? The name and contact info for your confederate at ABM."

The more he considered it, the more sense it made. ABM couldn't be using legitimate means to acquire stolen research. Who knew how far the woman he'd spotted visiting the servers might go to keep her illegal dealings secret?

"She may be guilty of murder," Greg continued.

"Murder? Now wait a minute. I haven't had anything to do with any murder."

"A young woman is dead and your business partner has secrets to keep. How much are you willing to stake on her good moral character? Your own life if she decides you know too much? Being counted as an accessory to her crimes? You'd better decide whether it's worth it to you."

"You're nothing but a damned self-appointed vigilante." The professor straightened, facing Wonder Guy with a scowl. "You have no legal authority here."

"No." Greg smiled. "But I can get the people who do have the authority over here if you'd rather deal with them. I can see letting the matter go if you give up your partner and return the stolen research. The authorities may not be as willing to deal."

The professor looked shaken, despite his belligerent manner. He glowered. "I'm not admitting anything," he said. "My relationship with Kathleen Pederson, who happens to work at ABM, is purely social. If she's done anything illegal, I know nothing about it."

"We can return to the issue at any time," Greg growled. "And we will if you don't produce her contact info for me in the next sixty seconds."

Stevens stared darkly back at him as he dug in his jacket pocket and produced a cell phone. Clicking through a few icons, he proffered the device. "Here. This is the only number I have for her."

Greg studied the number, committing it to memory. He initiated a call, but Pederson's phone sent him immediately to voice mail. Now what? He handed Stevens his phone.

"Thanks for your cooperation, Professor," he said, keeping a warning note in his tone. "I'll check back on the status of the student work, and ABM will be warned to establish the provenance of their research."

The professor said nothing. Until Wonder Guy took to the air, when his super hearing caught a bout of muttered, though ardent, cursing. At least he had Pederson's name and number. Now he'd have to figure out whether she really was connected to Jo's murder, making her a threat to Gloria.

Chapter 21

Elysha relished the woodlands at night. Especially on nights like this, with the wind dancing ahead of a brewing storm. She sensed the world through her skin, through the lush, moist air of a June night in which the rising breeze carried scents of wild strawberries, rain to come and the distant taint of gas and tar.

She wove her way between roots and brambles and stabbing branches as if she were herself a tendril of the wind, as much a part of the wild as any tree or vine. The wildness churned even in these shallow scraps of woodlands that once had wrapped this region in wilderness as thick as a grizzly's winter pelt. At the verge of the open lawns bordering the narrow road running along the creek for the length of the park, she met her contact.

"What are those?" Pederson asked, staring wide-eyed at the creatures all too visible even in the shadows of the open area between wood and road.

"You've done well." Elysha nodded to her. "Did you bring the weapon?"

Still casting nervous looks to the side, the woman turned her attention back to Elysha. "I brought that chunk of brick and cement, if that's what you mean. It's not much of a weapon. I'd rather have an automatic."

"This weapon has surely kept at least one of our enemies from interfering with you in the course of your errands." Elysha nodded to another minion, one looking more like a gnarled knot of tree roots come to life than anything else.

Pederson lifted the chunk of masonry from the back seat of her vehicle and the creature grasped it. The woman flinched from contact with the minion, quickly releasing her grip.

"What about the girl? She might still be trouble." She wiped her hands down the sides of her business suit.

"The girl will cause no trouble. Once she's of no more use to me, I'll dispose of her."

The captive in question struggled, despite her obviously dazed state, as the minions dragged her from the rear of Pederson's conveyance and carried her into the deeper darkness beneath the trees. Here, along the rippling laugh of the creek cutting to the south of the city, poplars and maples still stood tall and drew the darkness in around them, enclosing everything in night except for odd glimmers of lesser darkness between the masses of undergrowth. It took four of the stronger creatures to carry the girl from the road.

They took the duty with ill grace, complaining of having to go near the burning metal and noxious fumes. Elysha sniffed in disdain. Her servants should be calloused to such duty by now. Perhaps she needed to expose them to cold steel more often.

☆☆★☆☆

It's a nightmare. It must be. In the darkness beneath clouded night and leafy woods, Gloria caught only glimpses of her captors as they'd dragged her from the car. Whatever they were wasn't human. They seemed more like strange combinations of roots and toads, or insects and thistles in vaguely human shape. Aliens? Monsters? Nightmares. The 'hands' clutching her felt as unyielding as the branches of scrub trees growing up beside the garage. Ike needed to root them out or cut them back every season. Perhaps she dreamt of their revenge.

Her journey became a series of slaps and stinging blows. With hands and legs still bound, she couldn't protect herself from the lash of branches and trailing brambles sweeping past as the creatures carried her deeper into the woods. She tried to shield her face by tucking her chin into a shoulder. The gag made breathing difficult, but at least it protected her mouth. Squelching underfoot and the sound of flowing water told her some stream ran nearby. Minnehaha maybe?

At last, her bearers released her and she hit the ground with a jarring thump. Half-stunned from the impact, she lay on uneven turf where the roots of a large tree protruded and stinging nettles grew thick. She flinched from the nettles and wriggled to find some softer place among the roots.

Someone loomed above her, a darker shade among the shadows.

Something prodded her in the ribs.

"Such bait seems a poor lure for our fish. We must display you to better advantage than this." A woman's voice. Gloria lay at the feet of a woman.

Gloria gurgled in the effort to speak around the gag. She wanted to scream. Shout. Demand answers. Who was this woman? Bait to lure a fish? Not good. Not good at all.

"I cannot trust you not to scream." The woman's voice sounded thoughtful. "We're still too near human habitation. Still, a small spell will serve better than that nasty rag and you must be able to plead to your hero when he comes."

One of the twiggy creatures reached toward her face and Gloria flinched. With some tugging, the thing managed to tear away the cloth from her mouth. She drew breath and let loose what should have been a hell of a shrill scream, but no sound issued from her throat.

What? She tried to speak, to say, "What have you done to me?" Her lips moved. She did exactly as she'd always done to produce speech, but now only silence resulted. Panic warred with the awareness of how ridiculous she must look, mouth working like a stranded fish. She closed her lips into a firm line and glared at the looming shadow of her captor.

In her distraction, Gloria had barely noticed her other bonds changing form, not until her hands were drawn apart, dragged forcefully from their bound-behind-her-back position. Duct-tape no longer held them together, but she found each wrist wrapped separately with what felt like heavy, prickly cord. Unseen forces dragged these cords behind the tree at her back. She found herself pulled up and back to a seated posture with her arms awkwardly spread to encompass the width of the tree's trunk, solid bark scraping her spine. Her legs were freed for a moment and she squirmed into an upright posture with their aid.

The earth beneath her softened. The roots of the tree writhed below the sod, coiling up and around her legs, drawing them below the dirt, until it seemed she stood, buried to the tops of her legs in the earth and pressed back against the tree. Overcome by horror and helplessness, she screamed soundlessly, over and again.

☆☆★☆☆

Flying not far above the neighborhood roofs, Greg spotted the flashing lights of a police car lighting up the night. Several squad cars parked in front of Aggie's house. He landed behind the house, changed from Wonder Guy's costume back to his normal slacks and t-shirt, and only then went around to the front of the house at a run.

He found Aggie sitting in her wheelchair on the front walk, watching a pair of men in police uniform at the Torkenson's front door. One pounded the door intermittently while the other spoke into a radio. Greg's heart lurched.

"What's going on?" He came up beside Aggie.

"It's Gloria." Worry impressed new lines in her brow, drew down the corners of her mouth.

335

"Did you call her? Warn her?"

"I tried. Someone's got her, or at least, someone has her phone and claims to have her. When I tried calling, some other woman answered. She said Gloria will die if Wonder Guy doesn't come for her."

"What?" It came out at a much higher volume than he'd intended. The police looked his way. He took a breath. He had to think clearly. More softly, he asked, "How is Wonder Guy supposed to find her? How were you supposed to tell him?"

"I don't know." Tears stood in Aggie's eyes now. "I didn't know what else to do but call the police. They're deciding now whether she's gone, whether to put out an APB and try to contact Wonder Guy."

"You have to tell them to find Gloria's supervisor. It's Kathleen Pederson. I'd bet the farm she's one who has Gloria's phone."

"We don't own a farm, and why don't you tell them yourself?"

"This is no time to teach me to be more independent, Mom. The police would ask me questions I can't answer."

"I can't answer any questions about it either."

"You won't have to. You've met Pederson. You can tell them you recognized her voice, it only took you a while to put it together. They won't push a poor helpless cripple lady too hard," he added in a teasing tone he hoped would take some of the edge off the worry showing clearly on her face.

She socked him in the arm with the considerable strength she'd gained by wheeling her chair everywhere she went. "All right, I'll tell them, but I'll want the whole story later."

"Don't worry, Mom." Greg moved in close beside Aggie's chair as the red and blue police lights cycled across the scene, painting their faces, the neighborhood houses and street all with the same lurid colors. The rising wind and scent of coming rain only added to his sense of urgency, but he put a hand on her shoulder. "It will be all right. I'm sure Wonder Guy will come through." He said the words, and she nodded as if reassured, but he wasn't as sure as he'd sounded. How could he save Gloria when he had no idea how to find her?

"I hope you're right." Aggie kept her eyes on the officers next door. They stopped banging on the door and turned to face the new arrival, Ike Torkenson, emerging from a battered SUV pulled up at the curb.

"I hope you're right, but how can we even tell Wonder Guy he's supposed to follow the creek if we can't find him?"

"What creek?"

"That's all the kidnapper said. Just, *tell him to follow the creek.*" Aggie looked as confused and helpless as he felt.

He needed to talk to Serafina. If anyone knew how to find Gloria, she should. Why hadn't he heard from her already? She'd warned him about other situations where Wonder Guy was needed.

Ike strode up his sidewalk to the house, already in full righteous-indignation mode, shouting, "What are you people doing there? Get off my stoop. I'm a law-abiding citizen! You've got no business with me! And you gawkers--" He turned on Aggie and Greg and the Nelsons who'd stepped out of their house on the other side of the Torkenson's property. "This is no circus. You people mind your own business."

Greg couldn't leave Aggie alone in the midst of this awful sideshow. She started to wheel forward into the heat of battle, but he held her back.

"Sir." The taller, gray-haired officer turned to Ike. "Are you the property owner?"

"Damn right, I am." Ike thrust his stubbled jaw forward.

"We're here about your daughter," the officer continued, one thumb stuck in his utility belt, near the oversized flashlight hanging there like a billy club.

"Gloria?" Ike's shoulders slumped and his voice lost its bluster. "What about Gloria? She's a good girl, she wouldn't do anything wrong."

At her insistence, Greg went with Aggie then, helping move her chair across the bit of lawn between walks.

"Your neighbor here called it in." The other policeman, younger and shorter, gestured to Aggie.

"I tried calling her, Ike." Aggie drew up near the Torkenson stoop. "Some strange woman answered, saying she has Gloria, saying she's in danger."

"No." Ike dropped to sit on one of the steps as if he'd suddenly lost use of his legs.

"Sir, can you let us into the house to check for signs of violence or forced entry?"

Ike looked up, shaking his head.

"Give them your keys, Ike." Aggie moved up beside him.

Greg hung back. Staying here did no good. Aggie would reassure Ike. The police would do their part. He backed off, into the deeper dark between the houses.

"Serafina?" Greg called softly from near the garage, in the darkened back yard.

"Yes, dear?" He started at her voice. She stood at his elbow.

"Someone's got Gloria."

"I'm so sorry, dear. We couldn't interfere directly." She laid a hand lightly on his wrist, and he felt her sympathy flow into him like hot cocoa on a winter's day.

"Why didn't you call me? Let me know she was in danger?"

"You wouldn't have been able to do anything, either."

"Why the hell not?"

"Tsk. Language, dear."

"I'm sorry, but why couldn't I have helped her?"

"The enemy has a weapon, something taken from your birthplace. You could never have approached her in time."

"So where is Gloria now? How can I find her?"

"I'm sorry, but she's been taken by our enemy Elysha. We can't see into the creature's areas of power. You'll have to find Gloria on your own.

When you do so, we can come to your aid and deal with Elysha. I know you can do it, dear. You're not alone in this, as much as it may seem like it right now."

☆☆★☆☆

Aggie maneuvered her chair to the side of the stoop where Ike sat bent over, head in hands, apparently oblivious to the uniformed strangers going in and coming back out through his front door.

"You okay, Ike?" She put a hand on his shoulder, half afraid he'd shrug it off and more concerned than ever when he didn't. It seemed he wouldn't respond at all. She gave his shoulder a squeeze to offer comfort if he cared to take it.

"I'm a selfish bastard," he said no louder than if talking to himself.

"From time to time." She kept her tone light and conversational. "But you have your moments. Karen would never have married you otherwise."

He grunted. "The best part of me died with her."

"This is no time to wallow, Ike. Gloria needs us to be strong."

He sat upright, throwing off her hand. "My girl's in trouble and there's nothing I can do about it. I'm useless and now I'll be alone after all. I should have let her go a long time ago for all the difference it makes now. She could have been happier, but she was my baby girl. She was all I had left."

He slumped forward again. The scent of cheap beer overwhelmed her when she stopped close beside him, but this wasn't the time to remind him of his other problems.

"Ike. Stop that right now. Stop talking like Gloria's dead and in the ground. The least you can do is keep hope alive for her. Don't give up on her."

It's what she kept telling herself. Everyone had limitations. She had to focus on possibilities.

"I know you're not a religious man, Ike, but believe this much, we're connected to the people we care about. Our love and faith in them can make a difference, even if we can't explain how or why."

"I don't know," Ike muttered. "Karen used to talk like that." He drew a deep breath, straightened his shoulders. "Glory's not dead. I'd know it. I'd know it if she wasn't in the world."

"That's right," Aggie told him. "And so would I. Now let's talk to the police again. I want to make sure we tell them everything we possibly can about the situation."

☆☆★☆☆

Gloria struggled against the grip of her restraints. No one had the power to make roots and brambles grow and move at command. It was impossible. Could it be magic? She couldn't fight magic. She liked to imagine she had something special about her, but she was an ordinary human being, not some magic-wielding wonder woman or demon slayer.

She had never been this miserable in her life. Even after her mother died, she'd had people around her, offering warmth and comfort. She'd never been so cold and wet and afraid as now, alone in the blind woods at night. Especially now, while rain streamed down out of a heavy sky, undeterred by the thin canopy of spring leaves. Clothing adequate for a sunny afternoon now clung, soaked, to her goose-fleshed skin, no help at all. The muddy earth packed around her buried legs only added to her chill.

Worst, she lay helpless in the power of people-- speaking loosely--who didn't give a damn for her. They had some use for her now as some kind of bait, but she'd heard the part where she wouldn't live past her usefulness.

They weren't human. Inhuman monsters for their murderous intent alone, but also literally. She'd caught glimpses. She had no idea what to call them. From time to time one would come up to her, skittering like a huge insect or silent, with no warning of approach. They'd poke or pinch her, or stroke her bare arm or cheek with sticky, prickly or slimy fingers. Apparently for no better reason than to make her squirm or wince in pain.

The woman in charge looked most nearly hu-man. She could pass, but her preternatural beauty seemed like the rainbow sheen across an oil-slicked puddle, just as superficial, with nothing wholesome about it.

Gloria had never dreamed the world held such horrors. She'd done a good job of keeping life's known horrors at bay, managing to keep a bubble of light and warmth and comfort around her daily existence. Her nice quiet life had been primar-ily concerned with simple things: friends, family, work, home and making useful and pretty things.

Bad stuff--evil--existed out there in the world, but she'd always kept it at a distance. Lacking the powers to cure poverty, death, disease, war, or natural disasters, she focused her energies on the small things within her reach. She gave to as many worthy causes as possible on her budget, but giving constituted just another way of keeping the bad things at a distance.

Now, all Gloria's efforts at evading life's evils had come to nothing. The bad stuff had swallowed her whole. It held her alone in the dark, cold and wet, helpless in the clutches of enemies who meant to use and destroy her. Bound helplessly in place, it looked like all the choices had been taken from her. The bad stuff had her now. In tomorrow's news she'd probably be just another statistic. She should be a whimpering mess, but her mind worked overtime, soothing her panic.

A few tears had come to her eyes, and her arms prickled with goose flesh coming from fear as much as from the cold. Her jaw ached from clenching it against more silent screams, but mostly Gloria's thoughts seemed oddly abstracted from her reality. She strove for an analytic, objective perspective to help her find a way out of this fix. She might, literally, be rooted in the muck right now, but like even the tiniest seeds, something in her still fought toward the light.

Kathleen wanted her dead. Silenced. The strange, evil-sorceress person wanted to use her as bait. Who was this other female? Kathleen hadn't addressed her by name when turning Gloria over to her. When her odd servants addressed her it sounded like the shushing sound made even now by the rain in its descent through the canopy of leaves above.

But her name made no difference. Gloria had to stop the witch. She meant to use Gloria as bait to draw in her hero. That had to mean Wonder Guy.

The same Wonder Guy who had revealed himself to be Greg. Gloria, however upset by his keeping his identity secret from her, couldn't let herself be used to hurt anyone, whether masked stranger or the friend she'd known all her life. Greg was her friend, her dear friend, who'd been on her side forever. Wonder Guy had become her hero, and something more.

The best thing might be to end her life before her captor used her against those she loved. But how, with her movements so constrained? The sorceress held all the power. Maybe she could find a way to provoke the nasty creature. Without so much as a voice to taunt with, even that prospect seemed hopeless.

☆☆★☆☆

Staying below the storm clouds Wonder Guy shot high above his home neighborhood and angled south. Follow the creek? That must mean Minnehaha, the creek winding from Lake Minnetonka in the west metro all the way across South Minneapolis to Minnehaha Park and the falls before it finally joined the Mississippi river in the Southeast quadrant of the city. Miles of parkland. Most of it might be trimmed back and tamed, but the park included steep hillsides with tangled undergrowth and stretches of wooded and marshy land. What was he looking for? Where did he start?

The night may have turned rainy and overcast, but the added gloom constituted no impediment to Wonder Guy's penetrating night vision. Scanning below, Greg soon spotted the dark swath of the parklands stretching like spilled ink among neighborhood lights. He'd do this right. He'd start at the source in the west metro and scour its course from headwaters to the falls and on to the river. He'd do the whole route over again if he had to, as many times as it took. Greg would tear the woods apart stick by stick if that's what it took to find Gloria.

His heat vision showed him the sparks of living things, stray dogs, plenty of rabbits, birds, squirrels, even wild turkey, fox and deer. Not many human forms emerged in the darkness. The falling rain deterred all but the most determined dog walkers, joggers, bikers and runners. This near midnight, there'd be few enough of those even at the best of weather. The cars taking the scenic route along Minnehaha Parkway blinded him when he glanced aside from the darkness of the woods.

Within the hour, he'd scouted the creek's course past Bloomington Avenue without spotting anything out of the ordinary. Time and again he focused his telescopic vision on one of the few people out and about--just to be sure--only to be disappointed. No Gloria.

He followed the whole length of the creek, until he circled above the parkland where the woods grew thickest, between the falls and the confluence of the creek with the Mississippi. He must have missed something. Maybe if he flew lower? He angled into a descent, starting back along the path of the winding waterway.

Intent on searching the land below him, Greg was caught unaware when his power began to flag. He dropped, rapidly losing altitude and carried along only by his initial impetus. Once again, Wonder Guy's powers had departed him in midflight. He bent his angle of descent, trying desperately to backtrack in midair, but it did no good. Momentum carried him along until he flailed among the upper branches of trees, lashed by their limbs and the rain alike.

He clutched at the branches as he fell, finally bringing himself to a halt, high in a tree. His super vision had deserted him. His perch was in a deciduous tree, as far as he could tell by groping branches in the dark. Probably one of the Black Poplars growing thick along the watershed. He hadn't climbed a tree since he'd been fifteen.

As he recalled from his earlier, tree-climbing years, the poplars branched in a regular pattern, but it was hard to predict how far apart the branching occurred. Well, he'd have to feel his way. Clinging to the bole, Greg extended a leg, feeling with his booted foot for the next lower limb. He might be no stronger than the next man and blind as the next bat in these woods at night, but he wasn't stupid and time was wasting. Gloria needed him.

The lower branches of his probably-a-poplar had been trimmed, leaving Greg to shinny and slide down the last ten feet of the trunk. Still clad in Wonder Guy's costume, he escaped some potential scrapes, but a protruding stump of a branch caught him in a sensitive spot and he hit the ground bent double in pain, gritting his teeth against a howl.

The wind and rain might have masked the noise he made crashing through the branches, but he had to assume his enemies knew of his presence. Greg took a few long and slow breaths, letting the pangs subside, leaning back against the tree he'd descended and assessed his situation.

On the plus side, chances were he'd found Gloria's abductor or abductors. The question was, how dangerous were they? Something had brought him down just now. Obviously, his superhero powers would do him no good under the circumstances.

Serafina had warned him his enemies had a chunk of St. Mary's. Either Pederson's chunk of pseudo kryptonite was in this immediate vicinity, still in her hands, or someone else had another such weapon. Not likely. Might Pederson be the Fairy Godmothers' Union's enemy in disguise or be in league with their enemy?

His adversaries would have no interest in Greg Roberts. They'd used Gloria to lure Wonder Guy to this place. Someone must have noticed his interest in her, maybe observed their kiss. Great. They wanted Wonder Guy? He'd give them Wonder

Guy. Obviously, this was a trap. The only question was whether he'd yet sprung it.

He straightened. No superpowers. No rain gear. No flashlight and no more woodcraft than he'd picked up in his one year with the cub scouts. No point in being subtle.

"Hey," he yelled into the darkness. "Here I am. Where's Gloria?"

Chapter 22

Gloria woke with a start, the sound of Greg's voice echoing in her ears. She must have dozed off despite all the discomfort of her position. A hard knot in the tree against which she leaned dug into her ribs. Embedded in the earth, her legs felt so numb she could hardly tell if they were still attached.

She tried to call out, but her captor's spell silenced her. Her voice might have been swallowed in some vast abyss before it ever reached her ears.

"Ah."

An eerie purplish-blue light swelled around her, revealing the perpetrator of all Gloria's present misery, who appeared perfectly at her ease among the rain-drenched leaves.

"It's time to return your voice to you." The sorceress gestured with an out-thrust hand at Gloria. "Please feel free to scream and carry on now."

Gloria gasped in a breath, relieved to hear the sound of it and, out of sheer pent-up frustration, blasted out a scream, cutting the air with satisfying, piercing clarity.

What a relief to let loose everything she'd held bottled up for the past hours. They had to be close enough to the roads so someone would hear.

"Gloria!"

Her heart leapt when Greg called out, not far off. The sounds of heavy crashing through the brush followed. *Dammit!* She cursed herself, belatedly remembering her earlier conclusions and the danger to Greg.

"No! Run," she yelled, "Run! Get help!"

The livid light grew brighter. It revealed the tiny clearing surrounding her, her captor standing near, the strange servitor creatures shrinking away into the shadowed underbrush.

"Gloria!" Greg stumbled into the glade, slamming to a stop as if running up against a glass wall in the form of the tall sorceress, who held her stance, barring the way between him and Gloria. Dang he looked good in his form-fitting costume, even with that goofy look on his masked face.

"I said, run, you idiot," Gloria vented. "It's a trap. Get out of here!"

"Sorry, Gloria." He spoke around the woman standing between them. "I can't go. I can't leave you here alone with this...person."

"You may call me Elysha, Hero."

Hmph. Introductions for him, when there'd been none for her, hauled around and dumped here like so much luggage. This Elysha person obviously thought her no more than a tool. Gloria fumed at her own helplessness, itching to prove the folly of discounting Gloria Torkenson. She squirmed against the restraints of roots and brambles. With Elysha's attention turned to Greg, the roots trapping her behaved like ordinary roots again, keeping to their places rather than twisting to hold her. In the muddy earth, maybe she could work her legs away from their grip.

Meanwhile, Greg demanded, "Free Gloria. You've got me here now. That's what you wanted, right?"

"That is part of my plan, yes." Elysha stalked forward, circling him like a great cat. "Your powers are diminished while I have this." She gestured to a chunk of masonry the size of a football lying on the muddy turf near Gloria. "But you are still under the protection of my enemies."

She spun toward Gloria, throwing out her arm and clenching her hand in a fist. At the gesture, the thorny vines trapping Gloria against her tree tightened convulsively. Brambles cut sharply into her already lacerated flesh and she choked out a scream. Dragging her a few inches deeper into the earth, the roots holding her legs writhed back to life.

Elysha threw back her head and laughed a peal of ghoulish delight. "Yes. Good. Your beloved's pain, her fear, your anguish and desperation. I could feed from the two of you for a whole season. What a feast."

"Stop! You have to stop." Greg hurled himself forward only to fall back when he crashed again into whatever invisible wall Elysha kept between them. "I'll do whatever you want. You have to let Gloria go."

Gloria recognized Greg easily now, even masked as he was, the familiar eyes, along with his broad shoulders, firm jaw and the long, lithe lines of his bicyclist's form. How had she ever overlooked these qualities when he'd been clad in ordinary slacks and t-shirt or button-down plaid? She should always have recognized Greg as the hero standing before her now.

"No!" Gloria managed to yell around the constriction of the strangling brambles. "Get out of here, Greg! They'll just--" kill me anyhow, she meant to say, but the words choked off when the brambles grew even tighter around her throat, cutting off her air.

She gasped, struggling for breath. The cold mud reached higher, chilling her to the waist now. She shivered uncontrollably. Thought deserted her for the endless moments during which pain held sway.

Gloria struggled to stay aware of her surroundings.

Elysha laughed. "Oh, how delicious, Hero. Your anguish delights me. How great will it be when the earth closes over her head and the weight crushes her lungs as you stand helplessly by?"

"Stop it!" He threw himself again at the barrier and sank onto his knees from the force of his effort. It wasn't nearly the force Wonder Guy had exerted before. It must have come from St. Mary's, but it still seemed strange for a chunk of ordinary masonry have such a strong effect.

"Tell me what you want. What will it take to set her free?" Still on his knees, pleading, Greg turned to Elysha.

"You would deny me the pleasure of watching you suffer? Of enjoying your pain as your beloved dies before you, inch by painful inch?"

"Yes, damn it," Greg growled at her. He'd never looked so fierce, like a barely constrained and snarling beast. She'd never realized how powerfully he felt toward her.

"But your passion is so potent. The strength of your desperation to help her is like a drug for me. What more could I want?"

"There must be something. Did you lure me here only for this?"

Something lurched in Gloria's chest at his desperation on her behalf. She almost forgot the pain of the thorns cutting her and the chill of the earth gripping her. She longed to reach out to him, ease his suffering.

Elysha cast a startled glance her way and Gloria thought for a moment her bonds had loosened. The sorceress spun back to Greg.

"You're right," she said, closing on him, fixing him in her gaze as intently as a snake. "Let us waste no more time in this play. I want the power my enemies have given you. It is too much for a mortal man. You can't make such good use of it as I."

"As far as I'm concerned, you can have it," Greg said, "But I don't know how to give it to you."

"No!" Gloria cried out, renewing her efforts to pull free. She felt feeble with cold and pain, exhausted by the trials of the past hours. Her efforts came to nothing. "No, Greg. Think! She'll kill us both, then do awful things with the power."

He seemed not to hear her. Perhaps Elysha kept her voice from reaching him.

"Tis easily done." The sorceress spoke, waving a hand and the barrier against which Greg pressed vanished, and he fell forward onto his hands. "Give me your hand and say, 'I relinquish these fairy gifts to you.'"

Greg lifted his gloved hand. Elysha took it between both of hers.

Gloria didn't hear his words for the rushing in her ears. Everything in her strained forward, despite how her efforts pressed the brambles further into her wounds.

"No." He mustn't. Without his powers, the vicious creature would kill him. Her own fate was sealed. She couldn't escape, but Greg might. He should. She ached at the thought of her own Greg dying here needlessly. A thousand scenes of their shared past flashed before her mind's eye. Greg, so smart, so good-hearted and strong, so...dear. He mustn't die. She loved him. She was in love with him...her own dear hero.

Chapter 23

That was all Elysha wanted? These powers? He'd only ever wanted them to impress Gloria. Without her, they meant nothing. What a relief to know he could save her so easily.

Greg got as far as letting Elysha clasp his hand and saying, "I relinquish..." when he paused, pulling back at the thought of what the woman might do with so much power. In the same moment the dark woods exploded into light, he landed flat on his back with the wind knocked out of him. Voices, the sound of distant sirens...

Sitting up, he found himself back in his regular clothes and the costume gone. Looking around, the glade seemed at first to throng with brilliant beings of nearly blinding beauty. He must have knocked his head when he fell. He blinked and saw only a group of elderly ladies. He spotted Serafina among them. The Fairy Godmothers--and no sign of Elysha.

☆☆★☆☆

The glade exploded with light, dazzling in Gloria's eyes. It might have been a midsummer's day rather than a stormy spring night. Golden light turned the surrounding leaves to emerald jewels and the raindrops to diamonds. Her bonds loosened, the brambles fell away and the roots retreated back into the earth until she remained only loosely buried in the mud. Where had all these people come from? Greg stood among them, apparently at ease.No sign of Elysha. Gloria fell back against the trunk, her strength failing at last.

☆☆★☆☆

His gaze shot to Gloria. She slumped, propped against the same tree, head hanging forward, motionless.

"Gloria!" He rushed forward and finally made it unimpeded to her side. He took her hand, checked for a pulse and only drew breath again when he found it.

"She's just exhausted, poor thing. Don't worry." Serafina stood beside him.

"Are you sure?" Greg winced at the bloody scratches marring the creamy flesh of Gloria's neck and arms. No worse damage showed. Her breath came deep and regular as if she slept. The rain still fell upon them and her arm and hand felt cold to his touch. Being half-buried in the mud must have sucked the heat right out of her.

"We need to get her out of this hole, warm her up. Do you have a coat? Blanket? Anything?" He had only his slacks and shirt, already wet.

"Help will be here soon." Serafina gestured to the ground beside Gloria. "Why don't you sit down beside her? You can keep her warm in the meanwhile."

"Of course. Body heat." Greg sat close beside Gloria, his back against the tree, taking all he could reach of her into his arms, cradling her against his chest.

Only then did he ask, "What happened here? Where is Elysha?"

"We took Elysha into custody while she was weakened from the blow you and your young lady dealt her."

"Blow? I never touched her, but she sure knocked me back."

"Actually not." Serafina blushing? She avoided his eyes. "I must apologize, young man. It was I who pushed you aside just as you relinquished the magic I'd given you, before you completed the transfer of power. It was only proper that the energy go back to our FGU coffers. It was ignorant of Elysha to think herself capable of making use of it, any more than a housecat could make use of one of your people's combustion engine vehicles."

He let her go on, still stuck at the picture of the tiny woman knocking his substantial frame flat on the ground.

"You both did your parts perfectly in weakening Elysha." Serafina smiled, as bright as sunshine, at both him and Gloria.

"But we didn't do anything." He'd been about to do something, but that didn't count.

"Elysha was foolish enough to think you, and especially Gloria, would be unable to affect matters when you were physically powerless and immobilized," Serafina went on. "She thought she'd be safe if she kept you suffering and off balance with fear for the fate of your beloved. She always underestimates the capacity good people have for selflessness. We chose you and Gloria precisely because there was such great potential for true love between you. Elysha was quite staggered by the surge of energy when Gloria realized her true love for you."

For a moment, his ears rang with the sound of those words. Until he recognized the sound of distant sirens now growing nearer.

"Well, we must be going."

Greg looked around. The light once filling the grove like daytime faded to twilight now, like a dimmer switch setting the world back to night. The glade felt oddly desolate, the light and company of dazzling beings all fled. The other fairy godmothers had also disappeared.

"Wait. What am I supposed to tell the police?"

"Tell them Wonder Guy led you here, the bad guys ran off, leaving Gloria behind and you are trying to keep her warm until help arrives."

"Oh. Right."

Serafina vanished with the last of the light. Or not quite the last. Greg caught sight of more lights flashing in the direction of the nearest road. The sirens died away and the sound of car doors opening and closing carried through the rainy woods.

"Over here!" he yelled. Gloria stirred in his arms, snuggling into his chest as well as possible, still half buried in the mud. She was in love with him? Even after all the rest, that made this the best day of his life.

☆☆★☆☆

Gloria woke when jostled, feeling herself lifted up. Close to her ear at the same moment, Greg's voice reassured her.

"It's okay," he said. He sat beside her and held her hand as other people freed her legs grown so numb with cold. It all came back to her. Bizarre scenes. Vines and brambles and roots moving at the command of an evil sorceress. She would think she'd been dreaming, but, if it were a dream, how had she come to be buried to the waist in the earth?

At least she had Greg. Somehow, miraculously, both of them had made it through alive and well. Wrapping her arms around his neck, she clung fiercely to him.

"What happened?" she asked. "That woman meant to kill us, and then everything got weird. Weirder."

"It's okay," he assured her again. "We've been rescued. When the police arrived, Elysha took off and Wonder Guy left in pursuit."

"Huh?" Oh. Right. He probably didn't want the whole world knowing his secret identity. She'd play along, but she'd make him tell her the whole story later.

With a final sucking squelch, her legs came free of the mud. Several people helped lift her up and out of the pit. Gloria tottered, trying to stand, but was supported mainly by Greg's arm.

"There you go, miss." One of the EMTs who'd helped dig her out spoke, rising to his feet. "How are you feeling? Do you want a stretcher? We need to check you out. Can you make it to our vehicle?"

"A stretcher?" She felt awfully wobbly, her legs hardly supporting her. But she didn't want to let go of Greg. Her grip tightened around his neck.

He gave a laugh, adjusting her grip away from his windpipe. "I'll carry her." Greg hoisted her up into his arms. She relaxed against him. He was strong enough for this, even without his superpowers.

"No thanks." She smiled to the EMT. "I'm good."

One of the police officers who'd been moving purposefully around the glade came and walked beside them as Greg followed the EMT through the woods to a path and then to an ambulance parked near several police cars along the nearest road.

"I'll need to take your statement, Miss."

"Of course, but how did you find me?" Gloria asked.

"Your friend, an Agatha Roberts, suggested we interview your co-worker, a Ms. Kathleen Pederson. We found your cell phone in her possession and she confessed to bringing you here, where another woman, a Ms. Ellis, took charge of you. We're holding Pederson on charges of kidnapping and suspicion of conspiracy to murder."

"She killed Jo." Gloria shuddered, releasing Greg only reluctantly when he sat her in the open rear door of the ambulance.

The detective made a note.

"Excuse me, sir." One of the EMTs moved between him and Gloria, deftly slapping a blood pressure wrap around her bare arm.

☆☆★☆☆

The rain had stopped and dawn brightened the overcast sky to a soft, pearly gray by the time the EMTs had treated Gloria's various scrapes and cuts. They had transferred operations to the nearest precinct station where the police had finished taking their statements. Aggie would be coming to pick them up shortly.

The police insisted on questioning Gloria separately from Greg, and she pleaded confusion about much of what had had happened. If she mentioned the magic, they might want to keep her for observation. She told them about Kathleen and spoke only vaguely of what had transpired in the woods.

The whole time she kept wondering about Greg. Everything would be different now. She felt shy toward him. What would she say to him? It was almost as if he'd become someone new, a stranger she'd have to get to know all over again.

But when she left the interview room, there he stood, waiting for her. Their eyes met and in his smile, everything familiar appeared, and a whole future of light and love shone forth. She leaned into his arms again as if it were the most natural thing in the world and lifted her lips to his.

Yes. He had given up his superpowers for her, but all the magic of Wonder Guy's kisses remained.

☆☆★☆☆

Greg could hardly believe it. No masks. No disguises. No superpowers. And Gloria kissed him anyway. Her yielding lips and sly, slippery tongue ignited his senses, opened him up to the world of delight to which she held the key. The surge of sensation brought him to life in ways his studies never had. Love rang through his heart like a carillon of golden bells. Better than magic. Better than flying. He had everything he desired right here in his arms, and now that he held her, he'd never let her go.

Epilogue

"Serafina will present today's follow-up report to the steering committee." Philomena retired to her seat at the head of the table and her diminutive colleague stood.

"I'm happy to report an unqualified Happily Ever After outcome to the Superhero Sting operation," she began, pointing to the screen on which a PowerPoint presentation displayed a bar chart. "Here you can see the across-the-board drop in dark energies over the entire Upper Midwest Region following our curtailment of Elysha's activities." She paused when Euphonia raised a hand.

"I hadn't realized Elysha's influence was so widespread. How did we miss this earlier?"

"In her way, she was quite clever. We knew someone exerted a dark influence in the region, but on the surface, Elysha's activities appeared so innocuous we didn't, at first, suspect her. In retrospect, we traced her actions to see how carefully she chose her targets. Small amounts of her influence cascaded to cause a quite disproportionate degree of misery.

"For instance, a word in the wrong ear at the wrong time led to a suicide, impacting many other lives. Discord sown between friends and neighbors led to larger breakdowns in consideration and trust. She made introductions between potential abusers and their victims. Most recently we curtailed an operation beginning with an introduction between two ambitious and ruthless people, leading to a criminal collaboration that would have cut short the careers of many bright and promising young minds who might otherwise have gone on to do work benefiting much wider communities.

"Thanks to our operation Elysha's scheme has been short-circuited. I'm happy to report that one of the principal malefactors is in the hands of the proper authorities, and forensic evidence discovered in the trunk of her vehicle ties her decisively to the murder and the kidnapping for which she is responsible. Those authorities are also investigating the guilty woman's co-conspirator."

"Hear, hear." Several voices chimed in, with a tinkling of teacups and silver spoons.

"Best of all, the activation of the True Love cascade between our principals not only caught Elysha in its blast, but repaid our investment of magical energies in the operation many times over--a 'gusher' so to speak, promising to continue its yield for years to come."

She clicked to the first in a series of slides depicting the happy couple at their wedding ceremony: hand in hand at the altar, the groom lifting aside the bride's veil for a kiss, greeting guests at the reception and a shot in which the bride tossed her bouquet of mixed wildflowers straight to her new mother-in-law's waiting hands.

A chorus of happy sighs greeted each photograph.

Proof

19455126R00196